TILTING

— WITH —

LIPS

WILLIAM D. SULLIVAN

ARCHWAY
PUBLISHING

Archway Publishing books may be ordered through booksellers or by contacting:

Archway Publishing
1663 Liberty Drive
Bloomington, IN 47403
www.archwaypublishing.com
844-669-3957

ISBN: 978-1-6657-1146-3 (sc)
ISBN: 978-1-6657-1148-7 (hc)
ISBN: 978-1-6657-1147-0 (e)

Library of Congress Control Number: 2021917708

Print information available on the last page.

Archway Publishing rev. date: 09/21/2021

This is no world
To play with mammets and to tilt with lips.
We must have bloody noses and cracked crowns,
And pass them current too.

—HENRY IV, PART 1

DRAMATIS PERSONAE

James "DP" Keating	douchebag police and founder of the feast
David "Quotes" Connelly	movie aficionado, inventor of the Beer Goggle app
Matt "Smitty" Smith	a lawyer, Duke University enthusiast
Riley "Riles" Shaunessy	a base footballer
Jack Taft	a professor
Rosalind Taft	his daughter
Declan Kelly	an apothecary
Tracy Smith	Matt's ex-wife
Dr. Shubert	a professor
Ackerley	a driver
Steven Cavanaugh	a vicar
Reva Clarke	an antiquities expert

1
CHAPTER

Saint Declan combined the Sun Cross with the Christian Cross hundreds of years ago, and the irony of those two things standing prominently on the public house entrance remained lost on almost all who entered. The cross also served as a burial marker in many Irish cemeteries, and that sentiment resonated more apropos. "Cead Mile Failte," read the inscription above the carving, a hundred thousand welcomes, and for Jack Taft it meant he had overstayed his welcomes. As he pushed into Kelly's Pub, the light dimmed and awareness heightened; everyone in the joint gazed in his direction, a requisite glance to see if yet another regular was in the house. Recognized and unknown described Jack fittingly, and while he was very much a constant patron, he was neither acknowledged nor ignored. Only Declan Kelly, who still worked every dayshift despite the success of his lucrative investment, reacted and began pulling a Carlsberg.

The July heat, forgotten a few steps into the cool darkness of the room, made it feel less like eleven thirty in the morning. The contrite colloquialism "it's noon somewhere" wouldn't receive the slightest chuckle in a place like this, where it was, in fact, noon *everywhere*. Four men occupied the corner booth constructed from an old church pew, while scattered others sat at the bar dividing their attention between smart phones and the English Premier League match on the screen above the bar. The EPL was a regular fixture in pubs across the states, even if it could be found nowhere else. Everton held a one-nil lead.

Ignoring the cowboy trepidation of sitting with his back to the door, Professor Taft preferred the corner stool as the best angle to peruse the pub and eavesdrop into more conversations. While Jack had little family and no friends outside Declan Kelly, he was always comfortable, even at the experienced age of seventy-three, with Will and a tall stool. As Declan slid the lager across the bar and gave him a welcoming nod, Jack reached into his weathered shoulder bag for two books. The first, depending on how you date it, was over four hundred years old and known the world around. The second was his daily sounding board and known only to him. The leather-bound journal he set on the bar held all his thoughts on his own particular brand of bardolatry. Next to it was William Shakespeare's *Coriolanus*.

Obsessing over Shakespeare hardly separated Jack from countless others who searched for the meaning of the greatest prose and poetry among limited clues and long-dead connections to the world's greatest known author. In every sense, the man from Stratford long ago reached the status of a deity for those to whom he mattered most. Hamlet is the second most recognized literary character in the English language—behind Jesus Christ. Shakespeare arose from modest beginnings, disappeared for a while, and left behind legions of followers and doubters long after the time of his death, as did Jesus himself.

As sure as the canon had been Jack's religion throughout his adult life, Kelly's had been his church. From the end of the spring semester to the last days of summer, there were three months of reading; writing; research; and, of course, pints. *"If sack and sugar be a sin, God help the wicked."*

"You gotta be kidding me." Jim Keating's voice reverberated from his normal spot in the corner pew.

Lifting his lager, Jack could hear conviction and inflection intimating a clear confidence in the subject matter at hand.

"You seriously think that game wasn't fixed? The sun hasn't reached its peak, so I know nobody can be that drunk. It's all fixed, Abraham Drinkin," Keating continued.

"Listen, Alfred Bitchcock, I'm just saying they had all their starters back from a team that made the Final Four the year before. There's no reason they couldn't win that game," Matt Smith replied. "They were no joke. Laettner is still one of the best in the history of college basketball. Hurley was a legit point guard. And Grant Hill was as talented as anyone on the court."

"Do they ever argue about anything other than sports?" Jack asked Declan.

"Occasionally about which of them is paying the tab," Declan said as he returned to slicing limes. "But this one's personal. Smitty matriculated from Duke, professor."

Matt Smith, recognized around the pub as Smitty, had fought this fight more than once in his life. As a Duke undergrad, he'd waited patiently in Krzyzewskiville outside Cameron Indoor Stadium on many North Carolina evenings for his chance to taunt opposing players in the synchronized harmony that separated Duke fans from the normal catcalling collegians. Duke fans were better. Just ask them.

"Dude, I know attending *the* Duke University automatically makes you an expert on all things basketball. I'm certain you were right there when Dr. Naismith hung his peach basket. Obviously, being the least athletic black guy in the history of sports had nothing to do with you going to the greatest school in the history of nerds meet sports. And I'm positive tutoring Riley all through high school gave you some hope of entering into the upper echelon of a future NBAers circle by writing his papers for him." Keating paused to take a sip of his beer as Jack continued to focus his attention on the group. "I'm not arguing any of that. I'm saying that UNLV had all their starters back from the national championship team, which the year before beat Duke's ass by thirty."

"They beat us by thirty because Bobby Hurley shit his pants in '90. A year is a long time to live with diarrhea. That little bitch was ready," said Smith.

"Ready for Anderson Hunt to be in a hot tub with one of the most renowned game fixers in Las Vegas? What was that frickin' guy's name? Richard Petty, Richard Perry? Hurley was ready for one of the dirtiest athletic programs in the history of the NCAA to make a few bucks? What the hell was he ready for?" responded Keating.

"Domination. Get out of the hot tub and stop drinking the Kool-Aid. Anderson Hunt was the only guy playing who was in that stupid photo, and he gave the Devils thirty."

Jack observed Jim Keating waving off his friend's wry smile and sipping from his pint. "Nine point spread, brother. Somebody got paid."

Jack noticed how comfortable Keating seemed in the corner booth, almost as if the pub were built around him, with every beam and floorboard set, erected, and nailed to reflect him. He wore a gray oxford shirt and khaki pants that demanded you not notice him when you noticed him. As one of the many regulars, Jack had seen him in that spot many times before, but in some small way, he was more jovial than usual.

"Maybe it was the stripes. That charge block on Anthony went a long way to deciding the game anyway," said Keating.

Nicknamed DP, James Keating was known to many around

him as the Douchebag Police. This is not to say a policeman who was a douchebag but, rather, a man who policed douchebags. Jack often overheard stories of Keating's sophomoric Robin Hood-like antics. On this particular day, a construction lane runner paid the price for Keating's occupation.

"What the hell are you smiling at?" Matt asked Jim knowing it was more than just the Duke argument.

"I just don't understand what these idiots are doing," said Keating, pausing for moment of deliberation, as if deciding whether or not to get into the whole story. "It's not that difficult of a concept that construction crews close down one lane of a two-lane highway. This never causes a backup of folks frenzied with road rage. The crews always go opposite the flow of traffic. You guys know this. They work the road into the city in the afternoon and the road out of the city in the morning. They also strive to close one lane at a time and rarely hit a high traffic area during the day when they can collect perfectly good double-time laying tar at night. Drivers create backups. Regular as running red lights or failing to signal, there is always an idiot or two who waits until the absolute last moment to maybe set their blinker, cut off a driver like me who has followed the traffic signals, and slow down everyone who slid into the proper lane eight hundred yards back. The *construction lane runner*. You boys have surely encountered him.

"So anyway, as I'm rolling over to meet you guys, one of these ass clowns cut me off. Everyone else slides over when they see the blinking arrow, and this guy speeds past me in his shiny black Lexus and cuts me off. Now it's not like this hasn't happened a hundred times, but he has a vanity plate on his car that says, 'LEXMAN.' Do you really need that plate *on* your Lexus? Thank God I had just finished my coffee, or I would have dumped it when I slammed on the breaks. I was pissed." Keating looked over his Irish Breakfast Club before dropping the punch line.

"Jesus, DP. What did you do?" asked Smith.

Revealing he'd dropped more than a punch line, Keating answered, "I shit on his car."

"What the hell are you talking about?"

Jack had looked away briefly, disgusted with Jim's story, but could still hear the surprise in Smith's voice.

"I followed him to the medical building on Sycamore." Keating smiled. "And then I shit on his car."

"I thought you were adamant that the punishment fit the crime," Smith said, preempting an argument Keating loved. "Remember the time the guy threw his McDonald's bag out the window of his car, and you followed him all the way home? Dumped your garbage in his tiny little lawn for the better part of a year. By the end, that bastard was skipping work trying to catch you. I was fine with that, brother. Who honestly thinks the earth is their garbage can? But this is a little extreme."

"The punishment fit," said Keating as he leaned back and relaxed his arms outward along the top of the bench. "My man in his shiny new Lexus believed his schedule is more important than all the patient people who actually read the signs and followed the signals. He believed that his time is more valuable than mine. The moment he ignores the flashing yellow bulbs crying relentlessly for the merge, he's asking to be defecated upon."

"Still not following the argument, DP." Riley Shaunessy had managed to keep quiet throughout the UNLV debate and Keating's story, while staring intently at the Everton match, but he had heard enough.

"Would you drive a car with a pile of poo on the hood?" Keating asked rhetorically. "I didn't think so. When he heads home today, he's gonna lose the time he cost everyone else this morning. Agreed?"

"I absolutely do not agree on this one, brother. You're out of your mind," said Shaunessy.

Jack had noted over the years that Riley was the quietest in the group, but it didn't mean he went unnoticed. Even though his eyes may have conveyed his full age of thirty-plus years, his biceps bulging through his Real Madrid T-shirt made him seem a man a bit younger.

In years of study, Jack of course had encountered the crossroads of brilliance and insanity many times, and assuming you didn't currently have human feces hovering over your engine block, Keating's passion was compelling. Even with just another peripheral glance, Jack saw Keating smiling devilishly in the pew, anticipating no further discussion. Jim's controversial collection of laws had been discussed many times in that corner and defended tirelessly under his convoluted umbrella of "do unto others." The pint rested comfortably in his hand around relaxed fingers. He cupped the tulip-shaped glass gently and perused his usual group of friends. A pen and ink drawing on the wall above his head showed a street scene in Temple Bar, where Joyce breathed life into his *Ulysses*, and Keating, ever ubiquitous, fit perfectly in either scene.

"Declan," Keating hollered, raising his glass off the table, fingers clasped stronger now, "pull me another pint, sir, if you would be so kind." With that, Jim tilted back and finished off the remnants of this day's first Guinness.

Declan Kelly, the founder of this feast, had owned the bar for as long as Jack had been coming in, which was back to high school days for the men in the corner. Rumors bounced back and forth whether he was actually a connected guy in the Irish mafia. No one could have offered any evidence to support the fact, but between his Irish brogue and complete willingness to break up any skirmish arising in the pub, stories swirled. There were several occasions over the years where one of his patrons needed a few hours work, a few extra bucks, or a ride home and Declan seemed forever willing. IRA, numbers games, *Baastan* mob—no one cared a bit. He was a good dude who poured a great pint.

Artists use myriad canvases, and Declan painted behind three and a half feet of shined pine. In spite of, or in concert with, his wealth and happiness, he took constant pride in his work, as he did in almost any task. He was willing, though less than eager, to mix fabulous cocktails for the high-tipping, happy-hour society gals; he knew his wines and conveyed that well and cleaned his lines and glasses meticulously; but most importantly, he pulled a perfect Guinness. Anyone who made it to the weekend high school kegger or the Thursday night frat party had poured beer from a tap, but a draught of the bitter black stuff requires precision. One hundred nineteen and a half seconds, six degrees Celsius, clean lines, and a man who took pride in his work—that was a pint.

A Guinness is poured in two parts. First, the room temperature glass is leaned at a forty-five degree angle and the tulip is filled two-thirds of the way. Once poured, the glass is set back upright for the draught to settle. This patient pause is often ignored and results in a subpar pint. Once black, the glass is topped off above the rim allowing the foam meniscus to ease down and the illusion of the cascade begins. Bubbles rise from the bottom of the glass in the center, pushing outward at their zenith and forcing themselves back down the sides.

"I hope your five-hole is OK." Keating's favorite joke.

"A little bit of five-hole friction goes a long way. Ask any lass after six or seven pints, and she's sure to agree." Kelly played along easily if not eagerly, as he was often a grown man among children. The five-hole restrictor plate in the pouring system causes friction as the fluid passes through the line on the way to the tap and creates the bubbles resulting in the famous cascade of a Guinness settling. The five-hole restrictor plate also makes for an enduring double entendre and endless jokes between boys in bars.

"Are you sure your five-hole is working properly?" Smith asked.

"No leakage at the moment."

"Nothing worse than a leaky five-hole," Shaunessy deadpanned.

Men were idiots when no one watched them, a great certainty in life.

"Kel, you need the professor to examine your five-hole? Guy's got a doctorate, Yale educated, fluent in the great books, and probably joined one of those secret societies. I'm sure he's seen his fair share of five-holes." Keating laughed but elicited no response from Professor Taft.

"Doc just got here. He needs a little more booze before I let him anywhere near my five-hole. Leave him be now.

Jack never looked up; nor did he turn his head back toward the pews. Shakespeare's Caius Martius, ready to topple friends and enemies alike, now had his attention.

"All right, I'm ready." The scratchy voice belonged to the man laid out on the pew adjacent to Keating and Shaunessy. Minutes shy of noon, there was no better place to recover from a night of too much libation than an Irish pub surrounded by the fellows who love you. "Where's the spit bucket?"

"Spit bucket?"

"I'm pretty sure I lost a boxing match last night. Could use the spit bucket because someone also defecated in my mouth," the disheveled man said.

"May have been DP. That seems to be his kind of thing, Quotes," said Riley.

Dave Connelly, known to his friends as Quotes, earned his nickname with his ability to accurately quote movies to fill in the missing dialogue in any conversation. For Dave, by far the hardest drinker in the group, marriage and family had neither been part of his life nor slowed his thirst. A genius by all accounts, Connelly was a chronic underachiever, known as much for his ability to enter seamlessly into any conversation as he was for his inability to focus on any goal. By the superlative degree of comparison only, as Dickens wrote, David Connelly and Declan Kelly were polar opposites—the hustler and the grinder.

"Barkeep. Shoot some brown stuff though your five-hole for me." Connelly ended the joke ... for today.

"How was the date, Dave?" Riley smiled, hoping for details.

"Not sure I could call it a date. The bloody internet chum trail that leads women like that to guys like me is at least a few floors below dating." He ran his hand through his hair spiking it up into a ridiculous, six-inch-high pompadour. His blond locks and two-day-old stubble suited him well, as he appeared to be half beach bum, half bum. If he'd produced a brown bag containing a bottle of Wild Irish Rose, none of the others would have been shocked.

"That bad?" Matt asked.

"We had a ten-minute dialogue on how I shave, which descended into whether or not I would let her shave me. And I wish, to all that is holy, we were talking about my face. In what world do I need a topiary surrounding my junk to make a woman happy?" Connelly shook his head in disgust.

"The digital world," said Smith.

"The digital world?"

"When they can log on and look at your salary, it skips a few steps in the timeless art of seduction." Matt smiled at Connelly.

"WYSIWYG," chimed Keating.

Jack had noticed the obvious change around the bar when Connelly secured his windfall. There had been a few rounds for the house and myriad jokes from his mates, but he never quite got the whole story. He did, however, have an omniscient bartender. "Remind me again, Declan, how Mr. Connelly made his millions."

Declan couldn't help but laugh before quickly recounting the story. "Well, David was able to use his propensity for social networking and bar patronizing to formulate one great idea—no, let me change that—one profitable idea. There is honestly nothing great about it. The Bar Goggle application, as David named it, combined the ridiculous safe haven of zero human contact with the possibility of leaving a bar with the woman of your alcohol-induced dreams. He actually asked me if he could use this place to try it out. By the time I stopped laughing, he was gone. The app lets you connect to the bar TV with your phone and send messages. It works the way all idiotic social media works, but you're actually present. Cute girl across the room likes your message and accompanying photo, she responds, and you never even had to buy her a drink. He started with ten watering holes, and soon enough the floodgates opened. In the beginning of Mr. Connelly's Objective-C plan, he was out to grab seven digits. By the time he sold it off, he got eight." The bartender shook his head conveying disbelief and, quite possibly, a little pride.

"Here you go, boys," Smith offered. "Best hockey movie of all time?"

"That's candy. *Slapshot*," said Keating, pinpointing the film best known for the ridiculous Hanson brothers, perhaps the earliest portrayers of the hockey goon.

"C'mon, dude, *Miracle* was legit. I thought Russell coached in the Olympics when that movie was over," said Connelly.

"Big *Mystery, Alaska* fan myself boys. 'If you don't play this game with a big heart and a big bag-o-knuckles in front of the net, you don't got dinky doo.' Mike Meyers is frickin' hysterical." Riley Shaunessy laughed as the words escaped with his best Canadian accent, which was, in fact, a bit sorry, eh.

"All right, Riley, you're not allowed to talk for five minutes for even entering that movie into the conversation. You're seriously comparing the Rangers in outdoor hockey to one of the best American sports stories of all—"

"Jesus Christ!" The shout came from the corner of the bar, where Jack Taft miraculously wrestled his attention away from Rome's banishment of their heroic son. The sheer volume of the cry interrupted text messages, stock quotes, Facebook updates, and the inane conversation of four immature men. The gaze of each and every patron fell on Jack at the corner of the bar. "Isn't it possible, lads, there might actually be something more?" He stared briefly at his journal before pushing his stool away from the bar and making his way toward Keating.

"I've sat here for years and listened to you boys pontificate on Magic Johnson or Larry Bird, Kathy Ireland or Elle McPherson? You've argued whether you'd rather have a hook hand or a peg leg; who would win a fight between Superman and Batman; the cinematic merit of Will Ferrell; and, my personal favorite, DeNiro's crew from *Goodfellas* versus the Corleone family." Taft paused for a moment and glanced at one of the other patrons in a manner that made all of them look away. It wasn't their fight. "The Corleones would kick the shit out of them by the way, Mr. Connelly. But couldn't you boys just once have an argument that matters?

"Anything that matters. Perhaps religion? Maybe the existence of God? Arjuna versus the Buddha? History? Wind on the Hudson or French intervention? Philosophy? Politics? Science? Hell, we'd all be happy to hear your thoughts on the existence of extraterrestrials given the fact that life formed so quickly here on earth once conditions were right. Maybe I'll learn you're a believer, even if a quilted multiverse seems like too much science fiction for you."

Matt continued to chomp down a mouthful of sausage with his back to Jack as if the old man had been stumping thousands of miles away. Keating and Shaunessy stared at the professor, lost between shock and wonderment, confused by the sudden outburst fired at them without warning or cause. David Connelly remained a revolting shade of light green, which indicated a most certain projectile vomit loomed large in his near future, but the smile on his face could not have been contained by *Slapshot*'s Hanson Brothers. The glimmer in his eyes made it seem possible that, for at least this second, in that corner, he loved Jack Taft.

"Is this really all you've got, boys? A few laughs and meaningless rhetoric. Isn't there anything you'd *care* to talk about?"

"What's the matter, Jack?" Riley inquired, smiling at the other men around the table. "Did some sexy coed dump you on summer vacation and move on to a bigger one with a lacrosse star? She was fifty years younger than you, Teach. I don't think any of those little sweeties would keep you around for too long."

"I thought I said five minutes, Riles," Connelly snapped without moving his attention from the professor. "Pick the topic, professor, and lead off. I'll give you to the end of my Guinness to put forth an argument, and I'll have my rebuttal ready."

Declan Kelly was already on his way from the bar. He set two pints on the table and uttered a barely audible, "Go."

Connelly put the glass to his lips but offered one last thought before taking a sip. "No English literature, please. And think fast. It's my first debate, not my first beer."

2
CHAPTER

The truth in the room was ignored, lost on David Connelly's challenge. Jack didn't care what the boys talked about and always liked them very much, but the professor had walked into the bar angry that day. He loved his work and enjoyed his passions, and recently both of them had been threatened. Long alone in his life, he possessed no current outlet for his rage and took a shot that his outburst might set in motion a series of events to right those wrongs. In the dim light of the pub, with men he knew less than well, he could never have guessed how perfectly this initial challenge would affect each of the men in that corner.

"Well, since I interrupted your didactic discussion by using his name, I should argue that Jesus Christ is the most important man in the history of religion, but I'm not certain it would be very sporting." Jack glanced momentarily at Connelly's pint on the table. "I'll take Mohammed instead."

From there Taft moved forward with his argument while Dave knocked back his pint. Despite his anger, Taft wasn't looking to embarrass anyone, and although erudite, his points were very straightforward and simple. Whether Mohammed was in fact a prophet who heard the word of Allah directly or he simply inspired millions of people and gave them hope, there was certainly no arguing that his influence was as profound as any man or prophet in the history of religion. Anticipating Connelly's reply, Taft brought up the strong anti-Muslim sentiment in the United States, drawing a clear and succinct line of separation between Islam and Islamic extremism. "Ultimately, David, people in the Middle East were thirsty, and Mohammed gave them something to drink."

After roughly four minutes, Connelly poured the last of his beer down his throat, thumped his chest twice lightly with the inside of his fist and muttered, "Very good."

Not knowing whether he referenced the quaff or the argument, Taft stared quizzically at his opponent. He then turned and headed to the bar, retrieving his Carlsberg. Three steps from the table, he started. "You should have an easy road, but I'm anxious to hear your argument, especially if it involves anything more complex than a film quotation. And just for the record, David, this is not my first beer either."

"Isn't all the argument a 'cuckhold and a whore,' Jack? Sorry, no English literature, and stop me, I've quoted again." Connelly took a deep breath and nodded a couple times if only to himself. "You're right, professor. This is better. Go easy on that Carlsberg, big fella, as I may need a moment or two to organize my thoughts while I duck under the shade of a rose apple tree. First, let me get semantics and prophets out of the way. You asked, Who was the most important man in the history of religion? I could trot down the path of prophets being more than just men, but that's cheating a bit, so I'll go this route." Connelly raised his arm toward the bar, prompting Declan to hoist a glass from the shelf, spin it 180 degrees, and pull down on the handle. "Professor, I can't argue with a single thing you said. It's 100 percent true, and it seems I should still have the means to win, as everything you said about Mohammed is also true of Jesus Christ. Everywhere you go in the world, the name of Christ is known. He is the center of not one but many religious faiths. His story, like Mohammed's, is well documented, and whether you believe him to be the Son of God or just a man, there is absolutely no arguing his impact on religion for two thousand years." Dave hesitated again, seemingly for effect but truthfully to make the argument last as long as possible. "There really is no questioning that, so I won't ask. Instead, I'll ask this. *Why* do you know his name?"

Now it was Taft's turn to smile.

"For a man of modest beginnings, Christ had an impressive following. He garnered that following by being accepting, one of the main tenets of everything he believed. He got folks to walk away from their lives, their families, their homes, their work, just to follow him, to listen to him, to revere him. But there's a real good chance, heck a great chance, you would have never heard of Jesus if he hadn't been martyred. Every Catholic church in the world, whether it was built four hundred years ago or eighteen days ago, depicts Jesus in the same way." Dave took a sip from his fresh Guinness almost as soon as Declan set it on the table. "Your five minutes are up, Riley. How is Christ shown?"

Riley felt a slight pressure in his chest, palm sweat instant and profuse, but he managed an answer as if he was making his First Communion, "On the cross?"

"That's right. On the cross. There is absolutely no denying that the image of Christ on the cross is the reason his light still shines so bright. The crucifixion and resurrection didn't inspire his teachings, but they defined them. By that rationale, I'd say the most important man in the history of religion isn't Mohammed, Lao Tzu, Gotama, or even Jesus of Nazareth. It's …"

"Judas Iscariot." Jack arrived there long before the other men surrounding Connelly, and his expression hadn't changed.

While Taft spoke the last word, Connelly clearly got it. Although his answer obviously wasn't *the* answer, each of Connelly's friends stared awkwardly at him, impressed by his argument. The afternoon religion lesson from David reminded them all of his capacity for original thought, his mind much more adroit at finding quality argument than quality work.

Jim Keating, more than the others, tried to hold the image for a second. He knew Connelly was completely hungover and working toward drunk again, but the picture of him flexing his intellect while casual in his regard for himself was something beautiful. Jim's friend sat there in a tattered polo shirt, insignia and, perhaps, crusted barbeque sauce over his heart, completely oblivious to the guidelines of civilized society. Dave cared about his friends and his beer in no particular order, but as his words hung in the air, Jim spotted a better version.

"The Nag Hammadi scriptures, specifically the Gospel of Judas, suggest he may have even done it *for* Jesus and, if that were even fractionally true, then he certainly did it for the millions who ultimately followed."

"Well done, David. I have no reservations you will die offstage someday. You deserve it." It was Taft's turn to smile. "I don't think I could have illustrated my point any more clearly than you did. Figure out what matters, boys, and try to keep hold of it. This is for you, Mr. Keating. I've been hoping to cross paths with you for a few days now." Taft removed a blank white envelope from the back pocket of his twill khakis and handed it across the table. "If you would be so kind, I'd prefer you open it tomorrow." Taft looked down at the draught in his hand, and his smile vanished. "Only half empty."

"You could say—" started Shaunessy.

"Don't," replied the professor, cutting Riley off. Then as swiftly as he'd moved into their circle, he walked back to his stool, passing a double-fisting Declan.

"You catch that, Dec?" said Smith.

"I caught enough," Kelly responded.

"Any idea what it was all about?"

"None. Seemed the same as any other day."

Smith and Riley stared at Declan. And as is often the case with bartenders, he was expected to solve their problem. Keating fixated on Connelly, who gazed at no discernible point of interest, possibly outside the beams and walls of the bar. His friend still looked somewhat ill, conceivably from the previous evening's drinks; this morning's lack of nourishment; or, quite likely, a lifetime of regret. Across the room, Jack Taft stacked *Coriolanus* on top of his journal and placed them both in his shoulder bag. Dropping fifteen dollars on the bar, he walked out of the pub without anyone initially noticing.

"Guy's been coming here, what, ten years, Dec? Just walks over and starts yelling at us," said Shaunessy.

"More like twenty," said Declan Kelly.

It was then that Keating's eyes moved from Kelly to the envelope in his hand and, finally, back across the pub. Now all five men looked toward the empty stool near the entrance. "Did he leave?"

In the hot July sunlight, Jack stood next to the driver's side door of his car and gingerly placed his leather bag on the roof. He felt much older than he had just five minutes earlier as he released an elongated sigh into the sticky summer air, and in that depressing breath of weakness, he acted his age.

The pistol he'd owned for thirty-six years and never fired felt heavy in his hand when he removed it from the bag. It felt heavy. That heavy feeling, and a Moor from Venice, were his last thoughts before he pulled back on the hammer and began raising the gun toward his temple. For just a moment, the most important moment, the moment when strangers in a bar gave him hope, not everything looked like a nail. "Wait and see," the professor muttered before decocking the gun, gathering his bag off the roof and climbing into the car. None of the confused men in the pub would ever see Jack Taft again.

3
CHAPTER

James Keating fell in love during the fall semester of his freshman year in college, and by the time undergraduates broke for the holidays, he knew he had met the woman with whom he would spend the rest of his life. In a lot of ways, she did stay with him forever, but in the important way, she broke his heart into many hardened and unforgiving pieces. When the spring semester began, Keating felt the same irrepressible jubilance as the first time they'd kissed, the first time they'd said I love you, or the first time they'd drunk too much and gotten too naked. Yet to experience any real heartache in a fairly spoiled existence throughout his own life, his glasses remained far too rose-colored to notice what lacked in her step that spring.

In the beginning, she studied on far more Thursdays than she had the previous semester, but it seemed easy to ignore. Then her sorority demanded more time. Then her room was empty and the door locked when he felt certain she was in the dorm. All the while, she convinced her new boyfriend she couldn't think of a way to tell Jim it was over. He was too nice. How could she break the heart of someone with whom she had shared so many immature, intimate times?

As it turned out, college football players are much less

aggrieved by the subtle way to let someone down. When Jim opened the door to his dorm room, the photographs were fanned out on the floor at his feet. He had never seen her in the black lace underwear she donned for her new boyfriend, but cornerbacks tend to be more persuasive than the average college student. The three pictures, clearly taken with a timer, were all in succession with the football player in the foreground, his girlfriend's face and scantily clad body close behind. Keating stared at the photos for a full five minutes. If the photos offered a reflection, he would have seen his metamorphosis for the first time. For in that twelve-foot-by-eighteen-foot space, a new Jim Keating was born. His friends would one day call him DP.

It took ten minutes to plan and two weeks to execute. First, he sought her out and explained the pictures were a little rough on him, but he'd felt less certain in their relationship of late and had started seeing someone else. More certain than ever, the lie strained his limited power of deception, and as is rarely the case among college freshman, he felt no interest in seeing other women. She assured him of her innocence in sending him the pictures and professed she was mortified that anyone had seen them. Keating guaranteed the pictures would be returned as soon as possible, and he was absolutely telling the truth.

An athletic department equipment room is a lousy place to work and an easy place to get a job. Sifting through compression shorts and sports bras before dispensing them into the proper cubbies is tedious work no one really wants, but for Keating it was perfect. The only perks that came with this kind of employment were the occasional stolen T-shirt and access to locker rooms. Eight days after seeing pictures of his girlfriend, Keating bought $250 worth of marijuana, and two nights after that, he put it in the football locker room. He briefly entertained a call to public safety but realized an actual investigation might follow. Instead, he made an anonymous call to the football coach letting him know that his defense, specifically, one of his backs, was dealing to the whole student body. There might be consequences, but D-I programs don't involve the police. They handled matters internally.

Keating withdrew from classes and packed his belongings on the eleventh day; he slept on a mattress with no sheets and explained nothing to his roommate. He simply told him to be out of the room all afternoon. Someone was coming to kill him. The first knock came at 4:05 p.m., almost exactly two hours after the call. The screaming started at 4:06 p.m., and just as the cornerback's shoulder screamed toward the door for the fourth time, Keating yanked it open. When the athletic, 190--pound man-child poured into the room, he skidded across an entire container of Vaseline spread out across the tiled floor in the exact place pornographic pictures of Jim's girlfriend had been scattered two weeks earlier. Revenge is, in fact, slippery but not always a slope.

Almost simultaneously, when his back hit the floor, Keating smashed him with an aluminum bat, another perk courtesy of the equipment room. The first strike was quite aimless, but the second lash struck just above the knee and served its purpose. At least one season on the sidelines.

"If you come at me, the next swing is at your head." A lifetime of violence should have convinced the writhing man on the floor to take one more shot at Keating, but he held his knee and rocked back and forth on the floor.

Keating reached for the recorder on the top of the bureau, quickly hitting rewind and then play. The screams of a testosterone-raged twenty-year-old were clearly audible as he threatened the life of the younger, smaller James Keating. "That should pretty much cover self-defense. As for the rest, it's up to you. Police. Public safety. Retaliation. Whatever you want. I looked up your stats. Could be an NFL guy one day. Who knows? I just want you to know that I dropped everything. I quit school. I packed up. I'm gone. I did all that so I could see you writhing in pain right now. I didn't even know if this would work. I only knew I didn't give a shit. At this moment, I don't care what happens to me. If you want that in your life, then come find me. Otherwise, this is it."

Keating walked out of the room carrying the bat, the tape recorder, and a letter-sized envelope addressed to his ex-girlfriend's home with a brief note inside. He rolled down the stairs from the third floor at the pace of a young man with nothing to lose but still looking back over his shoulder at least once every four steps. He crossed the quad toward his car waiting in W Lot. The cafeteria entertained the usual small crowd of a dozen students waiting outside the doors for friends to come and go.

At the east entrance, Keating opened the door of the post office mailbox and deposited the envelope inside. If brevity is the soul of wit, then the typed note inside represented wit well:

> Dear Mom,
> College is great. Thanks so much for dropping
> $15,000 a year.

Within forty-eight hours, his unsuspecting ex-girlfriend's mother would receive that note … and three pictures.

4
CHAPTER

"What the hell?" Keating wondered.

"Who knows, kid? Open the envelope."

Keating half-heartedly contemplated waiting a day as Taft had asked but instead tore away the top portion of the envelope. He noticed his hands moving at a slow and foreign pace. When his awkward effort finally pried the envelope open, a single silver key spilled onto the table, but he ignored the *clang* of the metal. The black-and-white photo Keating held gingerly in his hand lacked the treasure map feel the men expected, and none of them had ever been so irrefutably wrong.

Keating moved the picture into the light above his head, squinting as confusion pinned clarity in a one-sided neurological wrestling match. The family in the photo consisted of three people smiling carelessly with an ocean filling the background. Each of the men failed to initially recognize Jack Taft as the man in the photo, despite the limited effect the last twenty-five years had had on his countenance. It was the circle drawn haphazardly around a young girl's face immediately pulling Keating's gaze. The blond girl appeared to be no more than eight-years-old, and the happiness in her eyes made the red circumference superfluous. Even the great artist Giotto would have noticed the girl's face first.

Smith crept alongside Keating, and it was he who immediately recognized the father in the photo, although his reaction could have meant anything, "Isn't that ..."

"It sure is," Declan muttered.

"And what exactly does that mean?" Connelly, still on the other side of the table, was the first to see the backside of the photograph when Keating gingerly raised it on a parabolic path toward the ceiling. The same red Sharpie used to identify the young girl as the focal point in the photo scratched a single word on the back.

"What does what mean?" inquired Smith.

"Cardenio."

5
CHAPTER

The room was much cooler than they expected. Keating, Smith, Shaunessy, and Connelly met at the pub, as no other spot would suffice, and drove together to the Littlefield Funeral Home in South Glastonbury, Connecticut, to attend the wake of a man they never really knew. Death is hard when he comes for those closest to us, but funerals are much harder when they're peripheral. The ass-out-hugs and awkward handshakes between strangers in the shadow of floral arrangements and brass rails rarely make for a comfortable situation. Funeral rites vary throughout the world, but there is near universal agreement that only family and close friends belong. The overwhelming sentiment of "we should probably make an appearance" doesn't help anyone involved, and standing in line before Ishmael's lifeboat is unsettling. Nevertheless, the four men crept into the parlor, signed their names in the log to prove the deceased made a difference on this mortal coil, and eased into a small pond of tweed.

"They still make jackets with elbow pads?" asked Shaunessy.

"Jesus Christ, Riles."

"Not sure bringing him into it is appropriate either, Smitty." Connelly smiled as they settled into the room and then added,

"Although the old man was expecting him the last time we talked. Let's say our goodbyes and hit the road, lads."

The room propounded a distinct separation of ages as two clear groups filled the space, Taft's students and colleagues. While Jack taught an entire generation, it doesn't take long for students to forget their best professors. Most of the former students in the room ranged from twenty-two to thirty, and his peers all pushed a bare minimum of fifty. In two compartmentalized ways, it was a clear look into the future for most of the youngsters. If you were reading about the Macbeths or considering Hamlet's procrastination, you could well end up an accountant or a banker, but Jack's serious students were in a little deeper. Life in academia was the dream, death in a box the certainty.

"Holy shit," said Keating, noticing her first.

Two dozen people stood between them waiting to pay their respects, and a quarter century separated her from the envelope, but the woman waiting at the end of the line was the one in the photograph Jack Taft had handed to Keating two minutes before they'd last seen him. Suddenly, for the first time since arriving at the funeral home, and really for the first time since meeting Jack, Keating felt a connection to the man. There was no definable reason why he felt a sudden rush of adrenaline and no explanation for his heightened awareness, but in a room full of esoteric knowledge, Jim knew something they didn't. An octogenarian in a brown sports coat moved away from Taft's daughter and stepped toward the closed coffin. Jim couldn't help but notice when she checked her watch.

Incongruous was the word that came to his mind as he continued observing her. Too meticulously dressed, she did not have the appearance of suffering, rather the look of someone late for a business meeting. Her black pantsuit sent the message she was in mourning, but the expression on her face and the line of her body gave her away. It felt impossible this woman had known Jack at all.

"What do we do now?"

"We say we're sorry for your loss and hit the bricks," Connelly responded to Matt's query.

"Are you sure that's enough?" Keating pressed.

"Dave's right. I'm not sure we need to get involved. Whatever he was trying to tell us, I'm sure it's between them." Matt Smith already had one foot out the door.

"Can I ask you guys a stupid question?" Riley peered across the room.

"You just did," said Keating.

"Very funny, brother. I'm wondering what's in the box?"

Each of the other three failed to notice the discordance of the coffin in the front of the room. Declan had explained to the men two days earlier that the professor's sailboat had sunk somewhere beyond Long Island when he'd wandered off into the more tumultuous Atlantic, and neither the boat nor the body had been recovered. The search had lasted a few days, as the harbormaster in New London had logged Jack's exit, and several witnesses working around the docks had seen the old man meander into the sea. No beacon, no boat, and no Jack Taft.

"Phenomenal question, Riles. Not sure we will be able to ask that one, but still a good question."

Jim led the way through the line, and each man offered his own cliché, except for Shaunessy, who exacerbated the separation by saying nothing at all. After a cursory thirty-minute stay within the tension and whispering of the funeral parlor, the men politely stood up and headed for the car. Keating noticed Smith looking back across the room at the diminished line and heard him utter a barely audible, "Bad timing."

The same gentleman in the gray suit who'd ushered them into the room held the door on the way out. He nodded but said nothing, as, "Have a good night," seemed like bragging. It takes a certain kind of human being to surround himself with death and tragedy all his life and remain unaffected. Keating knew the gray suit didn't have it. The young man would be out of the business within a year he guessed.

"Time for a pint?" Shaunessy asked three steps into the parking lot.

"I'm in," Connelly replied.

"Not tonight, boys. I'm out. Rolling home," said Keating.

"Yes. More for me, DP." These days, Smith was always in.

6
CHAPTER

Keating pulled back into the funeral home parking lot, mildly ashamed for having lied to his three friends. Perhaps it was simply that Jack had handed him the envelope, and maybe he felt embarrassed by his own curiosity.

Keating knew well enough his inquisitiveness stemmed from the daughter in the parlor as much as the professor in the bar, and maybe that was the truth he could not reveal to his friends. Despite her obvious apathy, Keating felt drawn to the now auburn-haired woman in the appropriate pantsuit, and at the very least he owed her a few questions. When he sat in the last row of the room with absolutely no idea how to begin, he still somehow felt confident the answer would come to him. With fifteen minutes remaining for calling hours, there were only a few scattered mourners left in the room. The young woman finally broke away from the front of the parlor and headed toward the water fountain adjacent to the restrooms. Keating moved.

"Excuse me, we haven't met before. My name is James Keating. I was kind of a friend of Jack's. I was here before."

"I'm not exactly sure what that means," she replied.

"Well, I knew him for nearly ten years, but I guess I hardly knew him at all," said Keating.

"Then I guess I'm *kind of* a daughter to him. I'm Rosalind Taft."

"I don't know quite what to say," confessed Keating.

"Perhaps you could tell me why you came back, Mr. Keating."

"James." When the words escaped, Keating realized that almost no one in the world ever called him James. On occasion, he was Jim, often DP, but rarely James. The natural pervasive awkwardness existing in a funeral home was now supplanted by a new and less usual awkwardness in a funeral home. Keating and Rosalind were breaking ground, by offering a secondary discomfort to an already uncomfortable situation. "A bit of a mystery actually. Your father left this for me about three minutes before he left Kelly's for the last time, and I'm wondering if you could tell me why."

Rosalind paused before reaching out and taking the photo from Keating's extended hand.

"Who is Kelly?" she asked.

"Kelly's, not Kelly. It's just a pub." As soon as he said it, he regretted the *just*.

"No, I can't."

At the very least Keating expected her to give a cursory glance at the photo. Perhaps Rosalind would pause and consider the circle drawn around her eight-year-old self or even melt down into a tearful fit. She hardly looked at it before offering it back to him.

"Listen, Miss Taft. I have no desire to intrude on your relationship with your father—"

"Impossible," she said cutting him off.

"I'm sorry?"

"I had no relationship with my father." She said it matter-of-factly, like a San Diego weather woman reminding her watchers they were in for another day of seventy-eight degrees and sunshine. She didn't cringe or flinch. She just let him know.

"You're here." Jim stated it as evidence that the two clearly had some sort of relationship.

"His lawyer left instructions. Perhaps the possessive was inappropriate. A lawyer left instructions. I doubt my father had a doctor, much less a lawyer."

"I'm sorry—"

"You can stop being sorry, James. There really is no need."

"Fair enough. I can't help but think—"

"Therefore you are."

"Sor ..." And he caught himself before apologizing yet again. "I was just going to say"—he hesitated again—"this picture. Don't you think it's possible he had some regret, some thought or feeling that maybe he wanted to convey to you? This isn't normal."

"Mr. Keating."

He almost corrected her again but thought better of it.

"I'm absolutely certain that my father had some regrets, more thoughts, my phone number, email, and the internet at his disposal. If he wanted to get a message to me, he would have done better than a shipwreck and a Sharpie." She hoped this would end the conversation but could tell Keating needed more closure.

"About that. Do you know anything about his sailing? Was he on the water a lot? Did he often go by himself?"

"I know my father was named Jack, and his boat was named *Terence*. I know this only because a lawyer told me it was mine. My father left me a sunken boat." She motioned back across the nearly empty room. "Well, a sunken boat and an empty coffin, as if the rest of this isn't a total mess."

"I hope it's not too bothersome, but we were wondering about that. Why is there a coffin when there is no body?"

Jim looked quickly toward the ceiling and back to Rosalind, a move Connelly would have called "an Iceman." "I know I'm being intrusive, but I was curious."

"No worries, Mr. Keating. It is completely bizarre. My father had already purchased the coffin and his burial site. He left instructions with a lawyer for this as well. I guess a man who is both meticulous and alone thinks of everything. His last will included instructions for circumstances that allowed for an open coffin, a closed coffin, and even an empty coffin. He thought of everything. The lawyer said he called it his 'second best bed.' Some sort of joke that neither of us understood."

"So, it's just an empty coffin?" Keating asked.

"Almost. There are a few things that were valuable to him in there as well. They were to go inside, whether open, closed, or empty."

"Well, I'll be honest. I have no idea what the hell is going on." Keating's glance dropped to the ground as if answers might be found there and leaned forward, elbows to his knees, sighing at the futility of this mock interview.

"My father's specialty," said Rosalind, almost consolingly, "making people feel like they know less than him. One of my fondest childhood memories."

"The lawyer. Maybe there were other instructions."

"Walk away, Mr. Keating. My father knew Shakespeare"—she paused turning to the now empty funeral home without motioning toward it—"and no one else. Good night."

Once she meandered around the corner out of earshot, Keating mumbled an aggressively sarcastic, "Call me, Jim."

7
CHAPTER

"Look what the cat frew up," Shaunessy slurred, spotting Keating first.

"Gents."

"Careful with that word, DP," said Matt.

"No, I need to hit the gents'. Funny though, Smitty, that you'd mistake yourself for a piss." He slowed his walk just short of a complete stop and offered Matt a sympathetic glance. "I guess maybe *funny* is the wrong word."

"Yes!" Connelly celebrated. "Better to keep one's mouth shut, Smitty."

Connelly's retort immediately brought Keating to Mark Twin's famous line about fools. Though neither Dave nor Jim could know it, Jack Taft had never enjoyed the little idiom left behind by Twain. His classroom often required painful extraction of information from his students. The last thing he wanted was a student who worried about sounding foolish. Shakespeare needed exploration and a sense of adventure. Twain was also one of the early believers in the theory that Francis Bacon, not William Shakespeare, loaded the canon. The Baconian theory, shot full of holes through the years, unsurprisingly left Delia Bacon, fountainhead for the idea, in a mental institution. Jack preferred mental institutions to unfounded theories.

"Water cold?" asked Connelly as Keating returned.

"And dangerously shallow," responded Keating.

"Fooling yourself and no one else, DP. You're hung like the urinal cake, brother."

"Damn it. Felt like a good lie."

"All right, champ, we're in the midst of debunking aphorisms." Slowly and surely, aphorisms broke from the pack to encompass sayings; clichés; expressions; and, briefly, colloquialisms. If there was a chance to outdo one of your friends, a thesaurus could be found.

"Connelly just beat, 'the shortest distant between two lions,'" Riley stammered.

"A. You're drunk, Riles. Two. Fuck physics, Quotes." Keating wished he had a roman numeral three.

"My turn then," said Connelly, "and that was nearly a haiku, DP. 'We'll cross that bridge when we come to it.'"

"Can you cross a bridge before you get to it?" Keating answered, giving Connelly a stare to make sure he left Einstein out of it. He *burned* that bridge on the last one.

"Riley paid a girl three bucks to cross her bridge in high school."

"Sccchhmitty, the girl was no troll, en she ad a good body." It was getting harder to understand Riley at all.

"Let's just say she had a body and leave the adjectives out, homeboy."

"Always darkish before the drawn." A smart way out for the hammered Shaunessy.

"In Alaska?" inquired Keating.

"Probably is, but it's hard as hell to tell," said Matt.

"A fool and his money are soon parted," added Keating.

"Rarely acquainted as far …"

"All the world's a stage." Declan said it loud enough to interrupt Matt midsentence. His world, his stage and his hearing, which may or may not have been some sort of superpower outside of Kelly's, undoubtedly beat kryptonite within.

Declan stared at the boys until they all looked up toward him. Across the room, he pulled back on the Bass handle to start a black and tan and showed no signs of anger. Jim often heard him say it was the best way to ruin a Guinness.

"Not sure if that fits the mold, Dec," said Matt, first responder.

"We have a friend who would say otherwise," Declan returned.

"It's from Shakespeare." Connelly knew he had heard it before but never could have found his way to Act II, scene vii of *As You Like It*. With the exception of a glossy Riley, the fellas mentally worked their way to Taft but needed more information from Declan.

"Why would you bring that up, Dec?" As Keating spoke, he moved from their traditional spot up to the corner of the bar. Of the four of them, he remained alone as the intrepid one not yet finished with their argument over pints. He forced the others to follow.

"Jack came in here one miserable afternoon. Crappy day and a painfully empty pub. He launches into this long-winded rant about how kids learn all the wrong stuff in school. He starts rattling off this speech about the seven ages of man, and all I can remember is the first line: 'All the world's a stage.' He got flustered talking about how Shakespeare used the phrase ironically as a joke, rather than attempting to make some great point. Said the audiences in the playhouses got the joke, but no one has ever since. When you guys played that game, he used to break off all kinds of quotations. That's the only one I remember."

"Vich game?" said Riley, late to the play.

"C'mon, pal. When we were running off cliché's, Jack would debunk Shakespearean quotations. Based on our little confrontation the other day, I'm guessing our game pissed him off a bit as well."

"Not at all. He loved it." Declan headed off with his black and tan but fired one last shot. "Especially that you knew the word aphorism."

"What are we going to do?" asked Keating.

"'Bout what?" asked Riley.

"Smitty, you mind taking Riles home before I rip his head off?" said Keating.

"I got him."

8
CHAPTER

The pub typically felt empty to Keating and his friends. Whether throngs of happy hour patrons crammed half-priced appetizers into their gullets or tumbleweeds blew through, it was their bar; and lions don't feel crowded at the watering hole. A line at the main bar was always obfuscated with a wave over the top of the masses. Waitresses in the weeds swung by when their pints dropped below the halfway mark, and they didn't often need a quiet place to chat. Tonight, even minus Matt and Riley, James Keating felt cramped.

A man in Levi jeans and cowboy boots played a Martin acoustic guitar singing far better than anyone would have imagined upon first sight. Between covers of "Country Road" and "The Gambler," he mixed in a few originals and dug for the crowd's soft spot with some traditional Irish. The volume on the amplifier was proportional to the crowd, smoothly drowning one another out. Keating only heard a ringing in his ears.

"What now?" Keating asked.

"It's over, buddy."

Jim knew Connelly actually meant it. He was out. There was no picture, no red circle, no enigma, and certainly no boat accident. His friend could have walked out of the bar room without another thought about Jack Taft. Keating had to reel him in immediately. "You think he picked that fight with you for no reason?" Keating searched the bar for the right words staring aimlessly between twentysomething women in the requisite groups of four and the locals fighting gravity with every swig of their now warm beer. "C'mon Dave. The smartest guy we've ever met walks up to you and challenges you to a frickin' debate and then goes off sailing alone where no one can find him or his boat, and you think he didn't want you on the job. You've got nothing to do and a 140 IQ. I think it's possible you have some responsibility here."

"No. I don't." Connelly looked quickly over his shoulder, dropping his arm in the same fluid movement, and set his pint on the table in front of him. "I gotta hang a rat. When I get back from the hoop, this is over."

Keating could not deny he needed this search in his life, and without Connelly he'd never get Riley or Matt in the game. More importantly, he'd never get anything done. Hell, Smith was book smart and Shaunessy was a terrific foot soldier, but without Dave, the task felt Sisyphean.

Keating took the last pull of his pint as a brunette waitress named Dakota set a full one on the table. Her parents had done her no favors. They had to be excited she'd currently dodged pole dancing, but destiny cried for that to change. A girl could score double eights on the SAT, have the drive of Joan de Pucelle and the social awareness of a boatful of Greenpeacers, but if her parents named her Dakota, she'd be clearing two tops or showing them. Cowboy boots launched into "Dead or Alive," and within six bars, everyone knew the soloist would pull it off.

Dave returned from the men's room and immediately began an impromptu oration. "All right, so *Cardenio* is believed to be one of Shakespeare's lost plays. There seems to be debate about whether or not Shakespeare wrote it, but it's certain that he got credit for it. More likely that a dude named Fletcher did the bulk of the work. The play appears in the Stationers' Register, where all plays were reviewed by the Master of the Revels. All this happened before the First Folio was published and before Shakespeare died. The name *Cardenio* and theme for the play most likely come from Miguel Cervantes's more well-known book, *Don Quixote*.

"I figure we have three definite possibilities. One is pretty easy. Jack felt the end of life creeping in and drew a line between himself and Quixote. He used *Cardenio* as the link between himself as a professor of Shakespeare and Cervantes's knight-errant. If he looked at himself against the knight of the mirrors, he may have felt like a failure as a father. That would explain writing *Cardenio* on the back of the picture of his daughter. Maybe he got so caught up in his professional life he felt like the delusional knight who would never again find his Dulcinea. His professional aspirations led to his personal failure.

"The guy also spent his entire life researching Shakespeare, who as a matter of fact, died on the same day as Cervantes. If they're dying at the same time, then they're writing at the same time. He could have found some link between the two authors maybe leading him to some profound discovery about the play *Cardenio*. If we can figure out what that is, maybe we're supposed to pass it on to his daughter as some sort of dying gift to her."

"And you knew all of this?" Keating barely got the words out of his mouth, shocked by Connelly's inexplicable lecture through obscurity.

"Googled it in the can."

"All that?"

"Everything except details from *Don Quixote*. Always felt

an affinity with that crazy bastard, so I've read it more than once."

Keating thought about taking a full-on Ultimate Fighting Championship swing at Dave but decided to conserve the energy. "What's the third possibility? You said three. That's only two."

"Oh, yeah. It is also possible that I've had thirty-five pints of the deliciousness and zero idea what I'm talking about. Either way, we need to go see his department head. Find out if he was"—Connelly let out a massive belch—"working on any relevant projects."

9
CHAPTER

Riley stumbled across his front yard, nearly navigating the turn into his front walk. If not for a few festering annuals he stomped toward the end of his ninety-degree high-wire act, the entire effort would have been a staggering success. His modest house on the Glastonbury / East Hartford border reminded him that the gentleman who coined the phrase "money doesn't buy happiness" was either completely loaded or a complete idiot. Riley would have purchased the map, the magnifying glass, the compass, and the scope, perhaps even the cartographer, and found his way to happiness if his bank account allowed. He knew it. Unlike Connelly, Riley actually worked. Unfortunately, everything became more and more difficult as he floated away from those high school glory days. Like the Pioneer anomaly, it would take some time to figure why he'd drifted off course.

He'd married the homecoming queen, and each day since their wedding, he felt more certain the coronation was the highlight of her life, as neither of them quite lived up to their reputation in high school. Sharon, a cheerleader, had beat out an 800-meter runner from the track team and a center midfielder on the girls' soccer squad to reign over the homecoming court. These days, as she bounced from one diet fad to the next through her late twenties and early thirties, Riley occasionally wondered if he shouldn't have dated the track star. In all honesty, he would have hardly noticed the extra thirty pounds if not for Sharon's own severe self-loathing. Her mental change far outweighed the physical, and rather than suggesting professional help, Riley drank. It suited him.

"Think you could have made any more noise on the way in?" she said as he entered the bedroom.

"No question."

"How many nights have you come home drunk this month?"

"I just said no question, and clearly it's your job to creep tack of how much I drink. Pretty sure that's the agreement." Riley didn't want to fight. He was too damn tired, but he didn't want to stand there and take it either.

"How the hell are we supposed to have kids?"

"Piles of sex?"

"You know what I mean. We've been married for six years, and you still act like you're in high school. Four nights a week you're out getting hammered with your buddies. Three nights a week you coach at the club, which leaves zero nights for you to act like you're married."

In all honesty, he didn't mind the fire. It made him feel as if she still cared, and the possibility endured that he was someone worth caring about. At least in her anger he saw some passion, allowing him a glimpse of the woman he'd married. He only wished she would see the same person. "Really don't want to fight."

"Then make better decisions."

"You know we went to a funeral tonight, right?"

"Yeah, the funeral of someone you've never mentioned in your adult life. Not sure you were overcome with the tragedy of it all. I'm going to bed."

"Sounds good."

"You're going to the couch, buddy. I actually work in the mornings, and I'm not about to listen to you snoring all night."

Cursed with a lousy memory upon drinking more than five or six beers, Riley introduced a habit into his evening routine applicable any time he fought with Sharon over his drinking. Far too many nights ended with verbal pugilism, and almost as many mornings began with a rundown of his immature, inebriated, incomprehensible, incoherent rants from the night before—all adjectives she mixed in on a regular basis. Eventually, he decided he couldn't possibly win an argument in the morning if he didn't remember the evening. So, he started taking notes. As soon as she walked away, he would scribble down some thought or idea to keep himself prepared for the morning rounds.

She threatened divorce. "Well, you were the one talking about divorce last night, not me."

She accused me of cheating. "I don't mind you criticizing me over the fact that I drank too much, but if you don't trust me, this thing is never going to work."

The early morning battles evened out, and a few may have even gone his way. But on this night, the note favored the wife of Riley, reading simply, "Apologize in the morning and stop being an ass clown."

While the nationally ranked soccer team at Glastonbury High School may not have defined Riley Shaunessy as a person, it defined his employment. A disappointing and injury-riddled second half to his college career left a professional future just on the outskirts of pipe dream. However, towns still take care of their local legends, and his was a soccer town. Riley bought into the town's soccer complex and eventually became owner of the pro shop. While he absolutely hated that part of his job, coaching the premier teams made it all worthwhile. He believed fervently that "those who can't do, teach" was trumped in spades by "those who used to do, teach." Sharon was gone before he awoke.

The Glastonbury Soccer Complex consisted of six fields, four outdoors and two indoors. The third indoor field was transformed into a weight room and agilities facility. The push to be bigger and faster trickled down from the highest levels of athletics and pervaded youth sports as well. The removal of the third field swallowed some revenue initially when the adult night game schedule had to be trimmed down, but the club's reputation and cash flow went up, as they added a major piece to the development of the premier programs. In affluent towns, dreams of big-time sports ran as deep as Mom or Dad's pockets, and training sessions were not cheap. The big upside of all this for Riley was a venue to displace some anger.

The designers had left the playing surface intact over half the space when the area had gone through renovation. Nautilus equipment ran along one side of the open area, with free weights and racks lined neatly across the other. The beauty of the setup, according to the consultants, was in the trainer's opportunity to build functional strength. A parallel back squat of three hundred pounds indicated impressive lower body strength, especially for a young player, but what could he do after six forty-yard sprints? Riley trained more than a dozen elite athletes, and one of his favorite things to hear from any sixteen-year-old was, "That's impossible."

"Watch."

He set up an agility ladder on the turf surface six yards from one of the racks and placed a small orange disc six yards beyond the ladder. He cleared the bench and the bar, leaving the center of the rack empty and the pull-up bar accessible.

Six pull-ups are unimpressive for almost any level of athlete, but functional strength challenged that notion very quickly. Through the ladder, one foot in a hole, sprint six yards, turn, jog, and back through the ladder. Ten seconds rest and then six more pull-ups and back through the ladder. Two feet in each hole—samba, Ali, Icky shuffle, and on and on. Each round took one minute, including the rest and a long pause at the top of every pull-up.

Riley threw up for the first time after seventeen minutes. Most of the first vomit was a large hazelnut black coffee from Dunkin Donuts. He wouldn't vomit anything solid for half an hour. Even more than the bar, this was where Riley felt most comfortable—no one questioning him, no one second-guessing him, no one lying. Weights, reps, times—they all told the truth without any room for argument.

It took forty-five minutes for him to stop sweating, not forty-five minutes after the workout but forty-five minutes into it. That's when his body ran out of fluid, drained from the alcohol of the night before and the large coffee, now residing mostly in the garbage can under some other incompletely processed sewage. His one-rep bench press max remained a mystery, his high number of chins an enigma, and the leg press never held six plates on a side. But there weren't a whole lot of folks who could stick with him through what he'd just done to his muscles and his mind.

Riley felt better. He wondered how he could feel this way all the time.

10
CHAPTER

"Dakota, can I get a Diet Coke?" whispered Riley.

Keating choked on his Guinness a bit, watching the adjacent Matt Smith slap Riley in the back of his head. Connelly rolled his eyes without looking toward Riley, making it all the more difficult for Jim to swallow his beer.

"I gotta quit drinking, fellas."

Matt smacked him again.

"Christ, Riles!" Connelly shouted. "She giving you shit again, kid? People are supposed to marry what they want, not what they hope for someday. Nobody gets married intending to change the person they want to spend the rest of their life with."

"I think everyone gets married with that exact intention," said Matt. "It still sucks though, Riles."

"Yeah, well maybe it's not her."

"The fuck it isn't." Dave still wouldn't look at him.

"It's not high school anymore, dude!"

"She literally said that to you last night, didn't she? I'm not spitballing. I actually believe that word for word, she said 'It's not high school anymore.' Please tell me I'm wrong. You have to tell me I'm wrong, or I'm going to throw up." Keating honestly hoped for some sort of resistance, any kind of confrontation. He prayed to be wrong.

"Threw up twice today already." It was all Shaunessy could say.

"If I was you, Riles, that's all I'd ever do. On a more serious note, nope that's just a bad choice of words implying seriousness to anything Riley just said. Maybe if he threw up again, it would explain everything that happened in the last five minutes. One long, miserable vomit. Anyway, we have some work to do, boys." Keating took a deep breath, intending to continue, but one pause typically punched your clock with this crew and brought rebuttal.

Connelly jumped in quickly, taking ownership. "Keating won't let this thing go with Jack, so here's what I propose. Two weeks, and then we bury this nonsense for good. Riley and I learn everything we can about *Cardenio*. Since I know there isn't any text or even great evidence that there ever was a text, I know this seems a little daunting. What we need are all the angles for why Jack would have left that book in particular. I'll go talk to his department head at the school. Riley will track down anything he can find on the internet. Keating volunteered to try and check back in with Taft's daughter. He already left a message with the funeral home to get her address so he could send a note of condolence, but now he wants to go full stalker-style to try and run down anything she can provide. We good?"

Matt Smith looked confused. "Any particular reason you guys don't want me to do anything? Work is surprisingly slow right now, so I can kind of jump in wherever."

Jim sat motionless, staring at Smith in a way that left Matt slightly more bewildered. Keating couldn't hold his gaze any longer without a word, so he started, "You have to call her and—"

"No way in hell I'm doing it!"

"No choice, Smitty," Connelly chimed in. "It's over in two weeks, and we need all the help we can get."

"You might as well ask me to call Shakespeare himself and try and get some information out of him. You would have a better chance," said Matt, shaking his head.

"Guy's dead, Smitty," Riley deadpanned.

"He is. I'm not. How do you even expect me to approach her?"

"Go that way really, really fast. If anything gets in your way, turn," said Dave.

"*Better Off Dead*. Nice, Quotes. He was just talking about how he's not ... Yeah, nice usage." Keating stopped him for just a second.

"Thank you." Dave tipped his glass to the table.

"True. Well played. But, Quotes, you could have ripped off Cusack's whole speech from *The Sure Thing*. You know the one. He drives the van back from Mexico because the girl won't tutor him in English. If you tore that one down, word for word, dove into the pool, and got out of prison with very few teeth, there is still absolutely no way I would ask her for help. No way." Matt uttered the last two words with enough authority to convince no one.

"Way," said Jim. *Wayne's World*.

"I love the smell of napalm in the morning," added Dave. *Apocalypse Now*.

"Nowhere near as relevant!" said Matt.

"Victory!"

"*Vic-to-ry! Vic-to-ry! Vic-to-ry!*"

Your boys could get you to do almost anything, if they were your boys.

11
CHAPTER

Rolling his red Giant mountain bike out the front door of his apartment into the gray of the early morning and negotiating the few cement steps down to the complex loop felt gratifying to Keating in a small way. He'd last ridden his bicycle to work over a year ago, despite the fact his company endorsed a group insurance plan providing discounts for employees participating in fitness initiatives. Keating had remained thin after college but had piled on the fifteen to twenty around his midsection men his age were somehow allowed. The inequality trickled down from Hollywood, where actors needed acting skills and actresses needed hotness. No female Paul Giamatti or Steve Buscemi existed in the confines of Hollywood, and the stereotypes allowed men to carry a little extra weight without the same self-consciousness.

The first four miles consisted of typically busy roads, but the presunrise timing dictated a safe roll through town. Once off Main Street, a quiet ride of near solitude awaited him on the few miles of road ahead until he reached the bridge extending over the Connecticut River. He passed over the redundancy, never noting that Connecticut means *long river*, so the Connecticut River means the *Long River River*. Somebody screwed that one up.

He crossed into the city, weaving in and out of the few cars already within the limits before ducking into the garage. He should have felt an overwhelming appreciation for some fresh air and empty roads but instead reflected on his own anger that had recently left him shitting on the hood of a car most likely belonging to a physician. He still had a lot of growing up to do.

Keating should have hated his job, but he just never found the energy necessary to support the loathing. He'd begun as an assistant performing his work dutifully, if not enthusiastically and had then become an account manager and, finally, head of accounts. His team had dodged much of the financial meltdown as mortgage bonds and swaps were outside their field, and it certainly didn't hurt when they made a few real estate suggestions to their clients. Many folks thought it soul-sucking work, but Keating simply paid the bills.

He grabbed a polo shirt and khaki pants from his office before heading to the locker room downstairs. Shower, shave, and a quick cup of coffee from the mezzanine, and he was sitting in his chair by 7:30 a.m. His assistant, scheduled to arrive each day at 8:30 a.m., never left her chair empty past 8:00 a.m. Keating had at least twenty minutes for research. The blue power light illuminated, and he poured over Google for answers. *Cardenio.*

Connelly parked his Harley Davidson in the visitor's lot of the Wesleyan University campus and didn't feel the least bit ridiculous about it. In a rare circumstance, Connecticut's lack of a helmet law seemed righteous, as a middle-aged man carrying his motorcycle helmet under his arm across a liberal arts college would have embarrassed Dave's friends, the undergraduates, all motorcyclists, and the rest of the people on earth.

His luck doubled down this afternoon, as he walked across the campus with his brains intact after a bike ride sans helmet onto a campus with myriad coeds sans clothing. When Connelly had matriculated, flannel shirts and baggy jeans had adorned college girls from the student union to the cafeteria. On this afternoon, L.L.Bean lost the sorority pillow fight against Victoria's Secret, and Dave plowed through a campus of bare midriffs and yoga pants. He would have complained if he had an audience, but he walked on, slowly.

"Dr. Shubert, Department Chair" scratched into the glass square on the door in ubiquitous block letters let Connelly know he'd arrived at the Department of Non Sequitur, as nothing says "well-versed in the beauty and subterfuge of writing" like block letters. Dave felt a little lost in the hallway, and it suited him well. In the quantified worlds of book smart and street-smart, he never took sides, playing well for both teams. This could be the best of times and the worst of times.

"Can I help you?"

Dave had failed to notice the woman approach until she stood less than four feet away, peering over the front of her brown horn-rimmed glasses. Dave wished, like a crab, he could walk backward. She wore a gray pantsuit and a look of disdain. Dave refused to believe she wanted to help. "Looking for Dr. Shubert."

"He's finishing up class right now. And it is pronounced *Sue-bare.*'"

"That name right there on the glass? S-H-U-B-E-R-T is pronounced Sue-bare? In what country exactly?"

"Do you have an appointment?"

"No. I checked his summer office hours online and figured I'd just show up. Not sure how busy college professors get during July these days, but I thought he might spare a moment for me. I have a couple of questions about Jack Taft."

The woman's eyes dropped slowly toward the floor, but she recovered more quickly than Dave expected. "Was he a friend of yours?"

"That's a good question." Connelly thought back to their argument the last time Jack stood in the bar. "I would say, in the last days of his life, he became a friend of mine."

"Ted." She looked past Connelly's shoulder into the brief distance of the well-lit corridor, and Dave could tell she felt released from a conversation she did not wish to continue. "Ted, this gentleman has a couple of questions for you about Jack Taft."

Connelly spun to see Dr. Shubert, a man quite different than he'd expected. Ted wore a short sleeve, light blue, button-down shirt with a palm tree climbing up his left side and finishing just under his armpit. Tommy Bahama shirt, cargo shorts and flip-flops didn't scream department head, and somehow it put Connelly a little at ease. Perhaps disarmament was the point, or maybe progressive liberal arts schools just didn't give a shit.

"Ted Shubert. What can I do for you?"

Connelly reached for his outstretched hand. "Grab me a Corona?"

"Come on in." Shubert opened the door to what appeared to be a book storage closet rather than a department head's office. A laptop and empty paper tray were the only things on the surface of his desk, but the shelves were covered with all manner of collections of plays, poetry, and novels. Dave lacked the acumen to find any discernible order on the shelves, whether it was haphazard, Dewey decimal, Renaissance to modern, or by genre; he knew only that it was a lot of stuff he had never read. The feeling in his stomach was familiar.

"How did you know Jack?"

"I guess I hardly knew Jack at all. We spent a lot of time in the same bar. A few of my friends and I were the last ones to see him alive. Before he walked out of the bar for the last time, he left something for us. Then he took his boat trip." He found it difficult to maintain focus on Shubert, as his attention continued to drift to the random stacks of books on the shelves behind the professor or, for that matter, all around him in stacks on the floor. Dave needed to lock in, as he could hear himself speaking without being entirely certain of what he was saying. "I was really just wondering if you had noticed any change in Jack over the last few weeks."

"Hmm ..." Ted thought for perhaps just a moment too long, as if giving the appearance of engaging in deep thought rather than actually thinking. "No, I guess things seemed fairly normal. Of course, it was summer term, so we weren't meeting as a group with the same regularity we would during the spring and fall terms. The last time Jack and I really checked in with one another, we had a bit of a heated debate over the new blackboard videos."

"Sorry, blackboard videos?"

"Oh, of course. The blackboard website allows professors to put everything up online for the students. They can pull up syllabi or class notes. They can access their grades by putting in their student ID number. And most recently, we've added a video portal where they can watch the lectures. The idea of the video is for students to be able to see the lectures again, but obviously many of the teachers are concerned students will skip class altogether if they can simply log on and see the lecture whenever they want. Essentially, it would do away with waking up for 8:00 a.m. class. The professors are also able to block the content and allow only certain students access, so if a student misses a class, the professor could block him or her from that class video. Sorry, I'm going on a bit about something that I'm sure interests you very little. Anyway, that was our last conversation."

"So nothing about Jack struck you as odd or different the last few weeks."

"Many things odd but nothing different," responded Ted.

"OK then." Connelly pivoted and moved a half step toward the door before he remembered his last question. "Ted, what can you tell me about *Cardenio*?

"Cervantes or Shakespeare?"

"Your call."

"I'll stick with the mystery then. *Cardenio* may have been a play by Shakespeare and Fletcher. The name is a reference to a character in the first part of *Don Quixote*. The play was written into the Stationers' Register in London and ascribed to Shakespeare. That work and *Love's Labour's Won* were perhaps excluded from the First Folio or never existed at all, as there is no quarto edition of either play. A few men along the way boasted to hold a copy, most famously a fellow named Lewis Theobald, who claimed to have rewritten the play under the name, *Double Falsehood*."

Out of questions, Connelly failed to respond or move, making for an uncomfortable pause between the two men.

"Is there anything else?"

And that was what bothered Dave. He knew Taft had worked at the college for at least the last ten years and surely the department chair had paid his dues with some length of service. Why didn't Shubert care who he was or why he was there or, at the very least, inquire about the nature of his concern about *Cardenio*. Surely, the latter was esoteric enough to prompt a minutia of curiosity from an English professor. Unfortunately, Dave had nothing else. He perused the room one last time as if there were some untold story among the countless volumes, some clue or hidden surreptitious evidence waiting to untangle the story of a dead professor. Unfortunately, no such *deus ex machina* could be found.

"That's it."

12
CHAPTER

"Rosalind, Beatrice, Cleopatra, Imogen, Olivia, Lady Macbeth. What do these women of Shakespeare have in common? What is their purpose?" Jack asked his students.

"To get married?"

"It is true we see some of them married. Along those lines, is there anything in particular about those marriages that stands out, or in their courtships, or in their coexisting in any way? Look deeply, and you'll see a unifying theme in Shakespeare's coupling."

"We never really see them end well."

"Excellent. Anything else?

"Crickets, always crickets. Let's put together a bit of a biography on Rosalind since we dealt with her most recently. Tell me about her."

"She's fatherless at the beginning of the play."

"She's exiled by the Duke."

"She's a good friend."

"She's clever."

"She's far and away the strongest character in the play."

"There it is! Now we're talking. Well done. She's far and away the strongest character in the play. There are certainly instances involving language and some tangential problems where you might make a case for other characters, but Rosalind dominates the play for us in much the same way the ethereal Juliet owns her play and her Romeo, Imogen owns hers, and on down the line.

"Antony, for brief, shining stretches, has a chance to bring us close to him in Caesar. I wouldn't argue that he ever gets there, despite his opportunity, but he comes close. Will gives everyone a chance in *Julius Caesar*, as his title character hardly speaks compared to the other main players. But when you put Antony next to Cleopatra, he's a stooge. She is Egypt. He is … who knows? Adulterer, liar, deserter? The man from Stratford gives us Cleopatra on her barge so golden and beautiful we must shield our eyes from the lines, lest we be blinded. Antony bounces back and forth, never committing to his army, his love, his country, or even his own pride. In Cleopatra's presence, he is a child.

"In *As You Like It*, the play opens with Charles and Orlando demonstrating their amazing strength, the wily Orlando defeating the beastly charge in the ultimate test of manhood. The author then brings us to the forest, where one must live by the laws of nature to survive, certainly no place for a weak woman of the court. But once they arrive, and Orlando is cast against Rosalind-Ganymede, he wanders around Arden, lost in love and bad poetry, needing Rosalind to breathe life into his every move.

"And that leaves us with a nagging, unanswerable question. Among these bad poets, untrustworthy soldiers, weak kings, and music-loving dukes, why can't Shakespeare's men live up to their women?"

13
CHAPTER

Jim had hoped Connelly would have more luck with Professor Taft's colleagues at the university but was disappointed to glean no relevant information from Dave's back to school day. In the five minutes since his friend had entered the pub, he'd felt nothing but frustration. Finally, he asked in a voice that was almost a yell, "What about the key?"

"Jim, it's over man," said Riley. "Dec, you have to get homeboy to wave the white flag, extinguish the last embers in the pipe, and let go." Like water and sunlight to flora, Riley's negativity bloomed from equal parts apathy for the cause and his certainty that linking up at the pub would once again lead to a lecture from his wife. It's not that he minded the fight; he just preferred to drink his way into the fight, rather than debate his way in. When your body is used to one mode of training, one pregame warm-up, the change in routine leaves you sore.

"Smitty?" Keating asked.

"I told you I'm not talking to her." Matt never even looked at Keating. He spit out his answer and then cleansed his palate with a long pull from his glass.

"Any luck with Taft's daughter?" Connelly remained the

only one Jim could count on, if for no other reason than a wide-open schedule.

"The funeral home finally called me back, but all they had was a P.O. box for the daughter, so short of driving up to Boston and going door to door, she's no help. I guess I could stake out the post office as well, but that seems extreme. Did the guy at the college tell you anything else, Quotes?"

"I told you, pal. Not only was the guy useless, he couldn't wait to show me the door. Guessing I may have needed a little better education to hold that cat's attention." Dave shrugged his shoulders and looked to Jim for his next cue.

"So what do we have?"

"Dead guy you hardly know," the omnipresent Declan chimed in, "key to nothing, alienated daughter, a lost play, and a chance to make something right."

Keating felt a small hint of hope looking to his bartender once again for answers. He saw Connelly smirk, while Riley looked quizzically at Declan, but even Shaunessy finally understood. Matt Smith broke and bellowed, "Fuuucccckkkk!" He needed to make a phone call to his ex-wife.

"Bring that beer with you, Smitty," said Declan. "It will help wash down the pride."

Three years after graduation from Duke and just out of law school, Matt Smith enjoyed the best night of his life in lower Manhattan. For a brief gluttonous stretch a few years post-9/11 and before anyone anticipated the housing collapse, the finance industry lined a lot of pockets, trousers, suits, mattresses, and whatever else needed insulating. Anticipating the legal ramifications of the products they created, the leaders of the finance industry needed lawyers.

Matt Smith knew leasing his soul and working for these

jokers would be the equivalent of rooting for archrival North Carolina, but a two-day paid vacation in New York felt right. After what amounted to a half-dozen handshakes and cursory questioning, a small crew started piling down drinks. Matt possessed little to zero experience in the world of mortgage bonds, swaps, or tranche but was well practiced in big nights boozing.

"Jesus, look at that," one of the blue suits offered, "and damned if I didn't forget to floss."

A woman leaned over the bar less than ten feet away, and her thin red thong welcomed viewers across the room. Two long strides, and navy suit moved alongside, tapping her on the shoulder, certainly the last place he wanted to tap her. "Excuse me, Miss." She glanced back at him. "You know who won the game today?"

Matt awaited some sort of ridiculous punch line but instead witnessed true genius. Whether the woman rooted for the local ball club with unbridled fervor or didn't know a foul line from a blue line, the suit gave her instant credibility. The question was unaggressive, lacked sexual overtones, and guaranteed some sort of answer. If she spit out the score, then he had common ground, but this was even better.

"Sorry. What game?"

"Yanks were on the road today."

"I don't really follow baseball," she replied.

"Me neither. It just seemed better than, 'Can I buy you a drink?' And it felt fifty-fifty that you pulled for the Bombers."

Now she hesitated. The guy in front of her showed the bravado to approach a stranger in a bar but the confidence to distance himself from the most sacred of all male past times. He'd lied, but he was honest about it. If she did follow baseball, she would have told friends years later that her signals were crossed. "Yeah, but at least then I'd have the free drink."

"Keep the change, pal." Almost perfect. He'd misjudged the bartender's skill by a matter of seconds. In those two strides to move alongside the woman, he'd casually motioned to the bartender, pointing to the woman and giving the international signal for drink by tipping an imaginary glass to his lips. Then as she spun to answer his question about the day's game, he'd cautiously set a twenty on the bar behind her. The bartender, a little slow, was still on the move a full ten feet away from them with the woman's martini in hand, but the trick served its purpose. "I'm Steve," Blue Pinstripes offered with his outstretched hand.

His name was not Steve.

Research suggests each person experiences two real coincidences a year—only one déjà vu but two coincidences. If true, it probably didn't qualify as a coincidence when, in the very instant Matt shook his head at the magical pickup moves of the recruiter, a tall, dark haired woman walked right into his field of vision. It certainly didn't qualify as coincidence that he'd consumed just enough alcohol to seem charming and confident but not enough to ask about the club's policy on body shots. A bit lucky, Matt arrived at her table shortly after the waitress set a perfectly poured pint of Guinness on the table. And when he uttered, "They give good dome here," in reference to the foamy meniscus atop his favorite beverage, someone in the cosmic distance lost out on two coincidences.

"By far my favorite Guinness joke," she replied.

"Damn. Thought I might pass that off as my own."

"Sadly, no."

"A second chance, perhaps?" asked Matt.

"Go." And with her permission, he left his Bud bottle on the table in front of her, grabbed her pint off the surface, and slugged down half of it, his face disappearing in the glass.

"Got Guinness?" He queried through his foamy mustache. It was all or nothing now.

The six other women surrounding his future wife all focused on Matt when he reached for a cocktail napkin and, possibly, her approval.

"Two Guinness jokes seem like a lot for a guy drinking Bud bottles."

"Love the dark stuff, but it's hard to drink twenty-five of them."

"I'm not sure," she said.

"I'm not Steve," said Matt sardonically, echoing his recruiter.

At some point over the next few hours of talking, laughing, stories about not being Steve, and general inebriation, his future ex-wife Tracy mentioned she was a graduate student at New York University. She studied English literature.

"Tracy?"

"Hey, Matt. Not sure I could have been any more surprised when I saw your name show up on my phone."

Three years had passed since they'd finalized the divorce—a time span slightly longer than the marriage.

"I need a favor."

"Hey! How are you? It's been a while." Sarcasm unmistakable, she wouldn't let him off easy, despite knowing the difficulty of this phone call.

"Yeah. Not really calling to chat," he said.

"OK, Matty. What can I do?" The familiar *Matty* hurt a bit.

"A friend of mine walked into the bar the other day—"

"Where else would a friend of yours walk?" she asked.

"Trace," Matt responded contemptuously.

"Hey, you called me." Now they were both exasperated.

"Listen!" He raised his voice in a manner counterproductive

to his needs and knew it immediately. "Listen, please. He walks in and starts yelling at the boys and I about how we're sitting around all the time arguing about nonsense when we could be talking about more important things. Religion, politics, blah, blah, blah."

"I like your friend already."

"Thought you might. Here's the thing though. He walks out of the bar, and we never see him again. We get word through the bar owner he was in a sailboat accident, and he's dead. Before he walked out of the bar, he handed Keating an envelope with a key inside and a photograph of his daughter with the word *Cardenio* written on the back of it. A Google search later, we know about the lost play and the Don Quixote reference, but we're missing the context. I need to know how that particular play might be relevant to us, our last conversation, sailboats, bars, daughters, anything that might help us figure out what he wanted from us."

There was a brief pause on the other end of the line before she responded. "I really can't help you."

It was Matt's turn to hesitate. He knew well enough she owed him nothing, but she could at least differentiate between the arbitrary and the legitimate to actually pitch in and help. This was important. "Seriously? You don't owe me at least this? Shit, Tracy. You ruined my goddamn life. You're banging what's his name for a year while we're married, and I'm working eighty hours a week to pay for vacations through frickin' Italian vineyards."

"Matt," she said calmly.

"Nice waste of five soul-sucking, manhood-sapping minutes of my life."

"Matt!" It was her turn to raise her voice now. "It's not that I don't want to help you. I really can't. I'll tell you everything you want to know about shipwrecks in *The Winter's Tale* or *The*

Tempest, the bar in Eastcheap and Doll Tearsheet, or anything else that might help you with your friend. I just can't tell you about *Cardenio*. I'm not sure anyone can. No one knows much about it, other than the fact it was performed and attributed to Shakespeare, which really means nothing. A huge chunk of what we now consider to be Shakespeare was connected to him after he died. Anyone erudite enough to leave that single word for you would have known it as well. Can you think of any reason why he would leave a word with no meaning for you as a message?"

No bulb illuminated over Matt's head. He experienced no grandiose moment of clarity, but her last question was the only one he could possibly answer. Could this be the point? He left them an unanswerable question, not so they could find an answer but so they would be asking questions. "Maybe," he responded.

"Those eighty hours were my reason, Matt. It wasn't a good enough reason, but it was mine."

"Thank you for the help," he said earnestly.

"Anything you need, anytime you need it." Her phone fell silent.

14
CHAPTER

"From 1614 to 1623, the people of England felt a surge of panic derived from the threat of the Spanish Marriage Crisis. Young Prince Charles needed a bride, and England needed security in the form of an alliance with the best navy in the world. The Spanish Infanta Maria could provide the English monarchy with both if they could pull it off. What might cause a problem with such an alliance in Renaissance England?"

"Money?"

"Always a good answer, but the survey says ... *Ehhhh*! Wonderful parting gifts for playing though."

"Religion."

"That had an air of certainty to it. Wonderful. While England had its problems clinging to one definable church through this period, the general sentiment was of a Protestant persuasion and the Infanta Maria Ana of Spain, sister to Phillip IV, was a Catholic. Needless to say, this led to massive dissent among the people of England and, in particular, some brutal abuse of one Spanish ambassador.

"Despite Charles's aggressiveness in sneaking off to Spain to make the match in 1623, coincidentally the year of the publication of the First Folio, the marriage never happened. The prince and his friend George Villiers, 1st Duke of

Buckingham, returned home to England embarrassed by the futility of their efforts and promptly redirected their attention to a war on Spain.

"While the match would have made sense militarily and financially, the religious aspect never allowed it to take hold. What makes absolutely no sense whatsoever is why a prince and a duke surreptitiously fled their country under the assumed names of Thomas and John Smith to pursue a marriage with a small child.

"Why would Charles ever attempt this ridiculous act?

"Could there have been another reason for the trip?"

15
CHAPTER

Jim noticed the brick, the mortar, the arches, and many more small nuances in the craftmanship of the university buildings as he made his way across the campus. Two weeks had passed uneventfully for him and his crew, as the trail to Taft's mystery grew cold and his boys returned to their lives.

A fortnight without a fistfight set no records in Riley's marriage, but Jim knew it felt like something worth celebrating for his friend. Riley and his bride, Sharon, made dinner plans and felt brief comfort in their contract, as if maybe it wasn't always hard work. A few less nights at the pub. A little less complaining. Nothing more than a brief brush with nostalgia.

Matt felt no satisfaction from his shallow conversation with Tracy, despite Jim's efforts to convince him it was progress. Smith's feelings of betrayal and embarrassment had made good bedfellows in the weeks following his split with Tracy, giving him a little cushion between himself and the hurt. Anger naturally followed, and it was better than denial, always the longest and simplest phase. Tracy was to blame for the split. Matt knew it with great certainty, almost.

Connelly spent his time being Connelly and tried to offer Jim details of his latest debauchery, despite Keating begging him to stop. Jim read a lot of material he didn't understand and failed to move on. This was it.

"Dr. Shubert." Keating read the unintimidating block letters Dave had described and gave a slight rap on the glass.

"Come in."

"Dr. Shubert?"

"It's Sue-bare. And yes, he is me."

"My name is Jim Keating. I was wondering if I could ask you a few questions."

"Friend of Jack Taft," Shubert said, making a statement rather than asking a question.

"Yes. How would you know that?" asked Jim.

"Stock characters, Mr. Keating." The tone of his voice wasn't nearly as pretentious as the motion of his arm reaching out, palm facing up, gesturing at the volumes surrounding him in the room. "*Miles Gloriosus* you are not, but in my twenty-five years of teaching, very few adult men walk into my office pronouncing the sentence, 'May I ask you a few questions?' Until my run-ins with the law become frequent, I'll assume everyone else is a friend of Jack."

Once explained, it really was a simple deduction by the professor. Keating typically appreciated intellect, but for some reason, he felt torn between dislike and contempt for the man across the desk.

"What can I do for you?" asked Shubert.

"Two things. I'm assuming somewhere in the school there is information on Jack's next of kin or emergency contact, as well as his address. I need to contact his daughter first and go from there. If there is any personal information you could provide me with that can help me sort this thing out with Jack, I would really appreciate it." Keating knew the information he wanted should not be released to anyone who walked through the door, so he tailored his tone to convey a position of authority, where he actually had none.

"Certainly, you know better than that." Clearly, they both agreed on Jim's lack of authority, not the best of common ground. "You said there were two things."

"My friend Dave mentioned that all the lectures are videotaped and put online for the students in the class. I'd like access to Jack's lectures."

Shubert took a contemplative, deep breath and lowered his head, looking at no particular point on the emptiness of his desk. Keating stared at the recognizable horseshoe of male pattern baldness on the top of the professor's head and felt no pleasure finally finding a pattern in this mess. Instead, he observed the desk and thought of Einstein's observation: "If a cluttered desk is a sign of a cluttered mind, what is an empty desk a sign of?"

"Mr. Keating, students at this university pay upwards of $40,000 a year for their education. I cannot just grant access to an overpriced education for no particular reason. I would like to help you, but I simply can't."

Jim's frustration stemmed from so many separate channels, he couldn't be sure of exactly what prompted his current near volcanic state. If NORAD ran him, he would be at DEFCON 2. It could have been the debate with Connelly, his innate need to solve problems, the erudition of the professor, or maybe, just maybe, the face of a stranger in a funeral home, but he desperately needed to find answers. That contemplative pause kept him from tearing off Dr. Shubert's head and punting it down the hallway of higher learning.

Letting out a sigh, the professor pulled open a drawer on the lower right side of his desk. When he reached up, he set a plain manila folder on his desk and uttered in emotionless monotone, "I have a class to attend. I'm sorry I couldn't be of any help. Please close the door behind you when you leave." Then he rose from behind his desk and walked out into the hall.

Keating leaned forward over the desk and read two words on the tab of the folder, "Jack Taft."

—m—

Despite Professor Shubert's random act of kindness, Keating felt unsatisfied with what little he learned from Taft's folder. Certainly the home address he scribbled down offered a new starting point for his pet project, but he still needed more information. Ninety excruciating minutes passed slowly while he waited in the hallway of the Arts and Sciences Building, and Jim felt more and more like Ted Bundy.

He found time to run down a bagel and a cup of coffee before the class let out, and now he waited comfortably and conspicuously in position as the nineteen- to twenty-two-year-old searchers made their way down the tiled hallway. Somehow, he felt more at ease stalking a male college student than a female, but he was still weary approaching the young man as he reached the middle of the quad.

"Excuse me."

"What's up, man?" The kid wore a plain wrinkled white T-shirt and what could only be described as yellow board shorts, despite the lack of anything resembling a swimmable body of water in Middletown, Connecticut. His baseball hat shifted halfway between forward and backward, tilting as an appropriate metaphor for the motion of most college kids, halfway committed. Tufts of dark hair sprang from all sides of the hat, and Keating wondered if the kid's immediate future would lead him to a shower. Realizing he'd now imagined a college student and a shower, he relished his decision to follow a dude.

Keating, unable to manifest any plausible lie in the fecund history of untruths and misdirection, buckled down and gave the truth a shot to get this kid to help him. "Is there any chance you were in Jack Taft's class this past spring?"

"Nope. Took 288 in the fall. Probably the best class I've had here. Professor Taft was one of the few teachers I've had who explained the relevance of learning four hundred-year-old literature in the context of the modern world. It wasn't a class for appreciation. It was a class for betterment. Wesleyan will miss him."

Maybe Jim hadn't picked this kid at all. "Is there any shot your ID number would still access his lectures? I'm assuming you know Jack died recently. He was a friend of mine. I think it's possible his lectures might help me understand what happened."

"Am I on a crime scene investigations show right now?"

"Would it still work?"

"Doubt it. Maybe spring but probably not fall. Couldn't give it to you anyway, bruh. Not supposed to give our ID number to anyone. It accesses all our grades, personal information; even gets you into dorms."

The minor victory Keating experienced in Professor Shubert's office felt a bit hollow now. He knew there wouldn't be any magical answers in Taft's lectures, but he also knew they would bring him a little closer to the man from his bar. *College campuses and bars*, Keating thought to himself. *They are much more similar than different.* The man sitting alone, depressed and struggling, glazed eyes pouring into the dark omnipotence of his Scotch on the rocks had everything in common with the precocious computer whiz alone in the library late at night. The woman pulling the toothpick from the rim of her glass, feeding on olives, and staring flirtatiously past the group of men surrounding a graveyard of pint glasses, announcing themselves by the value of their watches and the brands of their tie, shared more than she knew with an eighteen-year-old filling out her first class schedule. *They are all asking questions*, Keating thought. *Who am I? Who will I be? What is my value in this place?* There are no real answers in the bottom of glass or at the podium in a lecture hall, only more questions—endless questions.

"Yo. My man. You all right there, buddy?"

"Fine."

"Listen. You got a business card or an email address? If I find anyone who can copy the lectures, I'll send them to you."

Keating handed his card to the crooked hat with a visceral knowledge he would never hear from the kid again.

16

CHAPTER

"Ted, you can't just dismiss it without thought."

"Why not, Jack? You know as well as I do the authorship question is Delia Bacon's crap derived many decades after Shakespeare's death. And she had a dog in the hunt. She didn't crack some code or unearth some truth. She just wanted Uncle Francis to be the author. There is absolutely nothing to it. Why now after all these years would you even entertain it?"

"That's our job, Ted. We look for the underlying truths in the verse. I'm sure I remember a time when Edward II dominated your life. You dug into every angle you could find to prove that Marlowe used Gaveston to mock his contemporary rival, William Shakespeare. Kit's countless uses of 'upstart' echoing Greene. *The Earl of Pembroke's Men.* Anyone could pretend to be noble the way anyone could bombast a blank verse. We've been here before, Ted!"

Shubert had waited patiently for Jack's 3:30 class to exit the room just shy of 5 p.m. He didn't want to allow Jack the home field advantage, knowing it would be easier to address him in the classroom, rather than his office. Jack was Shubert's intellectual superior in all things Shakespeare but could never match him in university politics. Living in Julius Caesar or Coriolanus, Jack would have been the first man down. He loved literature, research, and writing. The nuances of clout and obsequiousness were below his pay grade.

"Just look at the texts, Ted. Iago warns us 'I am not what I am.' Juliet tells her audience 'I am not I.' Cressida wishes herself a man so she can have the privilege of speaking first. Viola begs, 'I swear I am not that I play.' Hamlet tells Ophelia, 'God gives you one face and you make yourself another.' Ted, the damn theme is ubiquitous throughout the whole canon. No one is who she pretends to be. They're all disguised."

"Conjecture."

"What if it's not?"

"Jack, you took Philosophy 101 at some point, so you remember Aristotle's, *Nichomachean Ethics*. 'There is a difference between arguments from origin and arguments toward origin.' You're creating the context to fit your argument."

"And that's the quarrel?"

"You really think this is the work of a woman?" Shubert stared vacantly out the window without really considering the reversal. Students were supposed to lose their attention to the outdoors, not professors.

"Yes."

"Why?"

"You of all people shouldn't have to ask," said Jack exasperated.

"I'm asking."

"Jesus Christ, I can't believe I need to explain this to you. You know better than anyone that none of Shakespeare's men live up to their women. The Macbeths, Romeo and Juliet, Rosalind and Orlando. None. You can't find one. At best, you could argue that Benedict rivals Beatrice, but you know that isn't true.

"Damn, Ted, let's look at some of the strongest. Cleopatra won't disguise herself for anyone. And what happens to arguably the strongest woman in all the plays? You know it, my friend. Rosalind is right at the top of the toughest, but she's willing to disguise herself as the male Ganymede. She gets her man, resolves the conflicts, and everyone lives on, the realm back in the hands of the rightful duke. Cordelia will not cheapen herself by lying to her father about her love, even when she knows she will lose everything. She dies along with her father. Portia disguises herself; Viola will as well. Keep going down the line, Ted. To disguise yourself as a man when you're a strong woman, in Shakespeare, is not only the way to survive; it's the way to thrive. Can this be just a coincidence in over thirty plays?"

"Jack you've read these plays a thousand times. Why now? You've lectured young minds, written countless papers, chaired committees, contributed to the theater for nearly four decades, and now you decide Shakespeare didn't write Shakespeare? I don't understand. And the board most certainly isn't going to understand if you keep going off the map and teaching this craziness."

"Who gives a fuck about the board?"

"You should."

"Because of their scholarship in the world of Renaissance literature?"

"Because they will fire you."

"'You take my life when you do take the means by whereby I live,'" said Jack quoting Shylock. "Hell, it's too late to worry about that. We're old men, Ted."

"Jack, there simply is no proof."

"What if there were?"

It had never even occurred to Ted Shubert that Jack might have a secret.

17
CHAPTER

When the key moved the tumblers and the doorknob turned, Jim spared himself the suspense of opening the door slowly in horror film fashion, rather brushing it open intrepidly and crossing the threshold into Jack's loft apartment in the Old Mill. The pervasive thought filling Keating's head was simple; he knew more about Jack Taft dead than alive. He knew it remained not just possible but also likely he would never have known Jack had passed away if not for the Mohammed lecture and an envelope.

The picture of Taft's apartment loomed not as an exercise in impressionism or surrealism but paint by number. Everything looked exactly as it should—a neater, larger version of Shubert's office. Jack allowed himself the distraction of a flat screen TV on the wall running from the front door to the small porch on the far end of the apartment. Keating surmised there was no cable or satellite. The open floor plan revealed a kitchen in the far corner adjacent to the sliders with the granite peninsula protecting chef from patron. At the ninety where the stone countertop met the far wall, bookshelves began and raced the full length of the room, stopping at a reddish-brown stained wooden ladder. The ladder served as the room's centerpiece, contrasting perfectly with the apartment's former owner and meshing seamlessly with the room itself. Each evening in a knight-errant's battle against colloquialism and cliché, seventysomething Jack Taft climbed a ladder to get in bed for the short goodbye. In his lifetime, Jack slept six feet *over*, maybe eight to be exact. Perfect.

Keating's smile became a chuckle, and he stepped further into the room, observing all the four walls contained, especially Jack's lofted bed. While the room existed as a study in straight lines and sharp angles, the owner forced Jim to wander downhill toward the bookshelves. The actual physics may have proved otherwise, but those shelves created a tangible bend in space-time, and Keating tumbled under the pronounced gravity until he stood face-to-face with Jack's books. Jack read everything.

The books on the shelves were scattered in no observable order. Brian Greene's *Elegant Universe* sat next to J. K. Rowling's *Harry Potter*, making the insanity of an eleven-dimensional quilted multiverse or a preparatory school for witchcraft and wizardry seem well within the realm of possibility. *The Life of Edward II* snuggled close with *Primary Colors*, forcing the books to wish for personification so they might share anonymity with their authors. Great Britain's traditions and Spain's heritage were intertwined, as was often the case in Europe, but not quite so often in the libraries where you learn about them. The shelves displayed the look of a man's tool chest, where perhaps no one but the owner could find the three-quarter-inch socket. Keating stared into the volumes, searching for some metaphorical window into Jack's soul, finding only defenestration, as they appeared to be just a bunch of books.

Reaching the last set of shelves, the picture became only a bit clearer when he found nothing but Will. *The Complete Shakespeare, Volume 1* nestled closely with individual plays, surrounded by critics named Bloom, Jonson, Shapiro, and Bradley. On the levels below, both literally and figuratively, Jim found works by Marlowe, Kyd, Greene, Middleton, Sidney, and others. When he pulled *Shakespearean Tragedy* by A. C. Bradley from the row, Keating felt the formidable weight of both the book and Jack standing on the shoulders of the men who came before him. He thumbed through the work, stopping occasionally on the name of a play or the never-ending marginalia, realizing he'd never cared this much about anything in his life. He knew nothing of the Renaissance or the men who'd changed the way literature was written, viewed, and scrutinized over, but he had heard the word *aficionado* and knew this was it. Keating had never even bought a man a fish.

Jim may not have died in that spot without feeling pangs of hunger or need of sleep, but he drifted into such a tonic state he hardly moved when the doorknob turned. His feet never shifted and torso never swiveled; he simply looked over his right shoulder and gazed across the room at Rosalind Taft. Of course it was her, and naturally he stood in the room when Jack's daughter crossed into her own poorly written nonfiction.

"Wasn't expecting this," she said.

"I almost was."

Rosalind slowly poured into the room. Jim might have wondered how many years passed since she felt a part of her father's life or how many months had skipped by since she'd last thought of him at all. Instead, he simply stared. If asked under pain of torture, buckets of water, and a seven hundred thread count towel, he wouldn't have known exactly what he was thinking when she walked in the room.

"I guess there's no getting rid of you," she said.

"Just ask me to leave."

"So confident that I won't."

"I wouldn't call it confidence," he said.

"What then? Indifference?"

"Ha." He had not intended to laugh.

Rosalind moved forward, tossing her bag on the table and spinning a quick pirouette in the center of the room, surveying her surroundings. Jim watched her closely, knowing there must be a deep sense of longing for this woman so completely removed from her father. He wondered whether she felt fearful and unsure, carrying the load of a child deprived an irredeemable part of her adolescence or a more natural anger of abandonment.

"Where do you think he keeps the wine?"

Or neither.

His lack of any response earned him a quick, disappointed glare, most similar to his physician's countenance following the question, "How many drinks do you have per week?"

"Not sure I can do this without wine. I'll be back in ten minutes." With that, she dug her left hand into her bag, deftly grabbing her wallet and keys and then walking out the door.

Jim realized he was still staring and felt like an idiot. Gathering himself, he began viewing an invisible, destructive wrecking ball, swinging back and forth between the door and the books. He failed to take a single step in the three minutes since Rosalind left the apartment. It was a strange coincidence, and somehow not at all coincidental, that his first movement, Keating's first step back to Jack's pages, began a journey of a thousand miles … and then some.

Unbeknownst to Keating, Jack organized Shakespeare's individual plays by genre and in chronological order. As the chronology remained somewhat of a historical mystery, Professor Taft went back and forth, reworking the sequence without any real hope for knowledgeable permanence. In his last, as in most previous efforts, he'd placed *Henry VIII* alongside *Hamlet*, signaling the end of history and the beginning of high tragedy. While the comedies got all the modern theater play, Jack knew where Will did his work. It didn't matter that Jim knew nothing of this; it mattered only that he noticed the leather-bound journal resting sorely out of place between Folger copies of two plays. He cautiously pulled the journal from the shelf and let it fall open in his hands.

The ribbon dangling in the middle of the pages led Jim to a hand-drawn map of England, nothing mysterious or satisfying, just England. Keating noted towns and cities he'd heard of many times or not at all. Rivers cut through various points in the map, and small "greater than" signs pointed toward the gold accent at the top of the page. Keating guessed these represented mountains.

Jim flipped the small ribbon out of the center of the book and let his thumb flip quickly through the book, wishing for a small stick figure in the upper right corner to perform all manner of acrobatics. That would have been comfortable. Nothing about his current situation felt comfortable. If an ostentatious prep school had led him to the Ivy League, perhaps this would all have made sense, but he was ridiculously out of place in the apartment of a professor awaiting the return of his daughter and, hopefully, a decent bottle of wine. Hell, at this point Keating would have settled for a lousy bottle.

Keating finally stopped in the only place he could start. The beginning.

"Ducdame, ducdame, ducdame." The three words written on the first page.

Keating wandered through the pages, understanding little of what he read. Most of the fifteen pages he struggled through were references to the plays, specifically many of the women. But without the core knowledge of the books themselves, it was useless. It felt a bit like standing in a mechanics garage under a car on a lift with all the tools at his disposal and no idea how to repair anything but an empty gas tank.

"God damn it," said Jim, quickly replacing the journal on the shelf as Rosalind opened the door.

"What?"

"Your father gave me a damn key, and when you walked through the door, I thought I was headed for Pelican Bay," said Jim, happy no bodily fluids escaped.

"Pelican Bay is maximum security. I don't think purveyors of the English Renaissance get mixed in with the hard-hitting guys, but if they did, you'd be somebody's bitch in the first forty-eight. Hope you like red." Rosalind held the bottle up like a trophy as if she shot three under on Sunday to edge the field. "Why do I lie? I don't give a crap if you like red, especially since you don't even have glasses out yet."

"I found something."

"Wine glasses?" she asked.

"No."

"Then I don't care." She tossed her wallet and keys back into her massive shoulder bag.

"Then why are you here?"

"Someone has to be." When she finally found the right cabinet, she celebrated with a small fist pump in the air. Perhaps another championship.

"So, you were the only one in his life?" asked Jim.

"Been a long time since I was in his life," she said.

"No need to mock semantics. I can feel stupid all by myself"

"You'd let *me* control how *you* feel?"

"Any time you have three and a half minutes to spare," responded Keating.

"I found glasses."

"Score!" Keating referenced his escaping domination

much more than her having found glasses and then asked sarcastically, "Pulley Fussy '64?"

Rosalind flipped her long hair back over her left shoulder, and in that one second, Keating noticed again, but more fully this time, that it was no longer blond like the girl in the picture. He had known her immediately at the funeral home—but not physically and not geographically, as she was the one standing closest to the picture of the dead guy—but in her expression. It wasn't until she flicked her auburn hair that he realized how well that photo captured her.

"Sorry, I drink anything that's not in a box," said Rosalind.

"Hmmm. I'm inclined to disagree, on several levels. Can you really tell me why you're here?"

"You first."

"Done." After too long a pause, Keating continued, "Son. I'm still kinda young. I don't wear Adidas cuz my name ain't Run … I have no idea why I'm rapping. Perhaps, this will help." He took a long drink of the wine. "Honestly, I'm here because your father wanted me here. Something happened in the bar, forcing me to be a part of his life. And yes, now that he is dead, I know how ridiculous those words sound coming out of my mouth." Jim sniffed the wine briefly as if he cared, and more honest than Iago, he continued. "The real answer is I'm bored. I'm lonely. I wake up in the morning, and there is nothing driving me. I don't care about my paycheck, my responsibilities, my obligations, or anything outside of maybe my three best friends. I'm here because I have nothing else to do."

"Wow," she exclaimed.

"Sad, right?"

"No. Well, yes, but truthful."

Jim didn't yet know what the expression on Rosalind's face meant, but he would understand it eventually. People weren't just cliché captives of habit; they were creatures of fear as well. They were predictable; they were safe; and, for someone like Rosalind, it meant she could anticipate their words and actions before they really knew themselves. Jim pondered a look of surprise on the face of a woman who was rarely surprised.

"Your turn." For almost a full half second, Jim knew he controlled the situation as the combination of vulnerability and honesty swung the conversation in his favor. Before his newborn sense of security reached the age of a full second, his cell phone sounded off an annoying text message whistle, making him feel like a very serious seventh grader.

"Go ahead and check that. I have to pee," said Rosalind without a hint of self-consciousness. She moved across the room, not yet touching the glass of wine she'd set on the coffee table.

"Fucking board shorts," he celebrated as Rosalind peaked in the door of the bathroom, making certain she wouldn't pee in a closet. The crooked hat collegian came through for Keating, delivering to him a student identification number and password, allowing him access to Taft's lectures. Jim wasn't quite sure whether he should be honored the young man would trust him or angered he looked so harmless to be trusted with anything in the world. Most likely, the kid gave him the personal information of some ex-girlfriend or frat buddy who had done him wrong and couldn't care less if it resulted in a stack of fraudulent credit cards and the endless work that comes with restoring an identity.

Jim was in a strange place. Nothing else could describe the bizarre set of circumstances leading him to this loft apartment, with this beautiful woman and the excitement he felt having received access to what was likely the most boring thirty-nine hours of video he could possibly get his hands on. *Thirty-nine hours*, he thought. Is that why the economy is so fragile, the unions so strong, the unemployment lines so long, and each new conversation an unbearable mountain of fragments interrupted by incessant and lingering leers at a personal electronic device? Keating hypothesized that the folks who handle thermonuclear bombs or, more importantly, the guys who maybe disarm them tend to train for more than thirty-nine hours. Didn't you need ten thousand hours to become an expert in something? And there it was, a group of people lacking in expertise. College.

"You still here?" she said as she scooped the wine off the table and pulled a long quaff without the pretentiousness of swirling or sniffing. It was alcohol. Just drink it for the love of God. It helps with everything.

"Still here. I don't suppose there's any chance you followed in your father's footsteps and could break down thirteen weeks of Shakespeare lectures for me, because that would be a huge solid." Keating held his phone up in the air as if it could aid Taft's daughter in understanding exactly what the hell he was talking about.

"Sorry."

"Stop apologizing," he quipped remembering his discomfort at the funeral home and then shifted quickly, giving her no chance to respond. "So if you're not an English professor, what do you do?"

"Ah, small talk and crafty segues," she returned before finishing off the rest of her glass. "I'm an accountant."

"About as far away from your father's profession as possible?"

"You're almost a full glass behind by the way," she said, dodging Keating's observation.

"You don't have to try to get me drunk," Keating offered. "I can find my own way. Besides I prefer barley and hops to red and white." He paused in a useless effort, considering exactly who Rosalind Taft was and why she seemed both ancillary and critical in his ridiculous newfound pursuit. "Didn't want to chase the mysteries of iambic pentameter like Dad?"

He left it hanging in the air, inviting a response and hopeful she would divulge something about herself, but it remained dangling without even a nod of her head or furrowed brow acknowledging his thought. Perhaps Rosalind was just a peripheral piece in whatever game Jack posthumously played with his new friends from the bar, and Keating couldn't tell if he cared in a determined effort to win this game or in a more primal way. In either scenario, he hoped to end up on top.

"OK, then. Good chat," said Keating, disheartened.

"You're leaving?"

"Miss Taft, I can't tell if I'm bothering you, boring you, or just in your way; but this whole thing is hard enough for me to wrap my head around without adding you into the picture."

"I thought I *was* the picture," said Rosalind.

"And here we go again. Not only can I get drunk by myself, but I can feel stupid without any help either. Somehow this whole mess has turned me into an awkward teenager. I'm doing homework and sticking my foot in my mouth every time I talk to a pretty girl. Jack dumped this into our laps, and I have no idea why I care so much. But the old man left a trail, and I'll be damned if I can't find some bread crumbs."

"Fine, Jim. What do you know so far?"

18

CHAPTER

Keating, Connelly, and Smith let their conversation wander from the prospects of the Sox and Yanks to the ever-deflating economy, until Shaunessy finally wandered into the pub. Each man had completed his assignment with reluctance. But in the end, they all knew little more about Jack Taft and even less about this damn man from Stratford. The kid in the board shorts had given Jim a password but neither the lexicon nor the experience to know what the hell was happening. On the first assignment, the boys were attempting to break down *Richard II*.

"This blessed plot, this land, this England … Fuck, somebody get me a Bass Ale so I can pretend I had some idea what the hell I was watching last night. You boys gotta be kidding me that I'm doing this right now. I get that the dude walked out of the joint never to be seen again, but I can't go another night of watching this nonsense." As he sat down, Shaunessy ran his hand through his hair in a manner conveying much frustration and not enough hair. The men had watched Taft's opening lecture from the fall semester as homework for this new and monumental undertaking. Each of them had felt confused, even self-conscious as the professor rambled and ranted through the opening scenes of *Richard II*.

The modern pedagogy for collegiate Shakespearean study separates plays by those written before 1600 and the ones written after. This division remains a bit ridiculous, as dating the work is almost impossible, a chronology littered with conjecture and speculation. Common sense, and perhaps a touch of original thought, might mandate the classes be taught as Revenge in Shakespeare; Women in Shakespeare; or even by history, comedy, and tragedy. The reason comedies are staged in the theaters most often is that they are, quite simply, the easiest to understand. The tragedies are regarded as Shakespeare's high art, and the histories might just have to repeat themselves.

Jim suspected that Matt agreed wholeheartedly with Riley but left him on the ledge solo, waiting patiently for he or Connelly to chime in. Bewildered by everything happening thus far, Keating had grown no closer to a concrete understanding of why this was so important to him. Connelly took another long slug from his pint.

"C'mon, Jim. You have to give me an answer to why the hell I have to learn Shakespeare if I'm not getting college credit or at least a college girlfriend," Riley begged.

"Thought things were going better," said Connelly.

"Shut it, Quotes."

"Make me."

"Incredible comeback, but I can't dance to it." Riley half chuckled at Dave's ridiculous reply, wondering if his friend was getting a bit sleepy.

"*Dead Poet's Society*," responded Dave, clearly still alert and awake.

"What will your verse be?" Keating loved Robin Williams.

"Well played, DP."

A shallow ripple of silence fell over the group, and if not for that deep breath, someone may have stood up and simply walked away. The pub was home for Connelly, and nothing really meant enough in the way of mirth or dirge to send him out of the church pew. Despite being the fountainhead for this pursuit, Keating could have fallen off the task. Certainly Smith, the worker, may have turned his attention elsewhere if not for that one important pause holding them still.

Before Riley could get a second foot out the door and back to the welcoming arms of the normal idiocracy typically governing the bar, Declan spoke. "'The tongues of dying men enforce attention like deep harmony.'" He paused just to be sure. "'Where words are scarce they are seldom spent in vain.'" Then Declan Kelly moved on to his next pint, his next pour, his next rocks glass and away from his most recent keystone holding all things in balance for those who mattered most. The thought meant little to Declan Kelly, the reading even less. He breathed life into his bar room, providing a pulse for all who entered, even the dead men.

"Gaunt, Dec?" Dave didn't really have a question for Declan. He seemed to say it out loud just to give them a push and keep moving forward.

Shaunessy and Smith kept their eyes on Declan, perhaps waiting for him to continue or explain, but Jim turned to Connelly, knowing they were all in again.

"I had a little time to read last night." Dave said it to Jim as if it were the least important thing it the world, but for Keating it meant yet another chance to marvel at Connelly's intellect. One night of reading, and his friend could place not only the quotation but the speaker as well.

"All right, then. Who needs a pint?" Declan hollered across the room. Omnipresent.

"Dave and I could both use one." Keating looked away from Declan toward Riley and then finally leaned on Matt with a tired, perfunctory look.

"Make it four and pull up a chair if you're going to keep bullshitting us," Matt offered.

"Have to work," responded Declan.

Jim looked to Riley, honestly surprised he had not yet punched anyone in the face. Riley leaned back in his chair, a disgruntled Michelangelo, and perused the blank ceiling. *Blankness*, thought Keating. *Riley's specialty.* The quick look at Riley brought Keating back to a story Connelly had once told him.

Connelly was complaining about the sexual boredom of one of his internet conquests staring at the ceiling during sex and then shifted seamlessly, midstory, to the Sistine Chapel. "You know Michelangelo painted the chapel ceiling *bent over backward* and not lying on his back. It's a simple mistranslation of the Latin *resupinas*, and history goes down yet another trail of lies." Recalling that story in his mind, Jim marveled at Connelly's intellect once again and Riley's willingness to bend over backwards only where his friends were concerned.

"Here's all I got, kids." Connelly spoke first. "Nothing. I bet that helps. As you all hopefully know by now, he spent half the time talking about how Christopher Marlowe influenced Shakespeare's play, even though it seems the two men never met. Who knows? He spent another ten minutes talking about the history of the Henriad and quite a bit about the writer's liberties with historical accuracy. I don't think I heard one thing that helped with *Cardenio* or a pretty blond girl. Anybody else?"

"I have *Holinshed's Chronicles* in my head," said Smith.

"Does it itch? I might have a little bit of that on my sack. Thought it was my new detergent, but it could be what you have." Riley looked downward toward the greatest driving force in his anatomy.

"Glad to have you aboard, Matty. Riles you're still an idiot, but you're getting a bit funnier as I continue to drink." Connelly smiled at Shaunessy, quite possibly the highest compliment he'd ever paid him.

Raphael Holinshed, a sixteenth-century historian, published *The Chronicles of England, Scotland, and Ireland*, known less formally as *Holinshed's Chronicles*, in two separate editions of 1577 and 1587. The book serves scholars as a map and genealogy of nearly twenty kings and is most well known as one of the primary sources for many of Shakespeare's histories, as well as at least three other plays. Shakespeare took many necessary liberties with the historical record, including telescoping of time, invention of characters, and the manipulation of life and death in an effort to produce more manageable art.

"Does anyone have the smallest shred of an idea about something in the lecture that could point us in the right direction?" Dave, striving to abbreviate the amount of time and effort poured into pointless labor, got straight to it. If it was important to Keating, it was important to him, but he needed to focus on keeping Smith and Riles resolute. He didn't care if they produced one iota of evidence as long as it meant unlimited pints with his crew. He needed to come up with something relevant soon, or those two would quit, meaning a few less nights at the bar—the end of his truncated, immovable feast. "You sure there was nothing at the apartment, Jim?"

"I was interrupted," said Keating in a whisper.

"Why don't we give the apartment another shot and move on to the next lecture. We can give the boys here a night off. Sound good?"

"Sounds fucking spot on to me." Shaunessy smiled.

"Good enough. Reconvene tomorrow?"

"C'mon, Quotes. You know I can't hang out in the bar every night, brother. Let's just agree that we link up next week. You can even give me an assignment if you want." Riley could have spent every night in the bar but only if he moved out of his apartment.

"I think I have to side with Riles on this one, my man. Let's catch up next week. I got enough work piling up to keep me busy. I love a good puzzle, but I have to pay the bills too." Matt, the moderate voice of reason, was difficult to ignore.

Connelly could have goaded Riley into anything, but if Matt needed space, then he was good. It would wait a week. "As long as you never say, 'I love a good puzzle,' again."

19
CHAPTER

A teenage David Connelly slept soundly in the back of the room just five feet below the sign on the back wall: "Time will pass. Will you?"

The sign over the clock loomed as a reminder to students awaiting the ring of the bell removing them from the pain of Mrs. English's geometry class. No decision was ever reached on whether English-geometry actually qualified as an oxymoron, non sequitur, or just odd paradox, but the jury was back on the pain of a tenured teacher's tenth-grade class. The taupe walls best conveyed the mood of the room and the students who occupied it. Only a framed picture of Albert Einstein, who would have been monumentally insulted by the nonchalance presiding over his passion at the most rudimentary level, adorned the walls. If space was constantly expanding at an accelerating pace, this room was a waste in the experiment.

Mrs. English was early into her twenty-eighth year of *teaching* geometry. Running students through the highlights of each chapter for twenty painstaking minutes and leaving them on their own to complete each section's problems hardly qualified as teaching, but this was the beauty of tenure. Like the famous drawing of the princess and the old lady, students had only their own perspective to decide between beauty and ugliness. Most tenth graders chose the latter.

"Am I boring you, Mr. Connelly?"

Dave's head rested softly in his arms in the middle of the desk. The one-piece wooden desk with chair connected pleaded uselessly for one size to fit all. If the inkwell in the upper left corner were still in use, he may have occupied his time with pigtails. Of the many connections made in the history of education, desk to chair was the worst.

"Mr. Connelly?"

"Yes, Mrs. English."

"Am I boring you?"

"I think I may have answered that question even before you asked, Mrs. English."

Over the first two months of class, Dave had aced every quiz and exam. That fact alone kept him in the room on that October morning. Fair, but not equal, helped him through last period momentarily. School bored him throughout the early years of his life, as he understood more and more how little these classrooms, and many of the teachers heading them, contributed to learning.

"Very clever, David."

"Thank you."

"Perhaps you can conjure one more thought from that witty brain of yours and tell your classmates the area of the circle behind me on the board." Mrs. English was losing her patience.

He now lifted his head from his arms, exposing a blank look on his face and a deep crease in his forehead from the seam in the sleeve of his coat. "There is no circle on the board."

"Very observant. However, there is a radius of a circle. From that you should be able to answer my question."

He debated for a moment and then continued, "I need more information."

Exasperated, Mrs. English now wished he was already on his way to the office for the boredom comment. Stuck, she indulged him. "I'm certain you have all the information you need."

"I need to know if the circle is moving," Connelly said through a yawn.

By now, the rest of the class relaxed and enjoyed the brief break separating them from the inevitable problems at the end of the section. Perhaps he could drag the argument out for the remainder of the class, rendering chapter completion untenable. As the teacher-student diatribe continued, other heads rested on desks or turned toward the undeniable pull of the open windows, and indeed, time passed.

"I'm not sure how that is relevant, Mr. Connelly. I'm certain with just a few moments of your time and the tiniest bit of effort, you might be able to answer my question. Spare us all the suspense and tell us the area of the circle."

"All right. The area of the circle, if stationary, is approximately 301.6 meters squared. If it's rotating at a particularly high speed, say close to 186,000 miles per second, then theoretically, the Lorentz contraction occurs, and it's just a bit smaller than that. Any chance I could go back to sleep?"

There were twenty-eight other people in the classroom that day including Mrs. English, and none of them knew what the hell David Connelly was talking about. Intellect is a blessing and a curse, to be hated and respected depending on each person's particular perspective. Isabel Morgan's genius was appreciated greatly by her family when she interrupted her polio research, and Jonas Salk's genius was appreciated forever by the world. Not all stories work out for the betterment of humankind. Dave Connelly would go on to cure nothing outside of his own boredom. He wouldn't rescind greatness to raise a family, but he did pass it over to raise a glass. Dave would do nothing, and for quite some time.

As David walked toward the door of the vanilla classroom and out of geometrical apathy, he offered Mrs. English one last answer. "You know you should wear the clock Flava Flav style."

"I'm sorry, Mr. Connelly?"

"You know, the crazy dude from that old rap group Public Enemy that screams a lot. He wears a giant clock around his neck when he raps, or whatever the hell it is he's doing. If you wore the clock around your neck instead of hanging it on the back wall, you wouldn't have to worry about kids looking at the time. When they stared at the clock, they'd be focused on you. Just saying." Then David stepped into the hall.

"Geometry ass clown!" The shout came from behind him as he moved from the front doors of the building to the bus that transported him home each day. Getting kicked out of math class broke the monotony sufficiently, but a chance for actual teenage interaction had seemed hopeless just forty-five short minutes ago.

Connelly turned to see three members of the Glastonbury High School soccer team standing behind him, including a midfielder named Shaunessy. The team had recently won its thirty-fifth consecutive game, spanning three seasons and climbed to fifth in the USA Today High School Soccer standings. This completely arbitrary and useless ranking allowed the soccer players to exude even more bravado than usual.

"Fellas. How we doing?"

"Listen up, smart guy. If I kick you in the face at 100,000 miles per hour, what would the area of your black eye be?"

The other two cronies laughed along as if the comment were, in some small way, funny.

"Got you out of doing problems at the end of class, didn't I?"

"As a matter of fact, you didn't, jackass. English was pissed that you showed her up in class and fired a pop quiz at us. Thanks a lot," said the soccer star.

"It's a pop quiz in geometry." Condescending to high school athletes about academics is a terrible idea for a smaller kid who took the back way out of school. Connelly hesitated briefly as the three boys came toward him but fired off one good kick to his lead adversary's offspring thing before taking the beating of his life.

Soon afterward, two monumental things happened— one permanent and one temporary. David Connelly started pumping out massive amounts of push-ups each day, and Riley Shaunessy urinated blood for a week.

—ɯ—

Connelly hardly remembered the dialogue from geometry class years ago, but he never forgot his first encounter with Riley. It always made him laugh. The classroom never really suited him, though it was a necessary part of the path. Pulling into the garage at his home, he dreaded the idea of opening another of Jack Taft's lectures, despite his incessant need to learn. Something about Taft's big production felt unavoidably counterproductive. He gently placed his helmet, which he decided to don for this ride, on the handlebar of his Harley Davidson Fat Boy, smiling at 725 pounds of happiness. He never marveled at the air-cooled twin cam 103B engine or the electronic sequential port fuel injection system. He just enjoyed the breeze in his face. Neither the sensation of bearing down full throttle nor a patch of flat, open road had prompted his latest purchase; he was simply a dog with his head out the window. Placing his keys on the double hook just inside the garage door, he closed the bay and meandered into solitude.

He took three steps to the right, involuntary muscle movements, opening the stainless steel refrigerator door in a Pavlovian trance. The Budweiser can felt comfortable in his hand as he moved around the center island in the kitchen toward his living room. The granite surfaces were near reflective, and the horizontal spaces of the room were perfectly uncluttered. The walk represented a vivid, empty microcosm of his life, in which plans were most often made twelve to sixteen ounces at a time.

Meticulous and sad, Dave Connelly's home served as a fun house mirror contradicting its owner, a photo negative of the man who resided there. Too expansive for a single person, the home boasted outrageous breadth and width but little depth. There were white walls, drinking in sunlight or track light depending on the hour and deep, rich carpet repelling all stains. This home was not lived in. The first decorator had scattered color among the walls with framed modern art and worthless window dressings before receiving a check from Dave's one hand and a wave goodbye from the other. Her replacement got and sent the right message. The polar opposite of Connelly's second home, here visitors were offered a hundred thousand goodbyes.

When he sat down in the leather massage chair, stationed perfectly in the corner of the living room, his reach for the remote control felt instinctive. Connelly paused briefly, staring at the black emptiness of the flat screen mounted opposite him above the sound bar and floor speakers. Emptiness. More of the same, the shelves in the room boasted no family photos; unusual trinkets; or clever slogans about family, friends, and togetherness. This home showcased all bed and bath; there was no beyond. Dave set down the remote and readied for class.

CHAPTER 20

"Along with *Love's Labours Lost*; *The Tempest*; and, perhaps, *Cymbeline*, *A Midsummer Night's Dream* is one of the few plays without tangible source material for Shakespeare to draw upon. It is a rare example of the man from Stratford creating his own plot. Remarkably, he paints his first original work across four separate worlds, including the court of Athens; the woods, closely monitored by Titania and Oberon; a world of fairies, represented most notably by Puck; and the workmen preparing for their play within the play.

"With no direct source material for the play, there has been a great deal of speculation about the inspiration. While E. K. Chambers, among others, points to a pageant offered up for the queen by the Earl of Hertford in 1591, the general consensus leans toward a pageant at Kenilworth Castle in 1575. One of the queen's closest companions and possibly her lover, Robert Dudley, the Earl of Leicester, manifested the celebration at the newly restored castle. The eighteen-day festival was certainly the most lavish party the English countryside had ever seen. There is a problem, however. What does all this Renaissance history have to do with William Shakespeare?

"Let's back our way into this, as we've been through the

whole play now, and I'll ask the looming question … Whose dream is it anyway?"

The answers, as always, came from the front of the class.

"It was Bottom's dream." The girl in the brownnose seats, who appeared to be at least eleven years old in Connelly's estimation, began riffling through her notes. "He says, 'I have had a most rare vision. I have had a dream, past the wit of a man to say what dream it was: man is but an ass, if he go about to expound on this dream.'"

He could only see the side of the girl's face from the awkward camera angle, but he felt the sanctimony in her expression, and his feeling was jealousy. He knew the front row consisted mostly of those who applied themselves, people with a sense of urgency, people who walked across the stage and turned their tassel ready to run things. People unlike himself.

"Who is Bottom the Weaver? Hopefully we all know who he is in the play, but I'm curious to know who he represents in the play." The CliffsNotes dried up, and No Fear Shakespeare showed trepidation. "The richness of language in Shakespeare, the intellect of his heroes, the treachery of his villains, the despair of his lovers are all ultimately a vintage wine clothed in the brown bag of a director's errors. The problem with his language is not simply the inability of a modern audience to laugh at the right time; the problem lies in actually reading the plays. The great tragedy of the canon is not *Hamlet* or *Lear* but that the plays are easiest to understand when you witness a director's interpretation, another person's vision. Will layered his characters for each of us to decide on our own if they are heroic or tragic, in love or in lust, mad or wearing an antic disposition. Maybe the better part of valor is discretion, and maybe Bottom the Weaver is all of us, on a good day."

21
CHAPTER

"What's up, Dec?"

"David."

As much as Connelly loved drinks with the lads, there were days, or at least moments, when he preferred this. Sagacious bartender and devoted patron separated by the well and the wood, a wall like Tom Snout, the tinker in last night's lessons, his midsummer night's reading—space where they could maintain the barrier between them but share the stage. He could sit alone with his thoughts, still just a throat clear away from conversation with his wise friend, the stock character— an omniscient drink pourer. Choices.

Dave looked at the opposing wall below the Jameson mirror toward the bottles on the shelves. Those bottles were a scrapbook defining his misspent youth folded into a misspent adulthood and tumbling downhill into a misspent now. The Grey Goose silhouettes reminded him of a night mixed with cranberry when he first thought of the Beer Goggle application. And somehow it just occurred to him in that solitary second, he had produced his very own Golden Goose.

The tequila bottle below, bearing the name of his hermano Jose recalled an evening when Riley had invented his very own language. Unable to string together any coherent utterances, he'd muscled through just enough onomatopoetic syllables to let all the fellas know he needed the car to stop before he vomited up a gallon of Cuervo Gold into Dave's SUV. Five minutes of guttural rumblings served as the necessary precursor to curb the car just in time for a stomach cleansing. Somehow that sophomore year fight had created mutual respect, friendship, and communal liver damage.

He reminisced with red wine, recalling countless steaks eaten greedily while feigning interest in the ramblings of another Internet date relaying her life story across a pristine, white linen tablecloth. In most cases, he would have preferred watching Riley vomit. He recalled CC and Coke consumed as a high school staple, easily pilfered from his mother's liquor cabinet, where there were never less than three bottles of the stuff in his childhood home. A flask and a sixty-four-ounce bottle of soda equaled ammunition for whichever high school soirée he wandered off toward on the requisite Friday night out. The album went on and on. Jim and John were his brothers, while Midori, Galliano, and Chambord mixed well with anything for the ladies. Pour a dram out and mix it with a comical yarn. Those bottles were magic when you weren't interested in leaving the joint alone. If it were a first-person account from Connelly's liver, there may have been a pang of remorse, but Dave didn't feel that right now. He felt thirsty.

"There ya go, brother," said Declan.

"Sláinte, Dec." Connelly offered health.

"In the end, it's all you're really hoping for. And as much of it as possible."

"Dec, what do I do about Keating? He's meeting me here in half an hour, and I've got nothing for the guy. I'm all for being obsessed, but can't he be obsessed about money or strip clubs or golf? I tried with everything I had to get on board with this nonsense last night. I watched the professor's lecture and the

PBS movies and dug around online. I'm starting to think the old man was just losing it." Dave took a long pull from his pint without any interruption from his intrepid innkeeper. "I don't know what the hell they were saying, but I got four couples trying to get their shit together in the woods, and Taft is talking about pageants, a swan, and a dolphin; the First Folio; and a bunch of other shit having nothing to do with a dude with an ass head. I felt like the ass head. I don't know who the ass head is any more. Keating? Jack? Me? Bottom? I need somebody a little more versed in this shit to sort this nonsense out."

"Yet?" And that's where bartenders and psychiatrists make their living. If it's true that genius lies not in having all the right answers but in asking the right questions, then the couch and the bar are breeding grounds for genius. The alcohol helps as well.

"I'm worried that I'm a little obsessed now, too."

"Thought you might be," said the barman, looking back toward his taps.

While Declan's face didn't contort freakishly or turn a ghostly white, the inflection in his voice conveyed discernable surprise. "Holy, hell." And when Connelly turned, he understood why. Matt Smith broke the plane of the threshold two steps behind his ex-wife.

Most people have an innate sensitivity for awkward situations, able to simply turn and leave a room or look away from whatever particular struggle is happening. David Connelly was exactly not most people.

"What the fuck is this?" Connelly exclaimed.

"A pleasure to see you too, Quotes." As familiarity breed's contempt, Tracy Smith's use of the familiar nickname made Dave more contemptuous. He turned his ire to Mrs. Smith's former husband and glared at Matt in a manner demanding explanation.

"She's here to help, man."

"She could have helped over the phone because she sure wasn't a huge help fifteen months ago when I was talking you down off a ledge three times a day after she dumped your ass and took all your shit."

Matt smiled the contented grin of a man who had moved on, and whether feigned or real, he looked relaxed for the moment. "It was my fault, Dave, and we're past that. I'm pretty sure that means you should be too."

"Spoken like the battered wife you were."

"Hardly." Tracy calmly held her ground just a few feet from Dave as he leered at her one last time, before he turned back toward Declan. "Drinks for my *friends,* Declan."

"What can I get for you kids?"

"I'll take a pint, Dec, and a vodka cranberry with a lime." He recognized his mistake too late to correct it.

"Oh, we're ordering for her still?" Matt caught a break as Dave took offense before Tracy could, and his friend's anger, which had caused him problems throughout their friendship, came to the rescue for the first time.

"Sorry about that," Matt said, looking toward Tracy.

"No problem. Still my drink. I'm just going to run to the ladies' room. Try not to miss me, Quotes."

The moment belonged more to video than photograph, as a still frame would have missed the simultaneous movements in the jawlines of both Matt Smith and Declan Kelly, smirking in unison at the mocking tone of Tracy's voice. There was a time when they were all friends, but divorce, rarely the fault of one individual, created sides to be taken. When the philandering sports star is caught in a web of lies, some blame must be laid at the feet of the platinum blonde with fake everything. When a dutiful wife feels unappreciated, there is an excessive likelihood he never appreciated her. And when the magic fades, it's generally because you know all of your partner's tricks. Dave wasn't mad at Tracy. He was mad at Matt, and in fifteen seconds, he would be mad at Declan as well.

"Um, David, you'll pardon me for noticing, but didn't you say less than two minutes ago you needed someone who knows more about Shakespeare than you. I'm guessing that a teacher of high school English might be just such a person." They locked eyes like horns, before he continued. "Then again, I've been wrong before. How about a whiskey?"

"I'll take one," Matt answered.

"After bringing her in here, you better take two," said Connelly.

"Still sore, Dave?" Now Tracy almost seemed to enjoy it.

"Back already?"

"We only take a long time when we go in pairs. You're right, though, we'll take two," said Tracy.

"Nice," exclaimed Declan, "sure you want to be the odd man out, David."

"Evidently."

"How about a Crown Royal? You love that stuff."

"I'll stick with the brew."

"Small beer," mumbled Declan.

"As long as it's the reason I'm here, I don't mind saying it. Thrice he offered you the crown and thrice you refused."

Neither of them knew what the hell Tracy was talking about.

"C'mon, guys. Mark Antony? Nothing?" She reached past Dave and grabbed the two shots off the bar before Matt even noticed the pour. "This may be harder than I thought." She quickly knocked down the shot of Jameson's Irish whiskey and slid the shot glass across the bar. "Matt filled me in somewhat—"

"Gotta do better than that, buddy, if you wanted it to last," said Connelly.

"Clever," Matt replied.

"You want my help or not?"

"Go," said Connelly, still debating the Crown Royal.

"Matt let me know what was happening, but I'm not sure I know what you and Jim plan to do, or exactly what you guys want from me. I'm at least partly happy to help if it leads to the education of you knuckleheads."

"Tell us what you know about *Cardenio*," said Connelly.

"Matt already asked me that. Cardenio is a character in one of Don Quixote's adventures, but I'm not sure how it applies to you guys. He said Professor Taft taught Shakespeare. There is a record in the Stationers' Register of a play attributed to Shakespeare called *Cardenio*. I've looked into it a little more since Matt brought it up, but there really isn't anything there."

"How did the Stationers' Register work?" asked Matt. "Jack mentioned it in his lecture when he spoke about the chronology of the plays."

"All the plays performed during that period were approved by the Master of the Revels. If the play was approved, it would be listed with the Stationers' Register. It's one of the few sources for attributing some of the lesser plays to William Shakespeare. Most of them were pulled together in what's known as the First Folio. Two guys named Heminges and Condell compiled most of Shakespeare's plays, and a few that may not have been his, into one volume called *Mr. William Shakespeare's Comedies, Histories, & Tragedies*. It's generally referred to as the First Folio. There was also a man named Philip Henslowe who was a part owner of the Globe Theater, and he kept a diary, which included some of the finances and operations for the theater. Between those three things and a couple of quartos, you get William Shakespeare."

Dave's frustration, most similar to that of a child at a blackboard with chalk and no answers at hand, continued to simmer in his newfound teacher-student relationship. "Why do you say it like that? You *get* William Shakespeare."

"Well obviously, they didn't keep a computer database of writers at Barnes & Noble in 1600. One of the reasons Shakespeare is so prolific now is the massive amount of work that survived. If you read *Edward II* and *Richard II* back to back, you'd have a hard time making an argument that Shakespeare is any more important than Christopher Marlowe, but when you look at thirty plus plays, he really starts to shine. The vast majority of what we know about Shakespeare is a body of work. The details of his actual life are a little sketchy, exactly like those of all of his contemporaries."

"My head hurts," said Connelly.

"*Holinshed's Chronicles?*" asked Matt.

"Nope. It's because you're drunk most of the time." Keating approached from behind them as Declan began filling a pint. "I'm not sure I was expecting to see you in here today, Tracy." He reached halfway around her waist and kissed her on the cheek, glancing briefly at his glass filling on the bar. Jim felt the exact same way Connelly did about their good friend's ex-wife. She was partially responsible for Matt's meltdown during the last miserable stretch of their marriage and the ensuing months. Matt was mostly responsible, but he was their brother, and that meant taking the appropriate side. Keating was fine with the cursory cordiality that society demanded in situations like these. Connelly didn't give a shit.

"You sleep here, Quotes?"

"Dec doesn't let me do that."

"Anymore," offered the Irishman as he set Jim's beer on the bar. "You know, they're trying to work here, pal, so if you're just going to get hammered and distract them, go sit over at the pew."

Dave rarely lacked a reply, but the confluence of events over the last ten minutes left him a bit off balance.

"Let's all head over," he finally responded.

"Sounds fine to me." Matt watched Tracy as she moved toward the corner, but Jim studied Matt.

The wide wooden planks of the floor were likely plumb and level, but like Jack's bookshelves, there existed a palpable gravity always pulling the lads toward that far corner. Jim contemplated the conundrum of that corner booth being both destructive and necessary at the same time. His friend Matt may have been feeling the exact same thing. Every object in the universe has pull on the objects around it. That pull can be necessary or destructive. Tracy was here now, and when she set her drink on the table, nothing in the room forced the glass to slide from its fixed position and crash to the floor. She just sat down and prepared to listen. Maybe Jim's gravitational theory was a bit leaky.

"So, where are you?" Tracy asked, bringing the conversation back to the man from Stratford.

"*A Midsummer Night's Dream*." Connelly smiled.

"Happy all of a sudden?"

"I would have bet good money those four words would never escape my mouth in answer to any question. That old bastard is smiling somewhere," said Connelly.

Jim considered that Dave was secretly enjoying all this.

"An old Irish toast to Professor Taft," offered Jim. "You're either sick, or you're healthy. If you're healthy, you've got no worries. If you're sick, you're getting better, or you're getting worse."

Dave and Matt joined in knowing the lines well. "If you get better, no worries. If you're getting worse, you'll live, or you'll die. If you're living, no worries: if you die, you'll go to heaven or hell. If you're in heaven, no worries; if hell, then all your friends will be waiting for you."

"DP, you want to toast the daughter?" Matt looked away, quickly distancing himself from his nonchalant crack at Keating.

"I think I'm good."

"Anything else you want to do to her?" Connelly buried his face in his pint after asking the question.

"Sounds like you boys might be leaving out part of the story," Tracy responded, and Keating sighed with exasperation.

"DP has a crush, Tracy. It's very collegiate of him," said Connelly

"Should have said very cosmopolitan." Jim knew Connelly hated a missed opportunity when it came to movie quotations and could not resist.

"Damn it," Connelly exclaimed.

"Anyone? To Rosalind Taft?" said Matt, interrupting the asides.

"Cheers, professor," said Tracy. "No idea about the rest." She looked at her glass and took a quick drink before turning to Connelly. "What do you have for me, Dave?"

Jim felt Connelly's trepidation as he hesitated for moment before answering. Connelly needed to make a simple choice between the past and the future. No matter where the fracture in the separation of Tracy and Matt, she'd decided to help, and it was enough for now. He looked around the table, knowing she represented the last time he and his friends would consider whether or not to move forward. They might fail, but the seesaw finally tipped for good, and they were in it together, wherever the path led. Keating was thankful Dave spoke. "I took a bunch of notes last night that would probably be helpful right now, but I'm still not sure anything got me a whole lot closer to Taft or *Cardenio*. For the most part, he sifted through the play within the play. He seemed really interested in the mechanical guys. He talked about them a lot, especially Bottom as sort of a representative for all of us."

Keating chimed in next. "He also went off the map quite a bit. He talked an awful lot about the duration of the play. Kept saying eighteen days, over and over again. Does that mean anything to you?"

"Honestly, it doesn't," Tracy offered. "I know Theseus gives Hermia until the next new moon to make her decision, but I never really thought about how many days it totaled. I guess it could be eighteen. I'm not sure it's super important to the play."

Keating waited a moment for Tracy, who seemed to be rifling through a lifetime of accrued knowledge rattling in her head. It was a different shake from the one David often felt. "Well, that's one of the things that really stood out. I've watched chunks of all his lectures, and he seems to wander off course a lot. I'm certainly no expert, but he started blabbering about Queen Elizabeth, some duke or earl, and this big pageant. Seemed like kids were paying an awful lot of money to not learn about Shakespeare."

"That part actually makes sense," Tracy interrupted. "Shakespeare stole the plots for most of his plays. He used some kind of source material for pretty much all of them, regardless of genre. *A Midsummer Night's Dream* is one of the plays following original plot lines. He's referencing a pageant held for Queen Elizabeth at Kenilworth Castle by one of her favorites, a man named Robert Dudley, Earl of Leicester. There would have even been a little bit of scandal in it, as there were rumblings among the nobles that they were lovers. Even more problematic were the mysterious circumstances surrounding his wife's death."

"Mysterious circumstances?" Matt was unsure if he actually wanted to know or if he simply wanted to be a part of the conversation.

"She fell down a flight of stairs and as the years go by, people always like to create a little drama from the history. At the time, there probably wasn't much speculation, but as Renaissance England has been studied and analyzed over the years, people make a bigger deal about these things. Christopher Marlowe was a spy. Walter Raleigh was a witch. The queen took a lover. Someone else wrote Shakespeare. Most of it is just an intellectual legal pad full of scribbles."

Keating looked at Dave, figuring he was thinking the same thing, "Jack seem like a doodler to you?"

"Not even when he was four-years-old," Connelly replied.

"Well, there is certainly a historical element as well. Teaching the kids about Kenilworth would be no different than teaching them about *Holinshed's Chronicles*."

"Itchy," Matt smiled.

"Enough with that, dude," said Connelly.

"It's a point of reference for the plays. It's important." Tracy looked at the faces of the three men as she lifted her glass off the table. "It's not like you have to learn everything about Shakespeare, guys. We just need to connect a few dots."

"I'm not sure any of us can connect two dots," said Matt, exhausted. "Kenilworth Castle, *Holinshed's Chronicles*, and Christopher Marlowe only add up to one reference per sentence that none of us understand. Stupid is as stupid does."

"Yeah, he couldn't have left us clues in obscure movie quotes? He had to go English Renaissance?" asked Connelly.

"Quotations," Tracy muttered.

"What's that?" said Jim.

"Nothing. And *Forest Gump*, Matty." Tracy smirked at her ex-husband.

"Doesn't matter. He knew we could do it." Jim said it with enough conviction to satisfy them for now.

"Who was Robert Greene?" asked Connelly.

"He was a contemporary of Shakespeare. He was most famous for a short piece he wrote called *Greene's Groatsworth of Wit*, where he basically insulted Shakespeare. The paper became famous because there aren't a whole lot of historical references to William Shakespeare as a writer. It's the ultimate example of bad press is better than no press at all. Shakespeare went on to become the most famous writer ever, and his only peer review is negative. Why do you ask?"

"Jack talked about him for a while as well," said Connelly.

"That doesn't make a whole lot of sense to me," Tracy replied.

"Shit, I wish I'd brought my notes," said Dave.

"Can you send me the link to the lecture?"

"You bet."

"Great. I think it's probably best if I get out of here anyway, before I have three more of these." She sipped the last drops of pale pink liquid from the bottom of the glass, and the sound of the cubes resetting drew Jim's eyes up toward Matt. There was no black or white in Matt's expression, just gray, or Dorian Gray. Keating couldn't tell if the afternoon was making his friend old, young, happy, or sad, but there was certain change. "I'll take a look at it and connect with Matt about getting together again in a few days." The importance of what she'd said was not lost on Keating. *Getting together again*.

Matt stood up and gave her a brief hug before she walked out of the bar.

"You good, kid?" Jim asked.

"Good."

"Fucking distractions," Dave uttered.

"Gonna go ahead and say she's a little better than a

distraction on several levels, Dave." Keating wanted to grab the reigns before Matt had a chance to put down the horse.

"Not what I meant, Hammerstein Ballshaft." Dave took a long satisfying pull from the tulip-shaped glass in his hand. The expression of his face intimated a deep contemplation of the sands of time and the efforts necessary to create the ubiquitous vessel. Or, maybe he just farted. "I'm sure this is pretty big surprise to you Matty, but I don't blame her one bit, and I'm not trying to belittle you either. I'm just saying there is a pretty damn definable reason why half of all marriages fail. I don't know that Matt or Tracy Smith can really be blamed.

"If you rolled out of your cave a dozen millennia ago, I'm not sure you had a whole lot of distractions in your life. You opened your eyes, and you prayed to some sort of something that your tools were still there and your fire was still hot before you put prints in the dirt and started looking for breakfast. If you were lucky enough to find a legit Betty or Wilma, she cleaned her tooth and rolled out to go grab some twigs and berries. Shelter, fire, water, food, belonging, rinse, and repeat. If you actually lived long enough to enjoy some naked time, you were so goddamned thrilled for the ass soup, you didn't care about quality.

"Fast-forward a couple thousand to Greece or Egypt. You better believe those bitches had a far greater gripe with the '1 percent' than any of us could ever begin to understand. Can you imagine the kind of life you led if you were a bargeman on the Nile or breaking bricks at the Great Pyramids? Not a whole lot of downtime when you're in charge of the Seven Wonders of the Ancient World."

"I think I found something that makes Jack Taft interesting." Matt chuckled, knowing that almost everything made Jack interesting now.

"Matt, you checked your phone three times in the last five

minutes. We live in a world of distractions. I'm just pointing out the simple fact that it's more than remotely possible these distractions, rather than some modern human fallibility, are the root of evil between two monogamous human beings. I don't care if Lysimachus was banging Hera or Hercules, he definitely didn't watch three hours of porn on his personal device in the hours leading up. They didn't text while they were driving or email from their pillow. We've become so close to the millions of idiots far from us, it's nearly impossible to not grow farther from those close to us."

The brief contemplation following Dave's last turn of phrase broke quickly when Matt pivoted with the most reliable of tactics. "You should have said further."

"What?"

"Finding Forrester, bitch. You should have said further. Drink!"

Keating smiled at Dave. "Well, at least we know he's not still thinking about the ex-wife."

CHAPTER

When Keating stepped into the Stop and Shop off Main Street, the monotony of trivial weekly tasks felt a little more melancholy than usual, as Jack Taft's enigma provided him with much-needed distraction. As a single adult, Jim found the tediousness of grocery shopping magnified when Ramen Noodles, mac and cheese, and a side of Bud Light cans begin filling the cart. The produce section was mainly a walkway he skipped along directing him to the terminal. Jim, like every model American, made himself countless promises to eat cleaner, drink less and spin the occasional salad. Change is hard, routines comforting, and food from a package, tasty.

Dave often reminded him the grocery store is a great place to scout women, as the requisite cart is as useful a window into the soul as anything. No ring and two half pints of Ben and Jerry's made for a dangerous woman, but yoga pants, a half zip and cart full of veggies, promised a lass that would take care of herself. Was she disciplined and organized enough to bring her own *little green bags* and grab a scanner at the door? Or did she haphazardly pile frozen food on top of eggs?

As Keating made his way past the dangling bananas, a virtual totem to banana hammocks, he noticed a well-dressed woman with a basket slung over one arm and a half gallon of milk in the other. Her business suit announced seriousness, but the charcoal skirt rather than pants showed extra effort. A random shot of courage prompted Jim to try what the boys in the bar would have called *a Connelly*. He grabbed a pen from the nearby register and wrote his cell phone number on the back of his business card, despite the fact he had never seen a successful pickup in aisle thirteen—not this kind at least.

"Excuse me, Miss, do you know where I can find kale chips?"

"Sorry?"

"Kale chips? Do you know what aisle they're in?"

"No, I …" She took a quick glance at Keating's cart and shook her head, knowing this man had never eaten a kale chip in his life.

"Damn, I thought I sold it," he quipped, beating her to the crunch. "I don't even know what a kale chip is, and I only have about three minutes before I need to walk out the door. Listen, I'm six feet tall. I have all my hair and some of my abs. I'd love to tell you all about the amazing catch I would make for any woman in the greater health food aisle area, but apparently my son had some sort of masturbation incident at prep school that is well beyond the limited skills of my ex-wife. My number is on the back of this card. Don't call the number on the front. I've moved to greener pastures since that bullshit money factory tore out my soul."

"Sorry, I—"

"No need to apologize." Ad lib courtesy of Rosalind Taft. "Listen if you never call me, I doubt you'll ever regret it, but if you do, you never will. Happy shopping." Then he simply walked off.

The subtle genius of Jim's first impression involved inferential knowledge. He never said women viewed him as marriage material or that he was a terrific father, especially as he'd neither married nor fathered. He left the impression of a caring man who had run off to help his son and ex-wife with a not-so-serious problem and the attitude of a man who would approach a stranger without a care in the world about rejection. She probably wouldn't even remember what he looked like, but she would have a clear image of him—just a simple image.

He hated the idea of the lie, but the game was fixed. Approaching with a name and a number meant losing before the opening whistle. It is a society of "no." Junk mail, cold calls, scams, and plain old apathy conditioned humans to answer no without ever really thinking about the question. Spin a sign on the street corner, and you'd struggle to hand off a fistful of twenty dollar bills.

Keating stood in line behind three other shoppers not long after the woman tucked away his business card and moved on toward the powdered peanut butter and Kashi whatever. While debunking aphorisms, the boys could have torn down death and taxes easily, as so many other certainties reared up every single day. Of those universalities, waiting in line seemed to appear at almost every turn, reason enough for taking paths less traveled. As the cashier moved at a typically glacial pace, her bagger slid over to open the next lane. A fortysomething man in front of Keating moved deftly to his left, bumping Jim's cart in an effort to save himself seven minutes and race into the virgin row. Jim looked from him to the septuagenarian still waiting in line.

"Hey, pal. Why don't you let this lady hop in front of you? She was next in line."

"Still is," the man replied, only half looking back.

"And gone are the days of common courtesy." Jim sighed.

Keating could have and probably would have let it go, but when the elderly woman in the brown cardigan sweater pivoted to smile at him, he really had no choice. "No worry, young man. It will only be another moment." A monument to experience, her face expressed the look of someone who'd traveled down this road before, defeated by all the idiots who disrespected her along the way. That was enough.

The *Wheel of Fortune*-style douchebag police Rolodex began spinning in his head, encouraging his blood pressure to rise and thoughts of consequences to ebb. Moving slightly to his left alongside the cart, he considered diving onto the mini-conveyor belt of the checkout counter in massive convulsions to slow the line lurker. A cry of, "Shoplifter," would likely stunt all the lines. A simple sneeze into the man's produce might force a detour, but having used the discharge of bodily waste so recently, it felt like a third option.

Lost between stealing a frozen pizza and implementing an atomic wedgie, Keating smiled as the answer simply presented itself. When the cutter moved to the front of his cart and emptied the first item onto the counter, Jim instantly grabbed the man's groceries by the handlebars as if it were Connelly's Harley and hauled ass for Sturgis. He ripped the line cutter's shopping cart away from the cashier's aisle, turning in a mad dash toward the deli.

Keating held an early lead as two grown men dashed past a tower of Ragu and a sale-priced outdoor furniture set with a lovely double glider. Turning up aisle 15, Keating began tossing objects out of the cart as the man closed in on him, waves of embarrassment crashing down over them both as onlookers paused to observe the ruckus. Keating's pursuer continued the chase, stunned by the scene unfolding before the evening shoppers. Jim's shame stemmed from not having thought of anything better. His incredible résumé of revenge built over the years was impressive. Resorting to *the shopping cart,* as if a dance floor had opened up, felt pathetic. What next? *The cabbage patch*? *The running man*? He was slipping or, perhaps, aging.

Keating hit the brakes, spinning for a final time like a dog giving up the chase for his elusive tail. On the last turn, he gathered all the *National Geographic* he could, stood tall, and growled to let the bear in pursuit know he meant business. Lie and play dead would not have suited the situation. As expected, the man froze in his tracks, never expecting a six-foot psychopath growling at him on the fringes of the refrigeration aisle.

"What the hell are you doing?"

"Policing," came the natural retort.

"What?"

"Wherever there is trouble, wherever there is someone in need," he was shouting now. "Wherever there is a douchebag cutting in front of a senior citizen in line, I will grab a shopping cart and run." Keating rolled the cart toward the man, but it made the usual, uncontrollable U-turn off the rotating front wheels and detoured toward the glass doors.

With more bewilderment than anger, the man pulled the handlebars toward him like a warm blanket, separating him from this chilly, bizarre encounter with the boogeyman of checkout line 12. Paper or plastic, motherfucker?

Jim moved toward the door abandoning the dozen or so groceries in his cart two hundred feet away, avoiding any unnecessary explanations for the store manager.

As he turned his back on yet another Sherriff of Nottingham, the charcoal suit maintained a glazed look, stupefied, and unable to continue into the adjacent paper aisle. Trash bags dangled as the penultimate item on her meticulous list. She reached only an inch or two into her pocketbook, where she'd stored his number and pulled the card out between her thumb and forefinger. The card stock made a metaphorical impression in her hand, and she noticed the quality of it in the way women in charcoal suits always notice quality. She knew, as we all know, that experience is a great teacher, and while *shopping cart man* wasn't a familiar type, *crazy* certainly was.

Experience is a great teacher … and we are all terrible students. She tucked the card into the front pocket of her jacket, now knowing, as Jack Taft knew, there might be more to Jim Keating.

23
CHAPTER

"Why does Mercutio have to die?"

"Honor."

"And what is honor to Mercutio? Does it mean the same thing to him that it means to people now? Please keep in mind that young Mercutio is fourteen or fifteen years old."

"Honor is defending his boy."

"Perhaps. Perhaps he is defending his boy, although his boy is 'dead'! 'Stabbed with a white wench's black eye; run through the ear with a love song.' Let's try this another way. Is Mercutio for love?"

"No way."

"How do you know?"

"He tells us. He says his bickering with Romeo is better than love. 'This driveling love is like a great natural that runs lolling up and down to hide his bauble in a hole.' Guessing based on most of the additional reading that may be a pun."

"What is Mercutio's dream?"

"That dreamers often lie."

"Well done. And who is Queen Mab?"

"A faerie."

"Cheater! Ha. Coming off *Midsummer*, that's too easy. Who is she? What is her purpose?"

"She makes people dream of love."

"And drives over a soldier's neck, 'And then dreams he of cutting foreign throats, of breaches, ambuscadoes, Spanish blades—'"

"And presses maids when they lie on their backs."

"Yes she does. Queen Mab leads us to whimsy, to love, to frivolity, and Mercutio leads us to ..."

"The truth?"

"Ah, yes. The skeptic I seek. So I ask again, why must Mercutio die? Come on, people. Someone will hazard a guess, or I'll make you read *The Comedy of Errors*. Don't make me do that! Please don't force me into bad Shakespeare when there is so much—"

"He'll take over the play."

"Why?"

"Bros before hos?"

"Now that you have dis-ingratiated yourself to every female in this classroom, I will tell you that you are absolutely correct. Mercutio must be removed from the play so Romeo and Juliet can be Romeo and Juliet. The author has absolutely no desire to send him on his way but has no choice. He even removes him from the fray and leaves it to our imagination, as the mercurial Mercutio dies offstage, one of the author's greatest compliments. Our fourteen-year-old Capulet may teach torches to burn bright, but Mercutio burns hotter. The man from Stratford must dispose of Mercutio before he takes over the play. The honorable warrior is dispatched, as he is so often within the canon. Before Mercutio can shuffle off, he must fire off one more insult at his friend. What does he tell him?"

"A plague on your houses."

"True, but what does he call him?

"Just when we were getting so close. Oh well. 'O calm dishonourable vile submission.' This death is dishonorable, the situation is dishonorable, and Romeo is dishonorable. And I broach this because I ask you, What is honor to William Shakespeare in 1595? Why must Queen Mab drive over the soldier's neck and make him dream of cutting throats? Soldiers, Spanish blades, and honor for the son of a glover? Oh courteous Tybalt is three times honourable, along with Mercutio. These boys are 'honor' to at least some degree, and honor usually dies in Shakespeare. Whether the characters are truly gallant like Hotspur, who dies for his father and country, or Laertes, who dies for his sister, they must die. The ironically honest and honorable, such as Iago and Brutus, shuffle off also, as there is no place for true or false honor in Shakespeare. The author is so obsessed with honor and the death of it that his greatest character in all the plays mocks it at every turn. We will need to examine why."

When the doorbell rang, disrupting his lecture, Keating knew for certain that pizza was better than grocery shopping.

24
CHAPTER

Riley Shaunessy slammed his laptop shut when the door opened behind him. He made his best effort to float away from the breakfast bar along the edge of his kitchen without a sudden movement, but Sharon, a secret service agent scanning a crowd with an informed eye, knew exactly when her husband was suspicious.

"Jesus Christ, Riley, it's just past dinnertime. You can't wait until I go to bed to surf the porn sites. I thought you're supposed to lose some of that drive as you get older."

"Maybe I was just fanning flames, awaiting your arrival."

"Ha. What flames? Unless you knocked back a twelve rack and plan on humping my leg like you normally do in your drunken stupors, I doubt the friction fire was for me."

"Mood killer." Riley moved the five steps across the room to the bathroom as Sharon deposited her bag on the edge of the bar. Not one for internet gratification, she did feel a tinge of curiosity as to what new website had caught her husband's attention. A small part of her flinched momentarily, as ridiculous bondage or Asian three-ways would have freaked her out a little, but the large part of her flipped open the computer.

"What the fuck is this?" If the bathroom door had been

supplanted from a missile silo launch facility, Riley would have heard her loud and clear.

Instinct led her down a short path from college website to college social media to a twenty-year-old sorority girl on the other end of her husband's internet connection, without even really considering other ends of him she may have been on.

Riley, on the other Holy palmer, didn't mind this situation at all, even stalling a bit, rinsing up slowly before exiting the bathroom onto high ground. He didn't really want to talk about Shakespeare and the limitless frustration of trying to understand what amounted to a completely foreign language, but climbing up that high road from porn to Renaissance literature, he wasn't feeling quite so embarrassed.

"What the fuck is what?" he asked.

"This! Why are you downloading videos from a college webcam? That's messed up even for you, Riley." Her exasperation grew, which had seemed impossible only seconds ago as he'd delayed again enjoying the ambiguity a bit too much.

"All right, all right, relax, Sharon. Grab yourself a glass of vino and plop down on the couch. It's not a long story, but it's at least a medium one. And since I don't think I'll end up in trouble at the end of it, I may stretch it out a bit."

"Open a bottle, please." She immediately relaxed, knowing her husband always thought he was in trouble. If he was this confident, she assumed he would offer a reasonable explanation.

Riley started his story with Jack Taft, the argument with Connelly, and the enigmatic note left behind for Keating. Clear and forthright about his own reticence in embarking on this little project, he also made clear Keating's desire to solve Taft's riddle. He mentioned the daughter, the department head, and even Tracy Smith—as well as his ridiculous attempts to understand *Henry VI* and *A Midsummer Night's Dream*. He glanced once at his wife's wine, noticing that he could have finished off most of a bottle of red in the time it took Sharon to finish half a glass. He wondered if that was her problem or his.

"Why did you slam the computer shut when I walked in?" she asked.

"Because I don't know a damn thing about *Romeo and Juliet*, and it seems like there are quite a few nineteen-year-olds who have their arms wrapped around it pretty tight."

"It's a love story, Riley." At least she smiled.

"I'm not so sure."

"What do you mean?"

"All right, I'm gonna sound like an idiot no matter what, because I'm a muscle head talking about Shakespeare. but the professor doesn't make it sound like a love story. He keeps referring to it as farcical, which got me fired up because I knew what that word meant. He started talking about this one speech Juliet gives, which I guess is pretty famous, because she says, 'if love be blind,' and most people recognize that expression. Anyway, apparently she used the words *night* and *black* like twenty times, and he makes the case that, once you say something that often, it becomes ironic; and Shakespeare's plays are filled with irony. Had to look that one up.

"Then he talks about all the sexual innuendo in the play, another word I had to look up. Would a love story about two kids be filled with references to cocks and pussies?" He paused recognizing the expression on Sharon's face. "OK, he says genitalia, but I'm less comfortable saying it that way. Pricks and shafts and pears and nothings all equal penis and vagina. Finally, he said it's only natural that Juliet dies by the blade, a symbol for male genitalia and Romeo dies by the cup, meaning the vagina. It just didn't sound like a love story anymore."

As he finished, Sharon drank the remainder of her wine in one full gulp, thinking how her husband really could dominate in the gym. Despite all his peccadillos, when he finished a lift or a run and ripped his shirt off, his biceps were still worth a glance. In his arms, she often saw the man she'd married—tough as hell; strong as an ox; and in all likelihood, at his best in high school. Those muscles made her want him occasionally. This was different. He sat before her vulnerable, self-deprecating, and surprisingly articulate in his ability to explain star-crossed lovers to her in a way her high school English teacher had never seen it.

"It seems like you know a little more about it than you're letting on." Her eyes looked greedy.

"Oh, Jack Taft I can understand. But that dude from Stratford, as he seems to call him all the time, I don't know what the hell he's talking about."

"I'm just happy you weren't on a sorority webcam."

"Never." Riley smiled. "Never before you go to bed."

"Very funny. So you finally found a reason to go that stupid bar other than alcoholism. Hard to believe a dead English professor could have that kind of influence on four children." It wasn't that she smiled at him. Her entire facial expression belonged to a time a decade old at least. A small glint in her eye and a pervasive feel of satisfaction elicited his response.

"Three children," Riley smiled. "Smitty still has his shit together even after the divorce. Can't make much of a case for the rest of us. Dec, maybe. However, we are usually under the influence."

"I'm just glad you guys finally found something to entertain yourselves other than movie quotes and supermodels."

"Son of a bitch if Taft didn't say the same damn thing," Riley replied.

"Smart guy."

"Smartest I've ever met anyway. Funny too, because I kind of feel like Dave took his ass down. Don't mean to trample on … well you know. But he went after Quotes, and my boy went punch for punch with old Ivy."

"Well, I'm just glad he has you drunkards thinking a little. I didn't even know it was possible." Sharon slid her empty glass toward the middle of the coffee table and leaned in closer to her husband.

CHAPTER 25

Tracy Smith toggled through chunks of Taft's lectures on *Richard II* and *A Midsummer Night's Dream*, reaching for absolute certainty she would be out ahead of the boys when they convened again. Keating meandered through the musings of Mercutio, while Shaunessy stumbled on, and Matt Smith's former betrothed caught up quickly. By the time Jack began speaking of "Juliet's play," Tracy felt her feet on familiar ground.

While reading the tragedy of *Romeo and Juliet* as a story of star-crossed lovers is completely enjoyable, the erudite know it more as a story of a young girl. Even if all the signs along the way are missed, Shakespeare hands it over with more than allegory in the final heroic couplet: "For never was a story of more woe, than this of Juliet and her Romeo." The young girl possesses both the story and the boy in the final lines. If it were a story of Romeo and his Juliet, the hero probably wouldn't be head over heels for Rosaline in the early parts of the play. When she is "too fair, too wise," she is also too *not Juliet.* Tracy loved this story of a young girl.

She squinted at the screen, rubbing her thumb and forefinger up the bridge of her nose and pushing her tortoise shell glasses up toward her forehead. Her brown hair hung over her shoulder covering the *U* on the front of her NYU sweatshirt. The last twenty minutes of film were a very good high school English class, nothing more. She imagined herself standing in front of a classroom full of fifth-semester English majors, chattering away, making arguments for a golden age of bygone genius, and warning them of the perils in this time of instant information and gratification. She briefly lost herself in the office of the home she and Matt had built together, wondering if anyone ever lives without regret.

Returning home for the first time after the divorce, she'd immediately felt small in the enormity of a house meant for a family. Square footage and the number of bathrooms had never bothered her in the less-than-palatial home, but the emptiness, not only of living without Matt but also of the absence of the family he'd always promised made her feel small. It was the first time Tracy had ever felt small. Life in New York City as an NYU undergraduate had taught her the art of invisibility, but she'd never made it her medium.

Suburban living suited her well, and teaching in schools with the most resources left no pang of regret. Students are challenged individually, while they are taught collectively; and she felt educators who miss this simple fact seldom have the ability to educate. The beauty of arts and humanities exists in the lack of right answers. Physics problems have one answer; they don't have ten, as any string theorist can explain. So if there is no right answer, then there is always a better answer. It naturally followed in her classroom that, if a better answer existed, so did a challenge for any student seeking to find it. Tracy liked to challenge her students.

"What does the author know of arranged marriages and the dreams of teenage girls? This is, after all, a play filled with dreams. Romeo dreamt a dream tonight. We've already discussed Mercutio's dream, Queen Mab, soldier's dreams, and courtier's dreams. And when young Juliet is asked about her disposition for marriage she tells us, "It is an honour I dream not of." Soldiers, courtiers, and the arranged marriages of teenage girls are unusual topics for a young playwright with little education still new to the scene in 1595."

—w—

She'd missed it at first skimming through the *Midsummer* lecture, but she knew he went on about Kenilworth Castle a little too long. Robert Dudley and Queen Elizabeth were relevant but not necessary. She closed the video window on the screen and hammered on the link for February 6.

A mermaid on a dolphin's back. Eighteen days in the play and eighteen days at Kenilworth. The rude seas grew civil at her song. The professor went on about John of Gaunt, Henry IV, and a girl who thrived after an arranged marriage at the age of sixteen.

A welcome breeze blew through the screen in the window and split the stickiness of the humid August air as Tracy listened again and again. The man from Stratford. The author. The Bard. Jack hardly ever said it—*William Shakespeare*.

—w—

"Matt, is there any chance I can meet up with you guys tomorrow?"

More than a year had passed since the house had suggested emptiness to her; it simply continued to be home. The vacant space along horizontal surfaces where picture frames once stood breathing life into the house were long since dusted and the hints removed. Closets once crammed with too many shoes, coats, and cardboard boxes cried uselessly, needing anything meant for the back of closets. They'd never decorated together. Tracy would have loved the chance to put *their* stamp on any part of the house. In the untenable dream world, they may have scoured a Pottery Barn or a Pier One, and perhaps if they'd just started on one project together, it may have saved them.

She always respected Matt's work and the passion he brought to every assignment. The difficulty proliferated in witnessing his relentlessness when it came to his office and then rarely seeing it when it came to his home, or its other occupant. She could have survived laziness, but to live with his tenacity and have no part in it pushed her out. This little scavenger hunt represented a last best chance to play a role.

Connelly switched on his computer overloaded with best intentions and, of course, found a road paved to hell. There were only three mouse clicks and half a dozen keystrokes between him and *Romeo and Juliet*. But *Tinder, Match*, and several less reputable web sites were also just a few strokes away. Dave had never fished in a barrel before internet dating, but afterward, he knew he would love it. He wondered often and aloud if connection sites like these were invented just for him. Midthirties with piles of money formed a simple equation never to be dateless again. These were dating web sites to him, not relationship ones. Maybe twentysomething anglers fished around for love and marriage, but Dave preferred catch and release, knowing Chunk or One-Eyed Willy from *Goonies* could have killed it on the Internet scene as long as they sailed a pirate ship filled with gold. The single greatest indicator for number of hits a man receives on a dating site is an income over $100,000. He was confident his own one-eyed guy would find success.

26
CHAPTER

Tracy entered the bar before Matt, and this concerned her on several levels. First and foremost, she had always wondered if Matt ever lost a race to the bar. She also considered her anxiousness, her motives, and the end results of spending time with a man she still loved. She also felt some intellective fear of a terrible joke where *an ex-wife walks into a bar.* Reminding herself to focus on one complex problem at a time, she took a deep breath and the first swing.

"Excited about this little project?" Declan couldn't tell if he'd tried intentionally to make her uncomfortable or if he'd completely lost the ability to play nice.

"And so it begins."

"Sorry. Couldn't resist. What can I get for you?" Perhaps the former.

"Just a Diet Coke."

"Get out." Declan pointed to the door, turned, and walked back into the kitchen. Maybe both.

She looked around the emptiness of the pub, not knowing what had just happened or how the hell she ended up here. The flags, Guinness posters, dartboard, and feel of the room seemed in line with every other Irish pub Tracy had visited in her life, and there were a few. But taking it in thoroughly, she observed the difference. It was the cleanliness and meticulousness of every corner of the room, so easily discernable—almost every corner.

"Should be just another minute." Dave's voice came from his usual spot, laid out parallel to the ground in his pew, surprising Tracy, who'd missed him in her initial scan of the bar room. "He texted me to say he was running a little late. Dec was kidding by the way. He does that every time someone orders a soda. He figures if he walks away and you're still here when he comes back out of the kitchen, you're determined enough to drink soda. If you leave, screw you. And if you change your order, he makes an extra buck. Don't worry about it, but make sure you don't leave. Too much on the line."

In Tracy's mind, Dave managed to hover perfectly on the edge of uselessness and genius, an *event horizontal*, never fully committed to one side or the other, suspended infinitely.

Dave began climbing vertically, and Tracy couldn't decide if that made her feel better or worse.

"You had to sleep here," she said.

"I did. Dec broke his rule for me. I'll be honest, I would have been fine on my own, but that girl was crazy. And I don't mean crazy in a twenty-selfies-a-minute way. I mean she masturbates to Lifetime original movies when the crazy wife," Dave gesticulated making air quotes above his disheveled head, "kills the crazy babysitter, so she can move on with the surprisingly normal and unaware husband."

"New shoe brand." Tracy sighed

"Still drunk. What?" Dave inquired.

"Sorry. Air Quotes." Now it was Tracy's turn to make them. "If you were some sort of ridiculous athlete, then Air Quotes could be the shoe brand." Funny how obvious the joke was, but the boys never got there.

"You kind of skipped over the part of my story with the crazy girl," said Connelly.

"This was intentional, and maybe you should have skipped that part as well."

"I haven't decided yet."

"Oh dear, David."

"Dec," Connelly shouted with guttural violence.

"Yes."

Declan startled Tracy, standing two feet behind her with a Diet Coke and merciless grin.

"Shit!"

"Quite correct, young lady. Diet Coke is shit, but I didn't order the damned thing, so drink it or throw it out the window. I don't care. Just make sure you pay for it." He shifted his stance and smiled in Dave's direction. "Mr. Connelly?"

"How's your five-hole?"

"Delicious," said Declan.

"Jesus, I could use a rabbit hole," Tracy mumbled.

"You're in it, Alice," said Declan. "Now saddle up; it's almost teatime, and you are the guest of honor. Glad you're not late."

Tracy felt naked, exposed among the professionals, the regulars of the joint. She was embarrassed, but at the same time, she knew and appreciated herself because they needed her. She felt value knowing they couldn't do it without her. *Naked is good*, she thought, *even if it's naked in a bar before noon.*

"So this crazy girl took her clothes off in my car on the way to dinner."

Naked is bad, she thought, as Dave pressed on.

"I know that I'm charming, but normally they take their clothes off on the way *home* from dinner. I honestly panicked that I was on some sort of a hooker site by accident—"

"Of course by accident." She smiled.

"Hell of an effort, Tracy, but we really live in a world where it is morally reprehensible to pay for sex anymore. And I don't mean in a holy sort of way. I mean it's so ridiculously accessible, the waste of money is totally unforgivable. I can't even begin to tell you the number of—"

"Got it! Reprehensible. No need to—"

"Kids." Matt Smith walked in the door well short of his hundred thousandth welcome and beyond the notice of the two reluctant conversationalists.

"Thank God I didn't have to hear the number." Tracy took two steps and fell gently into Matt's arms in a manner that was both too familiar and too uncertain for either of them to judge fully.

"What number?" Matt asked.

"You'll never want to know the answer to that question," Tracy returned.

"No, I was just telling Tracy that internet sluts represent the craziest kind of—"

"Bartender!" yelled Matt.

"Oh stop it, Matty. You know you love the deetz, bitch." Connelly said it almost thoughtlessly, yawning and scratching his head.

"The deetz?" Matt removed his suit coat and settled into the bench adjacent to Connelly without really thinking enough about Tracy still standing in the middle of the room. "Did you join a boy band and not tell me?"

"Legit question. And I'm honestly not sure about the answer. I'm positive that (a) I got crushed out like I was in a boy band last night, (2) I'm worried that the crazy girl who serviced me knows where I live, and (Roman numeral three) I passed out in the green room. Dec, do I have to play music to be in a boy band?"

Declan, always there with a pint. "Just before you passed

out you settled into my bagpipes nicely, so I would say yes, and you're a hell of a player." He deposited the glass on the table with a quick tilt that allowed the foamy top layer to pour over the side a bit. Dave knew passing out in the bar came with consequences.

For the moment, Tracy liked Declan the most. "When are the other guys getting here?"

"This is it, Tracy. Keating tried to skip a lunch meeting, and Riles runs workouts all afternoon in the summertime. Jim wanted to be here, and Riley is pretty happy to have workouts. Let's hear what you've got." Matt knew that the guts, heart, and mind of a human being are separate, stubborn entities engaged in a battle royal. He knew it because his heart spoke first, glad to have the buffer of Connelly in the room and fighting off the temptation of longing for the old days—whatever the hell those were. His mind laughed at him and his stupidity, for allowing a woman like Tracy, who never ceased to be the tough girl who mocked his first joke or the sweetheart who let him perform a second act, walk out of his life. His gut told him something was wrong with this day.

When she reached the front door of Kelly's Pub, Rosalind Taft laughed without ever really making a sound. She read the greeting at the front gate. A hundred thousand welcomes to a place she'd never planned to arrive. Breaking the threshold of her father's stronghold, absolutely none of the few patrons in the place noticed her—perhaps a first time for everything. She paused without so much as a creak from the floorboards and perused the public house, not knowing, never knowing, if her father had intentionally caused the incredible events that would follow.

When twins are separated at birth, they often live parallel

lives despite ridiculously differing cultural influences. SAT scores are unsurprisingly aligned with how much money your parents earn. And success in college is dictated by how many books your parents read. For all of Darwin's goddamned sanctimony, your own fitness relied heavily on the fitness of your parents, and Rosalind Taft currently cursed her fitness.

Now thirty minutes upright in his traditional position on the bench in the corner, Connelly spotted her first. As she passed into the house that Declan built, it appeared to Dave as the most natural thing in the world, *a small reckoning*. Dave watched her idle briefly, fixing her gaze on the three of them in the corner. She looked just a little bit lost to Connelly, delaying her advance, perhaps contemplating a last and useless chance to run. Whatever the reason, and regardless of circumstance, she now belonged to them, this place, and their strange *School of Day*.

"Pull up a chair." Dave stretched his foot from the opposing bench and kicked out the chair in front of Rosalind.

Matt and Tracy had failed to notice her arrival.

"I have no idea what I'm doing here," said Rosalind.

"You have some idea." Tracy spoke, surprising Dave, before he could manufacture any witticisms. "I've been patiently trying to stall while I was waiting for you." Tracy smiled at Rosalind, immediately making her more comfortable.

"OK, go ahead."

"I got her number from Jim and called her last night. I explained that you idiots haven't had a conversation about anything worthwhile since ... well, since you were born. I told her somehow Jack needed you, and now it was likely you boys needed her. I only know what I've seen in the lectures so far, but it's good enough to convince me." Dave could tell by her inflection that Tracy had found something, but Matt interjected first.

"What did you see?" asked Matt.

"I know this may sound a little ridiculous, but Jack didn't think Shakespeare wrote Shakespeare." Tracy paused again, leaving an opening for Dave.

"Really, Tracy? You think that sounds ridiculous?" Connelly was already experiencing the early phases of the shampoo effect. For anyone who has actually lathered, rinsed, and repeated, it's noticeable that no matter how efficient the rinse portion of the process, the last remnants of shampoo are still tangible. The same phenomenon applies to drinking massive amounts of alcohol. The first drink into the hangover, one begins to feel the buzz, but only if done right. Dave did it right.

"I'm guessing it won't sound as ridiculous when she explains, Quotes, especially as she's the only one who is even close to an expert on the subject!" said Matt.

"Shit, look who took the ex's side," snarled Connelly.

"So glad I came." It was only the second thing Rosalind said.

"Focus, kids." The voice of reason in a bar most often comes from behind it.

"I'm not really an expert, but there's an issue among Shakespeare scholars that no real evidence exists proving William Shakespeare, from Stratford-upon-Avon, ever wrote a damn thing. It's really not an important issue, but it is an issue nevertheless."

The light in the room bent around Tracy and despite a discourse more toward the ceiling, she had the floor. "Nearly two hundred years after the First Folio came to life, a woman named Delia Bacon pontificated from any pulpit available that her great-great-great—all right that's far too many greats. Anyway, she said that Francis Bacon actually authored the Shakespearean canon.

"Despite the young lady's efforts, or because of them, she

ended up in a mental institution leaving footprints on the road less traveled for others to follow. Folks have shaken."

Tracy's emphasis on the word shaken meant nothing to Dave, but he may have seen Declan Kelly smile at the turn of phrase.

"Kit Marlowe from the dead, the arbitrary avuncular uncle, and counts from the tower, all suggested as candidates, but no one has any real proof that William Shakespeare didn't write."

"So why the authorship question?" asked Matt.

"No one can really prove that he did. It's not like they had a Library of Congress in Elizabethan England. Authors scratched out plays as fast as they could to keep pulling in audiences and tons of them were lost over the years. The reason Shakespeare is so famous is because two guys published his plays after he died."

"Ha. Something I actually knew," said Matt.

"She mentioned it last time, brother," Connelly intercepted.

"Killjoy."

Ignoring them, Tracy continued. "There are lots of records of William Shakespeare as a churchgoer, playhouse owner, and even as an actor, just not much about him as a writer. I think this pretty much goes ignored by most academics, but it seems like Jack believed it."

"Any reason it would have something to do with *Cardenio*?" Dave asked the question with legitimate curiosity.

"I have absolutely no idea," said Tracy.

"All right, square one then."

"Don't be a dick, Quotes," Matt interrupted.

"Don't worry about it, Matt. No surprise from Dave. I actually need to get going anyway." Tracy stood up and avoided eye contact with Connelly.

"Me too," said Matt. "I'll walk you out."

"Whoa, whoa, whoa, brother. We have work to do. You just got here."

"And now I'm leaving." Matt rose from his chair and walked side by side with Tracy out of the barroom.

"Damn," Connelly snorted.

"All right, then. Obviously, glad I came here for this." Rosalind slid her chair away from the table.

"C'mon," Dave whined. "Just because none of my friends like me, it doesn't mean you can't stay for one drink. You came all the way here."

"I actually need to go to my father's loft. When Tracy called me, it seemed like a strange coincidence. A wasteful, strange coincidence," she muttered almost to herself.

"Well, at least let me come with you."

"Not before me?" Rosalind smiled. "The morning buzz has your confidence high I see."

"Not at all. In fact, my confidence in women is at an all-time low."

"I meant confidence in yourself."

"I got that."

27
CHAPTER

"The dichotomy in the first part of *Henry IV* is defined in two distinct worlds personified by the two juxtaposed characters of Hotspur and Falstaff. Young Henry Percy exists only for the field and the court, while Jack obviously lives for, and in, the tavern. So how can we summarize these worlds? For example, how are men measured on the field?"

"By how they fight."

"By their honor."

"Easy enough and certainly correct. And the Tavern?"

"By how much they can drink."

"Ha. Typically true, but more specific to this play, how are they measured? And more precisely, what do they do?"

"Not much."

"They rob."

"They hide."

"OK. Also very true, but let's try this. Hotspur tells Glendower, 'I had rather be a kitten and cry mew than one of these same meter ballad mongers.' He tells Kate, 'This is no world to play with mammets and to tilt with lips.' So if these things are not allowed in Hotspur's world, then they belong to Jack. How do men fight in the tavern?"

"As cowards?"

"An idea, but cowards don't fight, do they? If they did fight, would they throw punches? Sling swords?"

"No."

"The first tavern scene is a place for 'unsavory similes and breakers of proverbs,' a place where Hal reminds us, 'how much better than *my word* I am.' 'Then we did two set upon you four and with *a word* outfaced you from your prize.' What is the main currency of the tavern world?"

"Their currency is words."

"There you are. Words, words, words, anticipating a Danish prince. The tavern is a place for words, and the field is a place for action. The court is something in between, as we learn in Act III, when Glendower and Hotspur have their own battle of words. 'I say the earth did shake when I was born ... at my birth the full front of heaven was full of fiery shapes.' Glendower will call the devil for us while Hotspur will move rivers. They will divide a world they never conquer. They fill their speeches with metaphor, hyperbole, hendiadys, and more shame than truth, all the while claiming to be men of action. In the middle of these two worlds we have?"

"Hal."

"Yes. Our prince is the bridge between the tavern and the field. And by the end of the play, we know a man is better off mastering his words than his sword, wonderful anagrams of each other. So it is that Hotspur must die with honor, while Falstaff will live with his cowardice. Jack knows that honor can't heal a leg. Survival in *Henry IV, Part 1* depends on 'argument for a week, laughter for a year and good jest forever.'

"So what is this to the bard? While a history play, Jack Falstaff is a complete creation of the author. Why would it be important to him to give us this division?"

"He was a wuss?"

"Most certainly. 'What is honor then? A trim reckoning!

Who hath it? He that died a Wednesday?' I wouldn't argue that at all. Would it all make more sense if perhaps he had a circle of friends who sat together in a tavern discussing their works? Several such groups existed. What if he had a brother who died of a wound to the leg? Perhaps if he knew something of an Irish expedition as mentioned in Act III, scene i. Then would this world begin to come together?

"And what of the tavern? England was full of little writers' groups who spoke of words while they met in pubs—the University Wits, the School of Night, and the Wilton Circle just to name a few of these illustrious groups corroborating in and around London. However, for all the historical evidence of words as currency in the pubs with these writers' groups of England, there is, yet again, no mention of a man from Stratford as a part of them. The Wits, as we have noted previously, spoke of him but never with him.

"With the massive confluence of talent so ubiquitous in London and outlying towns, all these household names working together, creating some of the best poetry and prose in the history of the written word, where is Mr. Shakespeare?"

28
CHAPTER

Dave entered the professor's loft with none of the trepidation Keating had felt just a few nights ago. Rosalind bounded across the threshold while Dave leered, as if she were the dutiful daughter rather than the estranged. He may have marveled at her carelessness, if not for the oppressive heat pervading the apartment on this August afternoon. Whether the thermostat was ignored or a cost-conscious landlord had shut down the air-conditioning, Dave found himself in an unusual situation. He was with a woman, and he felt the heat.

"Holy hell," offered Rosalind.

"Even hotter," Connelly replied. Shrugging his shoulders, he continued on into the room. Unlike Keating, only the heat made him uncomfortable. Much like Keating, the books pulled him downhill across the apartment. He suppressed the urge to look back and make certain Rosalind's eyes followed. Far from a stench, he noticed a subtle smell originating from the onset of mildew, irreversible in the heat and humidity.

"Thank God I bought two bottles." Rosalind made her way to the kitchen and retrieved the corkscrew she'd struggled to find on the last visit.

"Not sure red is the way to go on a ninety-degree afternoon," said Connelly.

"Show me a liquor cabinet, and I'll get more creative."

"Try the one over the refrigerator."

Rosalind laughed at Dave's guesswork, looking over her cork and across the room. Connelly stopped ten feet short of the bookshelves, giving himself a sort of picture box view, taking in the width, as the depth was beyond him. Still disheveled from the previous night's activities, his four-button, collared, short-sleeved shirt cried desperately for an iron, and his cargo shorts conveyed disinterest from the jump. David Connelly was a mess.

"Son of a bitch," Rosalind uttered from the kitchen.

"Not nice. You never met the woman," said Dave.

"How did you know he had the booze stocked away up here? I did a hard target search the other night." Even with one knee pressed into the counter, hands awkwardly outstretched, and a curious look on her face, she somehow remained relaxed.

"Could smell it from here."

The tilt of Rosalind's head and the contortion of her lips into a smirk exuded something more than amusement at Connelly's theoretical olfactory prowess. "I smell it too, but I thought it was bullshit."

"You know my cologne? Bullshit by Dior! God, we're practically old friends." Connelly turned to face her now and pointed toward the floor just beyond her. "There's a small step stool to the right on the floor just past the edge of the cabinets. The books are all reachable, so I could only think of one other thing that would be in that cabinet above the fridge. Not to mention, I keep the backup bottles in the same place at my joint."

"You could have mentioned the stool before I hopped up on the high wire, Sherlock Holmes."

"Ahhh. The Arthur Conan Doyle classic," said Dave, deflecting.

"Oh Lord, don't tell me I have another bibliophile on my hands."

"I consider myself more of an enthusiast. I really only appreciate the classics. Tough to handle any of that rubbish the houses publish today." Sarcasm dripped from his tongue.

"It's on the shelf in front of you, isn't it?"

"You bet," Dave smiled, pulling the book out toward him and dangling it in the air for her appreciation.

"And ... GFY," said Rosalind.

"GFY?"

"Absolutely does not mean good for you."

"Got it. Anything good up there?" He motioned to the door above Rosalind's head, now ajar.

"Let me grab my stool." She hopped up the two steps and perused the bottles. "Nice! Scotch, and the old man has the good stuff."

Dave turned his attention back to the bookshelves, allowing a soft giggle and pondered *grab my stool*. He visited plenty of homes where people displayed their reading preferences as if they were trophies awarded to the owners, congratulating them on the ever-impressive and unprecedented skill of reading for pleasure. Normally, he would pass by without so much as a glance, but the rows of bindings before him represented Jack's life. Standing there in the void, which had once served as Jack's hat rack, Dave finally understood what really happened that day in the bar. Jack wasn't angry, aggravated, or showing off. He simply felt the need to do the same thing he'd done the last forty years of his existence—teach. And in the countless chapters, acts, and scenes now available at Connelly's fingertips, this wall of words represented a small fraction of Taft's own education. The wall wasn't a library. It was a photo album filled with the friends and loved ones of Jack's life.

In the same manner families collect images from the

beaches, ski slopes, reunions, graduations, and myriad other momentous occasions they wish to revisit, Jack's memories lived in the words and worlds of the authors on the dusty shelf. With Rosalind and her mother gone, this wall was Jack's scrapbook. Dave ran his finger along the bindings as if some process of osmosis might occur, bringing him closer to the professor's mind. His hand reached for the leather-bound journal at the end of the line, sliding it carefully from its place alongside the others, wondering about Jack and loneliness. Perhaps the professor finally felt a hole in his everyday routine, something missing; and the answer was an argument with peripheral acquaintances. Before Dave could fall too deeply into the trance of great words, Rosalind reached his side.

"Neat?" she asked.

Startled, he spun quickly to his right. If the journal had remained on the shelf or Rosalind's hand had dangled along her side rather than bending up to ninety degrees or Dave had failed to notice the stool, everything would have been better … or worse. When Dave turned, the journal swung at the exact height of the glass in her hand. The moisture of the sweltering room and the force of the blow allowed her no chance to maintain her grasp on the liquor. They were now on their own private island—Three Mile Island.

When the nuclear plant on Three Mile Island went, well … nuclear, it wasn't just one thing bringing it to the edge of catastrophe but, rather, a sequence of events. The wrong guy at a desk, a small light malfunction, an obstructed view, and obvious physics that make really small things create really big explosions.

So when the glass fell from Rosalind's hand and detonated on the floor beneath them, any one thing would have prevented what now seemed inevitable. Dave's awareness when they entered the room, his distraction as he looked into Jack's soul, a damn carpet at their feet, and the glass never shatters on the floor. Therefore, when they naturally and thoughtlessly leaned simultaneously to begin picking up the pieces, Dave's forehead would of course land a direct hit on the bridge of Rosalind Taft's nose. Dave retracted backward away from the contact, but either the shift of her weight or the height of her heels forced Rosalind sideways toward the floor. At such a short distance from the ground, she would have caught herself easily if not for broken glass.

When her hand careened toward a few small shards. she leaned instinctively to her right and continued to fall toward the ground at the foot of the bookshelves. Momentarily dazed himself, Dave now watched the last few seconds of the spill in what appeared to be slow motion. Connelly took in the entire yard sale, scene by scene, nearly coming to life from the pages behind her. No longer a tragedy, the plot laid itself out like the main character, in full comedic form. And Dave knew *spill* was the wrong word now. Despite what could have been a broken nose and should have been a lacerated hand, Dave didn't see one drop of blood. In Rosalind's other hand at the base of the shelf was her full glass of Scotch.

"Holy shit." Of course when the words fell out of Connelly's lips, it seemed a reference to the spectacular fall rather than the amazing catch, but he followed naturally with a more appropriate sentiment. "Are you OK?"

Rosalind tilted her head and observed the glass in her hand through watery eyes. "Supposed to drink it first and then fall down. By the way, that broken one was yours."

"Let me help you up."

"I'm good here. Maybe you should come down." Lying on the floor of the apartment, propped up on one elbow, she took a long drink of her scotch.

Innocent enough in her reticence to rise from her fall, as

so many postlapsarian stories end, Dave's descent created a natural and unavoidable moment of togetherness. It took only a few sips of scotch and significant self-deprecating laughter before Rosalind leaned in.

Dave had played out this scene hundreds of times with a long, long line of desperate inadequate women he'd trolled on the internet, but this felt different. Whether the women of his recent past attacked him for his money or for their primal needs, he always felt control. In Jack's apartment on an engineered wood floor adjacent to a bottle of eighteen-year-old and along the window of Jack's soul, Rosalind Taft took control. She leaned across Dave, and his gaze briefly caught her thigh just above the knee where her skirt slid naturally up her leg. She grabbed the back of his head and kissed him firmly with the confidence of someone who was used to being in charge. As increments changed at the variable, Dave engineered some wood of his own.

Connelly sat in the leather armchair by the window along the east wall of the apartment. He didn't wonder if Jack enjoyed his morning coffee in this chair. He didn't know if he planned his day with the sun at his back in this very spot. He never considered whether a bottle of Scotch sat on the table at the professor's left hand while correcting the incoherent ramblings of second-year humanities majors. Instead, he tried to figure out what the hell had just happened.

There was really only one other time in his life when he had been so thoroughly dominated, and at least on that day, he'd gotten to kick Shaunessy in the nuts.

Rosalind had walked out the door five minutes prior, and her departure hadn't come with much sentimentality. She may have mentioned that it was fun, but Dave wasn't entirely certain she'd said anything at all. Dominated. Hanging his head in his hands and contemplating the full scope of the last hour, he felt a wide smile on his face, wondering if it had been there for all five minutes. Dave knew his world, populated with seconds, minutes, and days of meaningless alcohol-soaked drivel, was a fictional place void of direction. He now felt it all imploding from the center, reflecting Rosalind Taft. She was real.

Understanding there was still a matter of some alcohol to consume, Dave pitched forward out of the chair and immediately saw it again on the floor at the foot of the shelves—Jack's journal. He considered going for the book first but knew the eighteen-year-old Oban wouldn't drink itself. As the blood continued to redistribute throughout his body and the alcohol touched his lips, he felt lifeless—sort of hemophilia drowning.

29
CHAPTER

Keating sat in the bar exhausted from yet another brutal day at the office. He would have preferred diving under his covers and preparing for another full-on beating from his boss, but there was work to be done here as well. He'd started this whole thing when everyone else wanted to let it go, so when Dave called, ebullient and screaming with unbridled excitement, his choice was made for him. Smith and Riley walked in together, as was often the case. Sharon leaned into Riley pretty hard about driving to the bar after too many nights of excessive libation and excuses. She didn't really care that, *It's a short drive. I didn't have that many. I'm careful.* She knew Riley lacked any discernable willpower when it came to shutting himself off at the bar. This was one small step in the seemingly infinite journey toward adulthood for Shaunessy. Each of the boys doubted he would ever reach that destination.

"Carting Riley's ass again?" Keating looked to Smith, drawing his ire.

"Only way the missus will let him out," responded Smith.

"Why can't you just drink two beers instead of twelve, brother?"

"Why are you making me learn Shakespeare?"

"Fair enough, but you should at least think about a cab

ride every once in a while. I'm sure Smitty gets sick of hauling you around."

"He loves me. Where's Quotes?" Shaunessy's inquiry was simply an effort to change the subject.

"Hell if I know. Dude calls at quarter to ten and tells me we have to meet him. I literally haven't heard him this happy since"—Jim's pause represented the sentiment better than the last word could—"ever."

Declan meandered in at Riley's shoulder, representing both the angel and the devil residing across from one another placing three pints on the table. It never got old. For a beer drinker, a real one anyway, the *standing order* serves as a badge of honor. The corner bar didn't just mean laughs with your buddies; it meant no line for a drink, no line at the door, no cover, and a nod of your head when you felt thirsty. Declan took as much pride in it as the boys did. A rare breed, Kelly cared about customer service in the customer service industry. "Here he comes."

"I found it, bitches!" Dave's voice was loud enough to turn the heads of everyone in the bar as he floated across the room toward the church pew. The smile on his face would have been contagious if he hadn't offended the two dozen other patrons. "It finally happened. I actually spent three enjoyable hours reading about Shakespeare—well, the man from Stratford that is."

There it is again, thought Keating, *the man from Stratford*.

Dave dropped Jack Taft's leather-bound journal on the table in front of him and sat down across from his normal position on the wall mere inches from where the professor had started it all.

Jack had carefully placed the book on the shelf in his apartment right next to the copy of *Coriolanus* he'd thumbed through on that meaningful last day a few weeks ago. Neither

Dave nor Jim had noticed the particular placement. But where Jim failed, Dave succeeded—finding the real key to the mystery of *Cardenio*. If board shorts had never called when Jim made his first appearance at Jack's place, it may have saved them all a good deal of time. That phone call leading to the lectures actually slowed them down a bit.

"We need to go to England," Dave exclaimed.

"What the hell are you talking about, brother?" Jim asked the question they were all thinking.

"England. We're going. London, Stratford, Kenilworth, and Wilton House."

Riley and Matt both looked over the table at Keating, and the enigmatic gloss blanketing his face gave them no sense of security. Declan Kelly listened in a bit closer.

"I've spent the last three hours reading through this thing, and it's a road map to *Cardenio*. I finally know what it's all about. The only guy we've ever met who knows the writings of William Shakespeare inside and out thinks the author was a front. Tracy was right. This whole journal is about a woman named Mary Sidney, the Countess of Pembroke. Jack not only believed the play *Cardenio* is still out there somewhere; he thought it proved Mary Sidney was the true author of Shakespeare's canon.

"We have a few problems, but we're going to see this thing through. Mary Sidney was the leader of a group of writers called the Wilton Circle. Jack mentioned it in one of the lectures, but I hardly noticed. There were a bunch of groups like this all over the place in Renaissance England—the University Wits, the School of Night, and the First Friday Club were just a few of them. Jack thinks she may have been involved in more than one. There is a passage in the play *As You Like It* where the character Jaques rattles off a song that's the first clue. It's the first page of the journal."

Connelly opened the brown cover and read:

> If it do come to pass
> That any man turn to ass
> Leaving his wealth and ease
> A stubborn will to please
> Ducdame, ducdame, ducdame:
> Here shall he see
> Gross Fools as he
> An if he will come to me.
>> Amiens. What's that ducdame?
>> Jaques. 'Tis a Greek invocation to call fools
>> into a circle.

"Jack is all over this passage. The first thing is that stupid word that none of you recognize—*ducdame*. It's meaningless out of context, but the character quantifies it. Call fools into a circle, but Jack broke it down from there. *Duc* is a French word meaning duke. *Dame* is an English word meaning a woman the equivalent of a knight. Essentially the word means duchess. It seems like a big stretch until you realize the play is based on an older play, but the character Jaques is an invention of this author. So you have this dude with a French name in among a bunch of Englishmen. Why? Ducdame! Mary Sidney called fools into a circle. The Wilton Circle, her writers' group. Then she educated the fools. Not to mention the literal meaning, essentially a female duke, also known as a duchess. Mary Sidney is the Duchess of Pembroke—actually a countess, but it's the same damn thing."

Despite all their best efforts, it was difficult to ignore Dave's enthusiasm. They had known him for years, but this was the first time any of them had seen his passion match his intellect.

Three plus decades is a long time to find enthusiasm, but damn if she wasn't beautiful when she showed up.

"He runs all over the place from there, but basically the short porch is this. The Mermaid Tavern in Cheapside, London, burned down years ago, but he thinks it's possible the play may have been hidden somewhere in the bar. Henry IV spends a lot of time in the taverns, and he talks a lot about Falstaff and what he means to the authorship question. There's even a quote from that character about honor and whether it can mend a leg. It would be completely random, but Mary Sidney's brother Philip was basically the most honorable man in all of England, and you guessed it ... he died of a wound to the leg.

"The Mermaid Tavern was where the First Friday Club, a group of Renaissance authors, met and Jack thinks Mary may have surreptitiously been a part of the group. *Surreptitious* was his word not mine. Christopher Marlowe was most likely a part of this group, and there is another nod to him in *As You Like it,* where she mentions a 'great reckoning in a small room.' That line is universally accepted as a reference to Marlowe being killed over a bar bill. There's more to that as well.

"The Forest of Arden is next, but by far the least likely. We could be screwed again on this one, but I'm hoping we won't even need to pursue it. Depending on who you believe, the forest may not even exist anymore but there's good news as well. A character in the play named Orlando carves poetry into the trees in the forest. There are an insane number of references to poetry in the woods in the play, including the simple fact that the majority of the play takes place out there. However, Jack leans on a couple lines from Jaques and Oliver, another character the author invented outside of the original work. Jack thinks those lines make it possible *Cardenio* is hidden in an oak tree in the forest. Good news is the book has never been found, and there are trees out there that may be two thousand years old."

"Um, David, is it possible that you took some amphetamines?" Smith asked. "You're freaking me out."

"Smitty, a copy of the First Folio is worth six million dollars. If a copy of this play is real—and in Mary Sidney's hand or with Mary Sidney listed as the author—it would be worth $20 million to $100 million dollars. I may be underreacting. I don't know shit about it, but I can identify good research when I see it. This is a real thing.

"'That any man turn to ass.' In *A Midsummer Night's Dream*, the character Nick Bottom wakes to find he's got an ass head, kinda like you Riles, and wanders through the play in that fashion. The thing about Bottom is he represents everyman. He's everyone, and he's of course wandering around the woods when he's not rehearsing for a play. Jack wrote briefly about the idea that 'everyman' meant we're all capable, but he spent more time on a different idea. That play includes a reference to a mermaid and a dolphin, different mermaid than the tavern, but same idea. The reference points to a pageant that Robert Dudley held at Kenilworth Castle to honor queen Elizabeth. Shakespeare would have known absolutely nothing about what the hell happened at this event, but a young Mary Sidney, fresh off her return from Ireland, was actually there. Taft pointed to Kenilworth as another possible resting spot for *Cardenio*.

"We have more problems on the next hunt. There was a Spanish ambassador in England during King James's reign who made quite a name for himself by pissing off pretty much everyone. He hung with King James; arranged the beheading of a few folks, including Sir Walter Raleigh, founder of the School of Night; and rolled out of England not long after the publication of the First Folio. Supposedly, he purchased a copy of the folio before he left and may have brought it to his library in Valladolid, Spain. I remember the name of that town because it unearths an amazing coincidence. Don Miguel Cervantes lived there. Why does Cervantes matter you ask? The foundation of the plot for *Cardenio* comes from Cervantes's seminal work, *Don Quixote*. You can't make this shit up, boys.

"If Ambassador Gondomar left England with the First Folio, no one has seen it since, with the possible exception of a book thief named Gayanos, but Jack thinks he may never have had a folio at all. Jack thinks he may have taken a copy of *Cardenio* because of the hometown relation to Cervantes. He wouldn't have even known what he possessed at the time because no one really gave a shit about Bill Shakespeare. In fact, Gondomar would have been much more caught up with Thomas Middleton, because that dude wrote an entire satire beating the second Diego down."

"The second Diego?" Keating inquired.

"Sorry. Gondomar was apparently so tight with King James they were known as the two Diegos. Whatever. Anyway, Gondomar arrived in England to solve something called the Spanish Marriage Crisis. Royalty from both sides believed a wedding between Spanish and English Aristocracy might stop the fighting between the two countries. The count failed miserably, but it's relevant, because soon after he leaves with *Cardenio,* two noblemen, one of whom is a prince, head to Spain under assumed names to try and check out the Princess Infanta Maria and maybe put an end to the so-called crisis. But there really is no reason in hell they would have made that trip, no matter how big the Protestant-Catholic bullshit was at the time. However, if a countess wrote a play and it got out into the open, that might be enough of a reason— particularly if said countess was one of the most renowned and influential women in all of England. Jack connects a few more dots between a disguised prince in one of the Henry plays and the prince who actually heads for Spain. I don't think that's really relevant for us, but you never know."

"You know, Dave, some decaffeinated brands are just as good as the real thing," said Riley with a gun and a wink.

"*Real Genius*, bitch. Fits perfect. I loved Val Kilmer in that movie. Well done." Dave poured a staggering amount of Guinness into his face, perhaps refueling.

"Anyway, this one ends with a bit of trouble as well. You see, Jack can't really follow the book because he thinks the prince may have actually recovered it, and when you get your hands on something you're trying to keep secret, you really only have two choices. You destroy it, or you hide it. Need to hope he hid it. He's run this one down a bit, but the long and short is a quick question. There's one image from all of Shakespeare's plays that serves as the same kind of marker as Christ on the Cross. Anyone care to guess what it is? From Hamlet?

"Got it. Prince holding the skull," said Smith.

"Yes, Matty!"

"The full extent of my Renaissance skills."

"That might be us." Far from the first time in the last twenty minutes, the boys had no idea what he was talking about. "Shakespeare's grave is in a church in Stratford-upon-Avon. There is a warning on the floor about not disturbing his bones that is a little atypical for this time in history—hell, any time in history—and Jack thinks it's relevant. As we've talked about before, two cats, named Heminges and Condell, published the First Folio after Shakespeare died. The author was dead long before he would have seen all his works pulled together and before Gondomar ever rolled out with a quarto or a folio.

"A few years back, despite a four hundred-year-old warning,

scientists performed a scan of Shakespeare's grave and found a bit of a mystery. Seems his head may, or may not, be missing. There is a rectangular space where his spine tops off, showing his grave was disturbed at some point. This is where Jack got a bit copious in his journal. He thinks the Spanish marriage boys buried *Cardenio* in William Shakespeare's grave."

"You're gonna need a fedora and a whip, Quotes." Matt smiled, enjoying every second of Connelly's speech.

"That would be awesome—but not nearly as awesome as Jack's last idea for the final resting place."

"Finally," said Riley.

"Exactly what I said, Riles. Jack seemed to hate it, but he also thought Wilton House might be a possibility. And quite honestly, that would make this the easiest grail quest in history—well, other than some petty larceny."

"So $100 million dollars is petty larceny?" Keating asked a legitimate question.

"OK, larceny."

"What's Wilton House?" Matt inquired.

"It's where Mary Sidney lived. We need to go to England."

"I ain't going to no England," said Riley.

"You're going to England, Riles."

"The fuck I am."

"We're doing this thing together, kid. You're going." Despite Dave's best effort to Jedi him into submission, Riley calmly placed his finger on the side of his nose, offering the universal drinking game symbol for *not it*. All and all, it was a decent play by Riley.

"OK, Quotes, I love the fire. I absolutely love it. Hell, it's all worth it just to see you rolling like this." Matt couldn't possibly ignore the obvious question before him. "But if Jack Taft knew the path to find the most important book in the history of books, why the hell would he give it to us?"

Matt was right. Dave had consumed himself so thoroughly with devouring every word of the journal in an effort to understand *where* the play might be hidden, he'd failed to even once consider *why* Jack would pass this on to them. The look on Dave's face made Matt wish he hadn't asked the question, but before either of them could reconsider Jim stepped in.

"It's poetic."

"What?"

"It's fucking poetic," Keating said emphatically.

30
CHAPTER

"Don Diego Sarmiento de Acuna sailed into Portsmouth Harbor in 1613 with a small armada and the audacity of a man who knew his rank. In the next decade, the first Count of Gondomar would drink often and aggressively with royalty, order the imprisonment and executions of English aristocracy, fail miserably in his one defined task, and leave the kingdom as the most hated man in England. And why, your curious minds are really churning now to extricate this kernel of knowledge, is this man so important to a classroom full of 200-level Shakespeare enthusiasts? I ask you.

"Deaf ears. Deaf ears.

"All right. It seems this morning's class will be in lecture format. I'm sure you'd be comfortable pontificating on the avuncular Polonius or the virtues of Mark Antony. But once we get past anything you learned in high school or Introduction to Literature, we're reaching. First of all, Count Gondomar, ambassador for the Spanish king, representative for his country, edges into Portsmouth Harbor with his flags at full mast. Under any normal circumstance a ship in a foreign harbor would drop all flags to half-mast as a gesture of courtesy, avoiding any potential imbroglio. This is to say nothing of the fact that he's coasting past the first fortifications of the harbor built in 1418 by Henry V and the Southsea Castle, home of the English Navy, erected by the fornicating Henry VIII.

"This is an ominous and appropriate beginning for the man who will send Sir Walter Raleigh and the enigmatic Edward de Vere to their cells and coffins. While being carted around London in his 'chair of ease' in an effort to subvert the pain of an anal fistula—oh I see I have your attention now—Gondomar will make enemies with almost everyone he encounters. By the time Diego leaves England in 1623, coincidentally the year the First Folio is printed, Thomas Middleton, one of Shakespeare's great rivals, will have dedicated some of his own farcical propaganda to the count with all the grandiloquence of a punch in the face.

"All of this is irrelevant in the historical context of the man from Stratford unless you consider the timing of Gondomar's exit from Will's island. In 1623, the count headed for home. He failed in the general framework of the Spanish Marriage Crisis. The Spanish Infanta Maria would never marry the English prince, and the troubles of Catholics and Protestant would continue on throughout James's reign. Along the way, he disgusted all of England—with the possible exception of its king—and has rarely been heard of again.

"He is relevant to you and the material of this classroom because he purchased one of the very first copies of *Mr. William Shakespeare's Comedies, Histories, & Tragedies* produced by John Heminges and Henry Condell. The folio then disappeared from the face of the earth and resurfaced only once in the last 180 years. If you believed it exists and had the wherewithal to find it, it would be worth approximately eight million American dollars. Treasure hunters beware, however, because it burned in a fire somewhere between the years 1835 and 1843.

"Gondomar, however, did have another work from the same author. He owned a copy of a play that hasn't been seen since the early 1600s. And it's that quarto, rather than a mysterious folio, that makes Don Diego Sarmiento de Acuna the most important man in the history of Shakespeare."

31
CHAPTER

"I don't understand," Rosalind uttered.

"What don't you understand?" asked Connelly.

"Um, everything."

"Can you be more specific?"

"Well, we've known each other for three weeks, and now you're asking me to go to England with you. That's what I'm struggling to understand."

"Well, I don't want to undermine how much I enjoy sleeping with you, but I'm not inviting you as a quasi-girlfriend. I'm inviting you as Jack's daughter. That's the relevance of you coming to England. Your father probably made the greatest discovery in the history of English literature. It would be like discovering the Old Testament with an author page. I'm thinking maybe you should be there for that."

"Dave, I've enjoyed the time we've spent together. You're massively entertaining, better than average in bed, really nice to me, and incredibly fun to be around, but I can't go to England with you."

"Now I don't understand," said Dave.

"Quite simply, I can't go to England."

"No. I mean *better than average in bed*? C'mon. I'm incredible in bed and better than average to be around. Throw a dude a bone, metaphorically."

"Definitely entertaining." Rosalind looked down at her coffee and then judgingly across the table at Dave's pint. In half a lifetime of good decisions, could she really go out on a limb for a guy who drank every day, rarely shaved, took nothing seriously, and was the most passionate student of Shakespeare she'd met since the father she never knew? When Dave took a huge quaff from his pint, Rosalind shook her head incredulously, beginning to feel a disintegrating dis-ingratiation toward all things important to her father. "You keep saying, 'Follow the book.' Explain it one more time."

"Did you end up looking at his journal?" asked Dave.

"I didn't burn it. You're welcome."

"OK. Uphill from here. Your father believed that Mary Sidney was the real author of Shakespeare's plays, and the proof of this theory lies in the existence of the play *Cardenio*. He believed a quarto edition of this play, written in Mary Sidney's hand, fell into the grasp of Don Diego de Sarmiento de Acuna, the Count of Gondomar, a Spanish ambassador who spent a few years in England right at the end of Shakespeare's writing career.

"The play was derived from an episode in *Don Quixote* by Miguel Cervantes. This is relevant to Gondomar because he lived in the same town as Cervantes. It's relevant to Mary Sidney because the particular episode involves a married woman who falls in love with her doctor. Mary Sidney, the Countess of Pembroke, falls in love with her doctor, Matthew Lister, after her husband dies, so the story itself has a link to both of them.

"It's generally believed that, when Gondomar left England, he took a copy of the First Folio with him. That book also disappeared over the years, but folks believe that the folio may have been stolen from his library at Valladolid years later. Your father believed the *Cardenio* quarto never made it that far.

"Gondomar's real job in England was arranging a marriage between the Spanish princess Infanta Maria and Prince Charles of England. He failed miserably, but it gave good cover for pursuit of the quarto. Charles and the Duke of Buckingham chased Gondomar to Spain under the guise of investigating the marriage, but it is incredibly unlikely any prince or duke would traverse Europe to check into a marriage.

"It seems equally implausible they would leave to chase after a book, save one small fact. King James had just appointed Mary Sidney's son Henry Herbert, the Earl of Pembroke, to be Master of the Revels. It would have been a massive embarrassment to the king if word got out that he'd approved a play written by a woman. So Charles and Buckingham take the names of Thomas and John Smith, book for Spain, and run down the quarto.

"Once they recover the *Cardenio* quarto from Gondomar, probably by telling him all the lies he needed to hear about the impending nuptials between Charles and Maria, they can head back to England and bury the book forever."

"You should probably drink less," she said.

"The only thing harder than that would be drinking more, what with the anatomy of the … never mind."

"Dear Lord," said Rosalind, frustrated.

"What?"

"It just seems so thin."

"Your father was researching a problem that's four hundred years old. Four hundred years!" Dave said it incredulously, knowing not only the depths of Jack's research, but his own as well.

"Who said there is a problem? I've never once heard a

theory that Shakespeare didn't write Shakespeare or Einstein didn't discover relativity or van Gogh didn't paint *Starry Night*. Anyone can just write a bunch of crazy ideas on a piece of paper."

"It's not just the one play," Connelly opined, exasperated by Rosalind's disbelief. "He points to evidence in most of the thirty something plays. Over and over again, there are references that a glover's son from Stratford would have known absolutely nothing about. The women of Shakespeare are like some sort of Wonder Woman / Amazonian hybrids seen nowhere else in the English Renaissance. Scholars, teachers, and critics have said for years that the author disguised his females as males to make it easier for the actors of the time. Obviously, that makes perfect sense. But if that's the only reason, then where are they in Marlowe? If it was so commonplace, why doesn't Shakespeare's most heralded contemporary use the same device, when the man from Stratford cross-dresses Portia, Olivia, Rosalind, Imogen, and on and on. And of course, the ladies who don't get to cross-dress lose their faces by going mad or dying. It's not empty, Rosalind. Your father was on to something, whether that book exists or not."

"And you want me to come to England because my father was on to something? That's the best you've got?"

"It's everything I've got. I know Jack wanted this done, and I'm going to do it. And there's one more thing. Your father notes in his journal more than once that Shakespeare's sonnets were dedicated to Mary Sidney's two sons, Philip and Herbert. That's not just another clue; it's a damn reason. He didn't leave that photo as a keepsake. If we find this book, it doesn't belong to us. It belongs to you. This is his dedication to you."

If her father had delivered the speech, it would not have

been nearly as persuasive, but somehow Dave's dedication to this insanity moved her more than the thought of a gift from her father. Four men she'd never met and an undeniable passion. Did she even have the right to refuse them? "So where does he think the book is now?"

"Let me show you."

32
CHAPTER

Heathrow Airport is a jail in much the same way Dulles, Midway, or Atlanta are jails. When the boys stepped off the plane and began moving along the corridor toward customs, a glass wall separated them from the check-in counters for all the passengers awaiting departure. The setup made the tired travelers feel a bit like Hannibal Lecter divided from Clarice by inches and worlds all at the same time. The quarter-mile walk between the 787 and passport services imitated the beginning of a competitive marathon. A crowd essentially running to stand still, as Bono once crooned, fighting and bumping through the requisite roller bags generally far too large to sit in overhead storage and pulled by people far too cheap to spend an extra twenty pounds. Fortunately, the international flights offered a little extra legroom, but the same level of congestion when the throngs departed planes.

This would one day be the singular part of the trip that Riley Shaunessy did not regret missing. Despite four hundred years separating Riley from William Shakespeare, the bard may have managed to save Shaunessy's marriage. With renewed passion for his bride, Riley chose his wife over his boys for the first time in his life—even after incessant badgering and taunting of his old friends. Jim surreptitiously loved it.

Keating watched the Europeans skate through immigration, simply standing in front of one of the many machines scanning both their skulls and their passports, matching them up, and allowing passengers into Jolly Old. All other imports were forced to twist through the stagnant, serpentine line marked, "All Others." Perfect. The only proper alternative would be "Standing Room Only." The real hold up for *All Others* germinated from the apathetic epidemic at the end of the lines. Jim marveled at the molasses movements of security officers checking passports. It was a slo-mo show.

Curling through the queue, visitors witnessed several distinct methods of people processing passports. Upstart crows, surely days or weeks into employment, would move individuals and families at a productive pace of five or ten travelers in fifteen minutes. Lethargic veterans of the monotony might steal a glance, or ten, at their smart phones between travelers or engage in lengthy conversations with their adjacent coworkers, halting two booths at once. Learned behavior taught them well. If we can't bum around the countryside today, neither can you. One hour and fifteen minutes later, Keating, Connelly, and Smith were officially in a new country.

The true luxury of international travel is the discovery of all luggage off the carousel when visitors finally break through and enter the baggage area. Of the many wrongs righted by James Keating's alter ego over the years, he repeatedly crashed into the carousel creepers in airports of call. Like so many things, the setup for luggage collection is well designed, except for the people. If everyone simply stood fifteen feet from the moving track, it would be very easy to obfuscate traffic, step up, grab a bag as it came through, and escape the crowd with ease. However, somewhere along the way, one person and then many decided it would be easier to hover over the baggage wheel where there is never enough room for all who departed the aircraft. They hover with their children, with their giant carry-on, and with absolutely no regard for the people around them. Keating's answer to this was simple. Find the largest group of men and stand behind them at the proper fifteen to twenty feet until his luggage spun out of the dark rectangular window. Once his bag was in view, he carefully dropped a shoulder, grabbed his bags, and was certain to crash into each of them with his luggage on his way out. Fights don't break out in airports.

International was easier.

"Who did you rent from, brother?" Connelly asked.

"Ace." Smith made a good living, and as Dave picked up the majority of the travel expenses, Matt insisted on at least getting the rental car.

"Ace? What the hell is Ace?" Keating asked before Connelly could.

"We're in another country. It's not like everything is going to be Hertz, Avis, and Enterprise." Jim could tell Matt regretted the words at almost the exact moment they escaped his lips. Moving into the transportation area, and into view of the large signs for Avis and Hertz, Jim and Matt looked upward almost simultaneously. At least he didn't see Enterprise. Unfortunately, there was no sign for Ace either.

"All right, Matty, any instructions?" Dave asked.

"The rental agreement says the desk is at the airport Holiday Inn."

"And we get there, how?" Keating smiled, as Matt's Type A personality took a hit. Jim admired Matt's attention to detail and his stringent protocols for organization, especially as they didn't necessarily mirror his own. He finally leaned in with a parting shot to ensure Matt's Ace was lower than a deuce.

"I mean, there's a sign right there by the ladies' restroom for off-site rental cars, but no Ace rental anywhere to be found."

"Say anything about Joker's?" Dave asked.

"Eat it, Quotes."

"Gonna drink it instead, if that's cool with you. You wanted to be in charge of the car, so you got it, brother. DP and I are rolling into that pub right over there and taking down some bitters. Leave your bag with us, find your way to the hotel, and meet us back here."

"Sweet. Thanks."

"Rather have us making fun of you for the next hour?"

"Good point. Besides, it's been almost three hours since you had your last beer. I'd hate for you to shrivel up and die," said Matt.

"Can't have it," said Connelly.

Matt walked away from his friends and began a ninety-minute journey destined to end with much laughter. Instead of wandering aimlessly, he pitched pride aside and asked a very kind girl at the Avis counter the best way to reach Ace rental car. She directed him to bus loading area twelve and thirteen, where he would unknowingly watch his bus pull out of the terminal. A complex grid gave the listings for a full two-dozen stops running in and out of the terminal from these two gates on ten different buses. Bus H-1 departed for several different hotels, including the Holiday Inn M4, where the rental car company was located. A twenty-minute wait for the next bus felt longer, and the additional five minutes to load before departing made him jealous and thirsty.

The hotel was the first stop—his only real break, allowing Matt to settle down a bit. Turning the corner into the hotel driveway, his disgust returned upon witnessing thirty people pouring out of the rental car office, crammed together in a disorderly line. In addition, six or seven customers clawed, pushed, and shoved for the privilege of being number thirty-one, instead of thirty-eight. Matt considered the possibility of a rugby ball in the middle of the crowd. Scrum rentals. It crossed Matt's mind that maybe he could have left Dave in charge of transportation. Surrendering to the inevitable wait, he figured a trip to the gents might be the proper first move. He paused briefly when he passed a very suitable hotel bar but thought better of it.

Upon returning to the counter and the art of waiting, he once again confronted a Heathrow-like glass prison. Most of the line stretched out into the parking lot, but the full front wall of the building, comprised of glass, forced those waiting to witness the mess inside. While some of the customers took a meager five minutes pouring in and out, one mother attended to three children, asked myriad questions and never once called for her husband smoking in the parking lot. Hers was a twenty-minute session—free for all to see.

Between language barriers, first-time renters, computer glitches, and one upgrade, it took Smith a full hour before reaching the magical door to the actual rental counter. Despite a text message from Keating fifteen minutes earlier, Matt did not anticipate what happened next. With his focus on the counter, he failed to notice the minivan pull up to the hotel loop and seemingly ignored the sound of Jim's voice and Dave's laughter. When he finally turned, Keating and Connelly each held a can of Tiger beer in their hand and rested comfortably in the back seat of the van. While Matt had walked, Dave had dialed and arranged a chauffeur-driven car for the duration of their trip. Halfway between anger and thirst, Matt moved for the car.

"Jackass," uttered Matt.

"Beer?" Dave asked.

"You bet."

"Smitty, meet Ackerley. He can drive from the wrong side of the car on the wrong side of the road with his wrong hand on the stick. He has a minivan with a cooler and is available for the next six days."

"Could have just said he's the greatest man alive." Matt smiled. "That would have covered it. Nice to meet you, sir." Without another option, Matt surrendered and took a giant slug from the chilly can.

"You as well," said Ackerley.

Keating rolled back and forth between the van window and the small gap between the back seats on the drive into London, and each violent swing forced him to contemplate his own mortality. Traveling sixteen miles in one hour and twenty minutes is a long bicycle ride, but in a motorized vehicle it tempts you to slam your hand in the car door just to feel a different kind of pain. However, with a cooler full of beer and Ackerley dodging in and out of traffic, he survived.

The scenery wasn't much help, as it could just as well be a drive through Boston. But the last stretch offered some promise, as Westminster Abbey came into view and then the first sight of Big Ben, the palace, and Westminster Bridge. Ackerley's passengers all slid violently to the right, Connelly smashing his right shoulder into the window, as Ackerley made a sharp left turn into the Park Plaza Westminster Bridge driveway. With construction strangling all but one small lane into the hotel, it was a pretty solid move.

"Here, lads," the driver offered.

"Thanks, pal," Connelly responded. "We'll be on foot the rest of the day, so you're good. Probably won't need you tomorrow either, but I'll let you know for sure in the morning."

"Good enough. Ring me if you need anything."

Check-in at the hotel presented them with their final queue of the day, but a handful of incredibly motivated women in matching blue pantsuits moved everyone through quickly. In ten minutes, they were upstairs with Connelly in one room and Matt and Jim in the other, only fair as Dave footed the bill for both. Rather than closing the day down and submitting to the sleep they desperately needed, they agreed to meet in the lobby fifteen minutes later—or 11:30 a.m. local time.

The trip, the mission, and the motivation all still felt surreal to Keating. Less than two months ago, nothing could have convinced him he would be present in a modern-day search for William Shakespeare—or that such a thing could even exist. Perhaps, London would have some answers.

CHAPTER 33

Two massive revolving glass doors separated the lobby of the Park Plaza Hotel from the street and the River Thames not far beyond, so when the three men wandered through the exit, they were dazzled by arguably the best view in London. The street stretched out ahead of them into Westminster Bridge and toward the Palace of Westminster beyond, with the Elizabeth Tower and Big Ben calling their eyes up above the horizon.

Keating instinctively looked to the left before stepping out into the street, and his pulse jumped thirty beats when the smart car chirped its ridiculous horn, approaching quickly from the right. The good news for him was a collision between the two would have been a fair fight. A lifetime of crossing the street told him everything was clear, and as usual, experience was a tough teacher.

After safe crossing, a one hundred-yard stroll brought them to the south side edge of the river. At that point, the look of the city changed drastically. Viewing London to the east from the edge of the bridge, it looked exactly like the city that barely survived the bombings of the Second World War. The eclectic menagerie of Gothic, Renaissance, Modern, and just plain god-awful created a woeful skyline along the brown and busy waterway. The river walk, saturated with tourists, was a hideous cement walkway leading up to the Eye, the world's slowest moving Ferris wheel. Rome and Paris were spared this unsightly incongruity, as the cities remained marvelously intact through the war.

Making their way to the east, meandering through the throngs of tourists, the men would soon become familiar with the best part of the city—the people. Not the massive crowds on the Queen's Walk but the precious few in the menagerie of taverns, when five minutes into their foray, a familiar feeling came over Connelly. He was thirsty. "Anyone else parched?"

"C'mon, Dave. You drank a sixer on the plane, one at the airport, and two more in the car. Can't we at least make it to one stop before we begin the inevitable London pub crawl this will turn into?" asked Keating. He wanted to get to work.

"No."

"Five more minutes, and we'll be at the Globe. I'll count that, even though it was built in 1997. Good deal?"

"Can you really walk past that?" Dave pointed to a two-story brown building with light blue trim that belonged on an island. Any island would do, even this large one. The Wharf. The first of two dozen ocean-themed bars they passed on their walk called like a Siren. This particular building clearly wasn't a survivor but, rather, one of the few new buildings offering something attractive. The Swan, a few different Anchors, and the Walrus all filled in the edges of the river, waiting to quench their thirst before finally reaching the Seahorse, once the location of the famous Mermaid Tavern. But first, the Wharf, and another Connelly win.

"Cheers," uttered the barmaid when they walked in, the first of no less than ten times she would offer *cheers* while they knocked down one pint.

"Cheers," replied Matt.

"Oh, Americans."

"Is that a bad thing?" asked Smith.

"Nah. Cheers. Just observing. Who's first in the queue?" The waitress looked back and forth between Matt and an elderly gentleman approaching from the right.

"Go ahead, sir," said Matt.

"Wouldn't dream of it, young man. Believe it or not, I've got time to wait." His smile couldn't be denied.

"Thanks. Old Speckled Hen, please." Connelly came over the top.

She pulled down on the tap four or five times to fill the pint glass with bitters, a distinctly British beer served near room temperature and with less carbonation than an ale or a lager. Handing it over the dark wooden bar, she instantly offered another, "Cheers."

As Matt ordered his beer, Keating perused the pub. Still early in the day, the room was fairly empty, but a couple in their sixties or seventies drinking stouts at 11:45 a.m. sat comfortably in two leather chairs in front of a stone fireplace. Some manner of large poodle sat dutifully at the man's side, and Jim made a mental note on the scoreboard—England two, America nil. He awarded one point for seniors drinking in the morning and another for dogs in bars. No wonder they lost the war. The English were too busy being awesome to ever learn how to fight.

Keating recalled Declan once asking Dave if he would be *walking the dog* when he came into the bar. Having no earthly idea what Declan Kelly meant, Connelly required an explanation that was happily provided. In Ireland, men tell their wives they are taking the dog for a walk, a convenient excuse for walking to the local public house. Excuse for one is excuse for all, and eventually the rail outside the pub had ten dogs leashed to it. *Walking the dog*. The Irish almost nailed it.

In England, they invite the dogs in.

When Matt turned away from the bar, he failed to notice the mountain of a man returning from the restroom. The gentleman looked less like a rugby player and more like the inventor of it. So when Smith bumped into him, Matt stopped incredibly short spilling perhaps an ounce of beer on the giant's shirt just north of the man's hip.

"Oh Jesus, sorry." Matt craned his neck and looked up the beanstalk at the giant who appeared to be wearing more of a Manchester City tent than shirt. Jim knew the dogs in the corner could smell Matt's fear.

"No worries. I'll drink it later," said the Man City fan. That was all. No shove, no stare, no annoyance. The giant continued across the bar without so much as a glance back toward Matt.

It occurred to Keating that, in the United States, you might have this convergence once in two months. You could cross paths with someone who insisted you order before them, and you could bump into someone who didn't give it a second thought. It happened plenty of times, but both things in forty-five seconds would be like seeing a leprechaun riding a unicorn in Connecticut.

"Good people," said Matt.

"Indeed," confirmed Keating.

"So where we headed first, Captain Connelly?"

"The Monument, eventually." Dave almost whispered his response, still engrossed in the intricacies of the pub.

"What's the deal again, Dave?"

Connelly stared down into his glass of beer, perhaps reaching for mental reserves, before beginning another lecture of his own. "The Monument was built in 1667 as a memorial of the Great Fire of London a few decades after Shakespeare shuffled off this mortal coil. The First Friday writers' group met at the Mermaid Tavern. The sculpture on the front of the

Monument faces directly toward the spot where the Mermaid was located, between Bread and Friday streets. Jack suggested it as one of the spots he believed could be the final resting place for Mary Sidney's *Cardenio.* Apparently, there are three cuts in the concrete at the top of the monument that don't seem to really have a purpose. He believed the book may have been hidden in there as kind of a memorial on its own, a nod to the writers' groups in general and specifically to the Countess of Pembroke."

Matt Smith smiled. "I can hear the words coming out of your mouth, Quotes, but I still can't really believe it, brother. It hasn't been two months since Jack came at you, and now you're a frickin Shakespearean scholar. It's pretty impressive, my man."

Dave' s laugh was genuine. "I don't know a damn thing about Shakespeare, but Jack was pretty persuasive. That's what I know, brother—Jack's argument."

"It's awesome, kid," Keating chimed.

"If we find this thing, I'll let you guys take turns. But in the meantime, I'm just standing on Jack's shoulders."

Matt, Jim, and Dave had all studied Jack's notes and lectures in the weeks preceding the trip. But despite their intellect, the former two were in a different world than Dave. Anything he read, he retained as if he'd written it himself.

"The guy who built the column was named Christopher Wren, and nothing about the statue is particularly unusual. All the inscriptions are about the fire and the king. The top of the tower is a flame representing the fire itself. The height of it is representative of the distance from where the fire took place. All makes sense.

"But there's a sculpture on the side facing the Mermaid. The sculpture depicts a female figure as the central symbol, and in general, it's understood that she represents England.

She's a sad figure, as disheveled and distraught as the people of England certainly would have been. Again, makes sense." Connelly paused for just a moment, making certain neither of his listeners had fallen asleep, but also dramatically as he readied to reveal the more mysterious part. "Then there's another woman, a figure to England's side gently touching her, almost as if she is bringing her up. In her other hand, she holds a winged scepter. It was this woman who interested Taft. The entire sculpture seems to be understood pretty well, except for this one woman. While there are quite a few different surviving sculptures the artist completed in England, the one that really stands out is, you guessed it, a mermaid.

"Both men, Wren, and the sculptor Caius Gabriel Cibber would have been known to the elite in England, a circle including Mary's two sons. If the sons were involved in *Cardenio*'s disappearance, this seemed almost as good a spot as any for them to hide that quarto."

"Almost?" Keating said it to himself as much as anyone.

"He thought this was the least likely of the primary spots. He only considered it because it was in London. And based on what I've researched, it's really four spots. The Forest of Arden is either mythical or firewood, because the damn thing doesn't seem to exist anymore."

"Well we're not gonna find anything sitting in here, boys." Smith whacked down the last of his pint, and the three men began to move.

Making their way along the Queen's Walk toward the Globe Theater, they stopped briefly before a sign reading, "No busking."

"What the hell is busking?" asked Dave.

To their great fortune, another sign came into view just

twenty feet down the line letting the boys know that busking was, in fact, allowed but must be performed on the Southwark busking pitches. Busking evidently included all manner of street performances and some fairly overwhelming rules, which could be found on the sign or, if so inclined, at www. buskinglondon.com. The website, obviously fecund, housed the Busk in London Code of Conduct as well as the Guidance on Busking at Bankside. As it turns out, if one is inclined to hop on an eleven-foot unicycle and swallow fire, there are rules. Busking must occur during the proper hours, and if no busking pitches remain, the process of queuing must be observed so the juggler would cede his pitch to the xylophone-flautist after one hour, rather than juggle all the way into a 120th minute. The xylophone-flautist, however, must be certain to busk in the pitch marked BP for musicians, where perhaps the great baseball-playing classical guitarist, New York Yankee Bernie Williams, would have found confusion, never knowing whether to busk or take batting practice—excellent evidence that busking is not a Yankee term. With diligent research, an Englishman could feel free to go busk himself.

Crossing London Bridge is a bit of a revelation for pitifully uninformed tourists. Years of "London Bridge is falling down," combined with the images of the beautiful Tower Bridge accompanying every edition of Wimbledon, *European Vacation*, or pretty much any image of London seen on American television, naturally leads to the assumption that the two bridges are one and the same. The name of London Bridge is commonplace, and the image of the Tower Bridge is very much the same, making it easy to forget that London Bridge is an unsightly mess of steel built in 1973. However, it is the fastest way from Southwark to Central London, so Connelly turned left to cross, with Keating and Smith in tow.

Tourists can easily walk right past the Monument without

even knowing it exists. The monolith would have stood out against a 1667 skyline, but London filled in over the years. Turning onto the side street and facing the main facade, it still isn't all that impressive. But ostensibly, there's no designated amount of ostentation for devastation. Slowly moving down the hill on the creatively named Monument Street, Cibber's creation came into view. Without an explanation, it's a difficult sculpture to decipher, but Dave's CliffsNotes on the structure influenced all three pairs of eyes toward the mysterious woman consoling London. Moving around to the east side of the column, they could see the entrance and, for once, no lines. Apparently, five pounds to climb three hundred and eleven stairs seems like a terrible investment to most tourists.

"Heading up?" asked Keating

"Yes, sir," Matt confirmed.

As they walked through the narrow door, the space seemed too small for claustrophobia. The family of three exiting the structure forced them to turn sideways and press up against the wall just short of the collection desk.

"Good thing we didn't eat yet," said Connelly.

Keating handed over a £20 note and received his change from a teenager in a beige uniform shirt. There was no doubt the man held the worst tourist destination job in all of London. The dark spiral staircase only a few steps away signaled the beginning of their journey upward but offered little evidence that it was a long way up. Three or four turns in, they encountered another family on their way down, and this exchange proved even more arduous than that in the hallway. Despite the best efforts of all involved, there was unavoidable contact between the descending husband and wife passing the climbing Americans.

"Excuse us," said the husband.

"Of course."

"Long way up."

"No worries."

"That's what I thought." Then the gentleman disappeared around the next narrow turn.

"Ha." Connelly looked back down the stairs at Keating. "Damn, Riley would have loved this shit. Psycho gym boy would be doing push-ups at the top right now."

"Don't say nice things about Riley behind his back," said Matt.

"Solid point."

The walk up the stairs provided fairly uneventful sightseeing, as the arched alcoves all offered solid stonewalls, rather than windows that would have made for tough construction 350 years ago. Every thirty steps, a small slit offered limited views into the sunlit afternoon and office buildings beyond—London's stepchildren. Keating fell back a bit behind the two other men, who were happy to catch their collective breath waiting for him before they continued spiraling upward. The stairway felt like an angry, twisted reverse single helix, a reminder of the fire robbing London of her DNA. The only other noticeable features were cameras along the way, installed to monitor possible heart attack victims.

After twelve long minutes that felt more like half an hour, they saw light pouring in from the final turn, and just as Jack described, three small cuts in the monument on the low left side of the wall.

"We're here, you son of a bitch. You hear me, old man? We're here." Connelly said it loud enough for the others to hear, but Jim knew his friend was really speaking across a table from a church pew to a professor of Shakespeare.

The three slits were only a foot and a half high and maybe two inches wide, but they felt sacred to David Connelly. Small wooden edges surrounded the cuts at knee height where plaster and stone filled them in. At that height and size, it was hard to imagine a purpose and even harder to imagine a way to chisel through them and look for a four hundred-year-old book.

"So what do we do now?" asked Matt.

Before Keating or Connelly could answer, a young couple approached from below, forcing the men up the last few steps. Breaking out into the day should have presented a glorious view from atop the tower, but instead they found themselves surrounded by more office buildings and a scene further mired by a chain-link fence running the full 360 degrees around the circumference. The fence, installed fifteen years ago, was a necessary answer to six suicides and one accidental fall, a monument to tragedy atop a monument to tragedy. The threesome shuffled around to the east and found some space where they could press up against the barrier and consider options.

"Like I said, what do we do now?"

"I know, Smitty. I know. We studied his lectures, read his journal, enlisted your ex-wife, and traveled three thousand miles to look at a wall." Connelly paused. He seemed to struggle, perhaps hopelessly, to find some measure of beauty on the skyline. Then he looked to Keating and smiled. "But it's here. We followed Jack's lead and found the first spot."

"A spot that's five feet of concrete, brother," said Keating.

"Doesn't matter."

"That's a little optimistic, Quotes," Matt countered.

"I understand. But all I'm saying is, eight weeks ago, we were trying to figure out the best hockey movie of all time, and now we're here. And the first spot Jack leads us is exactly how he describes it. I don't think we can roll the guard, circumvent the security cameras, jackhammer the sides of a national landmark, and bust out of town." Dave smiled. "Well, maybe

I do. But I'm not saying we should. I just think if we can gather enough information to present a quality case, we might be able to enlist some help. Shakespeare was a damn English treasure. If we can connect a few dots and convince the right people, I think we may be able to do this."

Again, it was hard for Jim or Matt to challenge his enthusiasm, but they naturally glanced sideways at one another to find some sort of reality to counter Dave's persuasiveness.

"Quotes, people have been reading Shakespeare for four hundred years, and I don't mean just regular old people. I'm talking about people who have a higher IQ than even you, and more free time than ... well, you. You think three holes in a wall mean we're on to something everyone in the history of English Literature missed?" asked Matt.

"Jack didn't miss it."

"Jack also lost his shit, yelled at a bunch of virtual strangers, and sailed off into the shipwreck. Not sure he had his noggin screwed on tight, pal," said Keating.

"Then what the hell are you doing here, DP?"

"Being a friend." He answered instantly as if it were the easiest question he'd ever been asked.

Connelly smiled, knowing his three friends were most certainly the best part of his life. "Then just keep doing that, brother, and leave the rest to me."

"OK, kid. What next then?"

"For now, the Mermaid. Just in case."

The Mermaid Tavern burned to the ground in 1666, so when Connelly ordered a 1664 beer brewed by the Kronenbourg Brewery in Strasbourg, France, he meant no disrespect to the English, instead offering a nod toward nostalgia and a time when Friday writers met. An amateur bilingual smack-talker, he would have resurrected his high school French and uttered a, "Seize cent soixante-quatre, sil vous plait," if hurt feelings were his intention. The building bore absolutely no resemblance to its historic predecessor, as the front wall was an almost entirely glass structure. The only remnant of historical significance was the pub on the bottom floor, a sad shell of her ancestor, the Seahorse.

The significance of this tiny block between Bread Street and Friday Street would mean nothing to any of them if they'd wandered in for a pint just two months ago, but now Jim looked around the room as if some scrap of idiosyncratic history remained. Ben Jonson, Francis Beaumont, and Jon Donne had all stood this ground, hoisted a drink, and engaged in argument; and perhaps, they'd occasionally mocked a friend. Despite the well-lit room, meticulously clean glasses, fresh air, and open feel, Keating felt sure he could see into the room's gritty past. He didn't know which group had come together first. Raleigh and the School of Night? Greene and the University Wits? Maybe Ben Jonson and the First Friday Club of the Mermaid were the fountainhead for all others. But he grew more hopeful as the day passed that Mary Sidney and her Wilton Circle perpetuated all others. It was still a dream, not unlike Bottom's dream, but it was his—his and his friends'. And if true, it would be for everyman.

Keating finally stopped spinning. "I'll have a Carling, please."

"No worries," said the young woman behind the bar, and the two words made her seem Australian to Jim. "This may sound like a ridiculous question, but do you know anything about the old Mermaid Tavern or the writers' group that used to meet in this spot."

"Oh, I'm sorry," the girl smiled. "I've only been here a few weeks. No idea what it used to be? Cheers." She handed the Carling across the rail to Keating.

"Of course." Keating felt a strange convergence standing, quite literally, in the middle of this quest and four hundred years away. The pub represented a marker reminding him how impossible this whole process was for a few men with little knowledge and less perspective on the inner workings of the English Renaissance. Could they find sixty sheets of paper a million others had missed?

Returning to the hotel later that evening, Keating felt completely exhausted, not from the walk around London on a hot day but from the time change and long hours of travel. He agreed with Dave that they would shut down the operation for the night and pick up in the morning with renewed energy. Keating could not muster a single productive thought as to what they would do in the city the next day, but all of them were happy to hunker down for the evening.

34
CHAPTER

"Let's get the hell out of here." Connelly didn't mince words when he arrived at the breakfast table.

Keating and Smith had hit the buffet twenty minutes earlier, pining for a Hilton Garden Inn and anything disguising itself as breakfast food. Baked beans and salmon made for a terrible morning combination, and the pastries on the end bar appeared old enough to vote.

"What?"

"We gotta get out of here. There's no way the monument is the final resting place for something like this. We need to get up to Stratford and see what Shakespeare's grave looks like. It just makes more sense."

"That's fine by me, but we need to see if the hotel is available and—"

"All set. I changed the reservation this morning," said Dave, cutting Matt off.

"Taking over, brother?"

"I think that happened a while ago."

—⁂—

Even with Ackerley's deft skill and complete disregard for human life, the road out of London was virtually impassable, a logjam of tiny hybrid cars maneuvering for nonexistent open road. The men traversed a mere ten miles of road in forty-five minutes escaping the clutches of the city. Somehow, optimism still filled the car, and omnipresent lagers filled the cooler, as the birthplace of the bard awaited them one hundred miles away.

The M40 ran directly from London to Stratford, and the highway architects had created an amazing feature by dynamiting a small passageway through a hillside separating the outskirts of the city from the country. The valley opened up, a wormhole separating them from modern London and dropping them into a bygone era in the English countryside. The dramatic shift of scenery gave everyone in the vehicle hope, as the driver finally reached fifth gear, and the van touched120 kilometers per hour.

This next stop would take them to Shakespeare's grave in the Holy Trinity Church of Stratford-upon-Avon and perhaps the most logical resting place for *Cardenio*, as the grave site provided plenty of mystery. One of several dozen graves in the church, an enigmatic warning was left behind for mourners:

> Good friend, for Jesus' sake forebeare.
> To dig the dust enclosed heare.
> Bleste be the man that spares thes stones.
> And curst be he that moves my bones.

Shakespeare paid a substantial sum of money to become a lay rector in the church hierarchy that allowed him burial inside the church, rather than the graveyard outside. The warning was left to prevent grave robbers and relic hunters from tampering with the bard's bones. After years of efforts to explore the grave, the church finally yielded, allowing a radar scan in 2016. The scan revealed Shakespeare's skull was missing and some sort of brick structure appeared in its place. The combination of the curse, the hollow, and the mysterious structure led Jack Taft to believe the grave may have been the final resting place for *Cardenio*.

While the enigmatic open space in the grave gave the fresh-faced *Cardenio* hunters this day's optimism, they readied for the same problem all over again. They were back at the Monument, history repeating itself. Someone would have to let them dig. All they could do for now was poke around and, perhaps, ask for help.

"What's the plan this time around, Dave?"

"Hell if I know," said Connelly.

"Awe inspiring," said Keating.

"Thank you." As Dave opened the cooler, Ackerley made a sharp right turn into yet another roundabout, and some of the icy water sloshed over the side of the cooler onto Matt's foot.

"Damn, that's cold," said Matt, retracting his now freezing foot helplessly. "Wide awake for sure though."

"Sorry, brother. I'll keep an eye out for the curves. Only appears to be a traffic circle every fifty feet or so. I'll adjust." Dave smiled and handed beers to Matt and Jim.

"Yeah, Ackerley, what's with all the loops in the road, my man?"

"Part of our charm," said the driver.

"Good enough for me," Connelly returned.

"Seriously, Dave. What are we going to do when we get there?"

"We'll look around and ask some questions. You guys know I'm not the greatest planner in the world. I'm just following Jack's research. I still believe he found something, and I'm willing to see this thing through. If nothing else, we're on a vacation learning a little history and knocking down a few more pints." He scanned the faces of his close friends, looking for approval, first Matt to his right and then Keating in the seat behind him. "It doesn't really matter if you guys think this is crazy. It only matters that you're here with me. DP, you know Jack struck a chord with me in the bar that day. He was right. It's not only possible, but it's damn certain there's something better. For me, this is it. And if it ends up being a worthless trip through the English countryside, then it's better than the bar and trolling the internet for yet another sexually transmitted striptease."

Keating smiled. He loved this David Connelly. "I can live with that, brother."

"Me too," said Smith

The post-and-beam facade of Mercure Hotel on Chapel Street in Stratford-upon-Avon poured charm out into the street. The black-and-white timber front hardly formed a right angle, as the years of gravity's harsh treatment caused soft sloping angles all across the building. Ackerley slowed the van to a stop at the front entrance, and yet another tiny hybrid car squealed its pathetic horn in disapproval. Dave would have offered a finger in return as he stepped through the van's sliding door, but damn if he hadn't fallen in love with the English people already.

Either way, it wouldn't have mattered, as the English had invented the ridiculous gesture and likely took pride in it. Often the case with English animosity, it began with France. The French had a nasty policy of cutting the middle finger off of captured archers to prevent them from ever returning to their craft. Better than death, but it still seems like it would hurt. So when the English defeated the French at the battle of Agincourt, glorified in Shakespeare's *Henry V*, the archers reminded them of the defeat by giving them the finger. *See, we still have them* is not really relevant anymore, but the gesture has remained. Matt and Jim hauled their bags through the van's rear door, while Connelly excused the driver for the day, promising to deliver plans in the morning.

The lobby of the hotel was cool and dark. The small windows allowed little light into the room, and the crouched ceilings forced the men to duck into the room. The floorboards sloped softly from left to right perfectly, creating a natural pull to the hotel's pub aptly named the Quill. Matt pushed forward toward the reservation desk, but Keating paused, looking into the pub. There were only a handful of tables scattered across the unpretentious room and one patron in a leather chair facing the fireplace. Jim stared in disbelief at the woman leaning into a book with a glass of Chardonnay on the table at her left hand. It was Rosalind Taft.

Walking into the Quill, Jim softly squeezed the words out of his mouth. "And there she was, not doing a thing he could see, except holding the universe together." He loved that line from Salinger and never could have found a better moment.

Looking up from her book, she smiled. "Funny, I'm a little surprised myself. I expected you tomorrow but without paraphrasing Salinger."

"What are you doing here?" Jim's confusion defeated his typical penchant for manners. He wasn't even impressed that she recognized the quote.

"I invited her." Connelly brushed past Keating while Rosalind rose to her feet to meet him. He only kissed her on the cheek as they met across the table, but the gesture seemed too familiar to Jim. "But I never thought you'd actually show."

"Aren't you boys a day early?" she asked.

"Tired of London pretty quickly," said Connelly.

What the hell is happening? Keating wondered to himself.

"Let us go check in, and we'll meet you back here," said Dave to Rosalind. "We can grab a drink or head right over to the church. It doesn't close until six, so we have plenty of time."

"Perfect. I'm almost done with this chapter."

"Anything good?" Dave asked.

Rosalind smiled sheepishly, knowing the title of her book sounded like a confession. "*Lost Shakespeare.*"

"Ha. Glad to have you on board. Let's go, DP."

Following Dave out of the room took more effort than Jim really wanted to muster. For some reason, perhaps the oldest reason in the world, Keating felt he was on the wrong end of a twelve-round title fight. He'd never anticipated this beating, but he felt it nonetheless. Connelly owed him an explanation.

"Dave, what the hell is going on?

"Upstairs. Let's talk about it upstairs."

Keating looked back over his shoulder toward the entrance of the pub. Rosalind had already returned to her book and the comfort of her chair. He didn't know how he'd missed it over the last few weeks. Somehow, it felt obvious now. Usually the first one to expound on the gory details of his love life, Connelly had failed to say a word about whatever had happened with Rosalind Taft.

After checking in, they crammed their bags and bodies into the tiny elevator, a vertical clown car designed for one passenger maximum. Claustrophobia piggybacked on ire, and the lack of space made Keating even more angry, though he still wasn't entirely sure why.

—m—

"OK, we're upstairs. Now you can tell me what happened?" Keating said it too impatiently.

"Well a few weeks back when she met us at the pub, the two of us ended up alone after Matty and Tracy left. I was just starting to get fired up about our little project, so I asked her if I could steal her key to Jack's loft. Turns out she was headed for the apartment anyway, and it just kind of happened from there."

"What *just happened*?" asked Keating.

"We did it on the floor of the apartment and have been hanging out ever since." Connelly chuckled.

"Why wouldn't you tell us this?" Keating continued.

"You never really cared about my escapades before. In fact, you have specifically asked to not hear about them," said Connelly.

"You don't think this is different?"

"You're actually confusing me a little bit now too, pal. What's the problem, Jim?" Keating knew he was in trouble when Matt asked the question, as he had no reasonable argument he could articulate.

"I didn't know we were inviting dates." It was the best Jim could muster.

"She's not a date, brother. She's Jack's only surviving relative, and we're looking for something that would make her father famous." Matt's response made it worse for Keating.

Connelly should have looked to Matt recognizing the support, but Jim could tell he really didn't give a crap. Keating knew with absolute certainty that his friend David Connelly did exactly what he wanted, whenever he wanted and asked permission from no one.

When they entered their hotel room, Matt continued his search for an answer. "C'mon, Jim, what is it really? Is it the girl? You pissed that Dave got there first?"

Jim looked at Matt, wondering how much he knew about Occam's razor. This was certainly a time when the simplest explanation was right. Still, he tried to deflect. "I don't give a shit about her. I just don't like Connelly making up the rules as he goes along. We started this thing together. The only other person who should be here is Riley. Anyone else is a tourist." Keating's emotions were transparent.

"So, it's the girl." Matt smiled, without fully understanding the entirety of Keating's feelings.

Of course Jim had no claim over Rosalind Taft and, therefore, absolutely no reason to be angry, but something from that night in Jack's loft stuck with him.

"Lets' go to the church."

CHAPTER

Jim walked down the hallway at a torrid pace, ignoring myriad paintings on the walls bringing scenes from Shakespeare to life. Viola's shipwreck, Falstaff's tavern, the ghost of a Danish King, and a cross-gartered man smitten with love were all ignored as Keating traversed the ancient carpet onto the old stone floor and ducked beneath the crossbeam entering the lobby. He needed a much longer elevator ride to calm down and reached the lobby still fuming. Never one to hide his emotions well, he did his best when he saw her standing by the front doors. Why did it matter so much to him?

She wore a loose-fitting, white sheer blouse and light green capri pants. It seemed impossible Rosalind could dress to impress no one yet be noticed by almost everyone. Plain beauty. A lost art in the modern world of photo shop, perfectly executed selfies, heels, makeup, and the land of pretend women all striving fruitlessly to be the girl in the perfume ad. Fake nails; eyelashes; breasts; and, of course, personalities. Fuck Dave.

"Ready to roll?"

"Of course. Still a little surprised to see you boys today."

"Not half as surprised as I am to see you." Jim let his tone get away from him briefly when he uttered the final word, but he recovered well with a subtle smile.

"I guess that's true," said Rosalind.

"Yeah, sorry to be rude, but what are you doing here?" Keating asked.

"Dave invited me," she said, not the least bit defensively.

"That's it?"

"Well, he made some pretty compelling arguments about what Jack was researching, and I figured maybe I'd see for myself. Even if I can't embrace his skills as a father, I can at least respect his intellect." Keating saw a small crack in the exterior as her last statement, perhaps pining for approval.

"OK," he said matter-of-factly, refusing to give in. Jim brushed past her out into the street, leaving Rosalind behind as Matt and Dave approached through the lobby.

"Is Jim OK?" she asked.

"All good," said Connelly, chuckling.

Matt Smith listened for answers in the six hundred-year-old floor and remained silent. This story didn't have an ending yet.

Stepping out into the gray afternoon, the three of them followed Keating to the left, down Chapel Street and past Othello's restaurant and the Chaucer Head bookshop. Over the first fifty steps, tourism revealed itself as the hamster driving the wheel in Stratford and moving much more swiftly than London's Eye. They made another left onto Chapel Lane after passing the entrance to Shakespeare's New Place, the author's home away from home as he spent the better part of two decades in London away from his wife and children. These four walls were really only a home to his second best bed.

Continuing down Chapel Lane, the wall of the Great Garden at New Place blocked the view of flowers, topiaries, and statues. Views of history rarely come free, but occasionally sounds might, as the laughter of children could be heard beyond the wall and, as always, the cries of parents yelling, "Don't touch that." "Don't climb on that." A late afternoon musical interlude. "We're not in our backyard, Owen." "Be respectful, Katie." Did parents never learn? Some things are meant for climbing, history be damned. Some things are meant for touching, antiquity be damned. And if you don't want them to be touched or climbed, then bring your children some place where they can touch and climb.

Keating continued to move swiftly and awkwardly, ten paces ahead of the others as the Royal Shakespeare Theater loomed ahead. A mere 130 years old, the theater made for one of the best monuments to the modern era in Stratford, surrounded by older cousins, brothers, and sisters, hundreds of years her senior. Despite her youth, the theater routinely offered some of the best productions of Shakespeare in the world. Fighting against Connelly's vehement protests, the boys were set to walk across a Renaissance, Einstein-Rosen bridge.

Jim finally paused at the corner of Chapel and Sothern Lane, waiting for the others. With his anger subsiding, he needed to diffuse the situation and break the tension. "Can you guys walk any slower? Let's head across the park here and take the river up to the church."

"We can probably walk slower," Matt returned.

As they moved along the brick path down to the waterside, a single swan meandered aimlessly across the park, pausing once to stretch her magnificent wings, warning all others to stay off her turf. Only Connelly understood the allegory of the swan as they made their way across the park. He couldn't quite put his finger on Ben Jonson's introductory poem in the First Folio, but he would have known right where to find it.

Sweet Swan of Avon! What a sight it were
To see thee in our waters yet appear,
And make those flights upon the bankes of Thames
That so did take Eliza and our James.

Moving south along the river, tourism jumped at the visitors from all angles. A pontoon boat moved along the water, man and microphone describing the bankside life and death of a bard. For a quieter expedition, there were rowboats for rent on the west bank, each vessel named for an intrepid Shakespearean woman—*Rosalind*, *Miranda*, *Cressida*, *Portia*, *Viola*, and *Ophelia* moored side by side. The owner of the rental company possessed ironic ignorance or a sick sense of humor. *The Tempest*'s Miranda grew up on a deserted island with her banished father. *Hamlet*'s Ophelia drowned in a river. *Twelfth Night*'s Viola barely survives her shipwreck. Perhaps Beatrice rowed on the river already, having survived her play and a drop to drink.

"Are we definitely going the right way?" Smith asked.

"You bet, Matty. It's only another hundred yards up ahead on the right. Who the hell are you texting back there?" Keating asked.

"How do you know I'm texting?"

"I didn't, but I do now."

"You're a regular private investigator, DP."

"Ha. I hope you're not picking up roaming charges," said Jim.

"Nope. Work has me set up for international anyway."

"Always forget you're a jet-setting lawyer," Connelly yelled from behind, having fallen back a few paces with Rosalind.

"Not exactly how I'd describe it, but good enough to get the bills paid. Guess you were correct. The church is right there. Looks like we'll have to go around front." Matt started to cut across the grass, rather than continuing to the stone path at the north side of the church.

"Whoa, whoa, whoa, speedy. You're not just walking away from that. Who were you texting?"

"See you're in a better mood all of a sudden." Matt leered at Jim.

"C'mon, seriously. It was Tracy, wasn't it."

"Yes. Since you absolutely have to know. It was Tracy."

"That's awesome, brother."

"Relax. I was just telling her we arrived in Stratford-upon-Avon. Obviously, this whole thing is a big deal to her. The last few weeks she actually started to believe all this herself. She just asked me to keep her posted."

"If I see a grave digger with a skull, I'll holler," said Jim.

"Alas, poor Yorick."

"Nice work, Matty. You are a fellow of infinite jest and excellent fancy," said Connelly, bettering his friend.

"Christ, Dave, your hearing is better than Declan's."

Jim looked at Matt with the thirteenth-century Holy Trinity Church framing him in the background, surrounded on all sides by history and gravestones. The churchyard graves marked the deaths of Stratford citizens who didn't merit or purchase burial inside. Observing his friend more closely, Keating wondered about mistakes, Matt's and his own.

"Sorry, brother. I always loved Tracy, and I know you weren't the one who wanted it to end. You always took responsibility for it, but you never wanted it. I know it." Keating paused, considering this might not be the time, so he marched past Matt giving him the obligatory bro punch on the shoulder as he pushed forward. "Let's check this place out."

"Seems like it's getting a little weird around here," Rosalind said to Dave, while Matt and Jim wandered ahead a few paces.

"Nope. This is perfectly normal. Whenever we investigate four hundred-year-old mysteries, everyone gets a little tense. Plus we haven't set foot in a pub today."

Keating looked back at Connelly, his words dripping with sarcasm. "Wow. It's half one. Assuming that's a vacation record."

"Might be a record for this year, but men drink while boys watch the clock," said Connelly, unfazed.

"Sounds about right," said Rosalind.

"Let's go. I know you're not here to be entertained by someone who's better than average in bed," said Connelly.

"No way I cross the pond for that."

"Ooooof. Was hunting for a compliment."

"One hunt at a time," said Rosalind.

Turning the corner toward the front of the church, they moved through the archway of lime trees covering the front sidewalk, offering a view beckoning for a stroll toward the street, but Dave and Rosalind continued to the left following Matt into the church. The detail of the stone and woodwork at the front entrance of Trinity Church is ignored by nearly all who enter for the first time as virgin churchgoers. Instead, eyes are pulled to the front door or, more specifically, the signs above the front door. As humans finally grew past Hobbit size, the five-and-half-foot entranceway started causing problems, forcing the church to place a comical wooden sign above the entrance warning, "Caution. Very low door." However, the sign failed to provide sufficient warning in preventing head injuries, so a second laminated paper sign hung over the sign hanging over the door, an admonition-apparition floating above. Occasionally churchgoers get a sign from above but rarely two.

Warning
One step down into church
Uneven floor
Floor may be slippery when wet

Entering a six hundred-year-old church anywhere in England meant entering a place of worship and a place of burial. Now Keating knew why. If you didn't watch your head, your feet, and the weather, the funeral you attended might be your own. Traversing the didactic and dangerous doorway to the Holy Trinity Church, most visitors' eyes are pulled to the right toward the gift shop, while the gorgeous stained glass windows; the Clopton Chapel; the altar; and, alas, Will's grave all breathed life and death far from the left. Like most who entered, Jim found his eyes drawn to T-shirts, coffee mugs, and three dozen white plastic chairs. The anachronistic sales center was designed perfectly and horribly. When Keating finally turned, he saw Rosalind grabbing Dave's arm and pushing east toward the center of the church.

The church, designed as a massive cross, stretched on for two hundred feet to the east ending at the altar. Moving down the west section of the cross, visitors could peruse the chapel of St. Thomas Becket or the Clopton Chapel of 1582, also known as the Lady Chapel, a nod to the statue of the Virgin Mary. William Clopton's final resting place can be viewed for free, but when visiting the man from Stratford, a £5 donation is expected.

Handing over a £20 note, Keating waved the other three into the middle portion of the crucifix beyond the confessionals and several tombs to the south. At the chancel near the head of the church were the Shakespeare graves paid for in full by patriarch, William Shakespeare. Beyond a thin yellow rope lay the graves of daughter Susannah; son-in-law John Hall;

first husband to his granddaughter, Thomas Nash; wife, Anne; and, finally, Will with a warning. Staring down at the two massive stones protecting a poet just three feet below, Jim wondered if Will had kept his head. Lectures, journals, plays and poetry had led them here to an answer underneath three feet, beyond a yellow rope, and again, still miles away. A crowbar, a crowbar, my kingdom for a crowbar.

"What the hell is that?" Rosalind's vernacular failed to match her venue.

"What?" Dave asked, still peering at the grave in front of him.

"That ridiculous cartoon on the wall."

Keating looked up at the bust of Shakespeare on the north wall, understanding the nature of Rosalind's inquiry. The bust dangled from the wall, a still frame version from *The Wizard of Oz* in color. It didn't look quite right, more commemorating a caricature of a person than an actual one. Pen in his right hand and paper in left, Will looked like a Claymation creation designed to come to life in short choppy movements. Mr. Heat Miser. Mr. One Hundred and One. His bald head, a Humpty Dumpty sphere, sat on a wall. Luckily, his acting troupe was once, appropriately, the King's Men. Maybe they could piece this shit together.

"This little pamphlet here says it's supposed to be the greatest likeness of Shakespeare in existence."

As Keating finished his sentence, Rosalind looked at him coyly, an auburn-haired Andrew Marvell poem, wishing he would define irony again.

"That's not true." All three of them looked at Matt, shocked by the declarative nature of his statement, unaware of his expertise on the church. "Sorry. Tracy told me about this. It's his funerary monument. That's what it's called. She made a big deal about it. Asked me to take some pictures." Matt paused for a moment, knowing he performed well in front of groups when practicing the law but felt like a sixth-grade spelling bee contestant when offering an opinion about a Renaissance statue. "The statue was designed and placed in the church the year Shakespeare died, but apparently a guy was hired to clean and paint it white a century and a half later. When he cleaned it, he literally wiped away all the features in the limestone, and the face of William Shakespeare was lost forever."

"You gotta be shitting me," said Dave, without letting his eyes leave the statue.

"Shit you not. Tracy showed me a few different portraits of Shakespeare during his lifetime, which isn't really the right way to say it since he didn't sit for any of them. He always has a receding hairline and a goatee, so you kind of think they all look the same. But really no one has any idea what William Shakespeare looked like."

"Not sure what I like more, Matty—the idea of you investigating *Cardenio* or the idea of you hanging out with Tracy. Too close to call," said Connelly.

"Lies. You hate her, Quotes," said Matt.

"You're an idiot, kid. I just hate when my brother is hurting. Tracy has nothing to do with it. That's all that matters to me, my man, how you feel." Dave looked away from Matt toward the back of the church, as sometimes, the truth forces men to stumble. "What's Keating doing?"

Jim stood at the center of the church speaking to the "five-pound lady," occasionally gesticulating toward different points along the church walls. Matt and Dave instinctively moved toward him while Rosalind held ground, looking around the altar.

As they moved into earshot, they heard Jim. "So the church

closes to visitors at 6:00 p.m., but you sometimes have services after that?"

"Not often. Generally, it's completely shut down."

"Even for worship? Can I come in to pray after hours? I'll be in town for a few days, and it's always nice to have a place to find my center."

Connelly battled to contain his laughter, holding it in only due to Keating's newfound perseverance. *Is Jim really trying to find a way to break into Shakespeare's grave?* Connelly wondered.

"No, I'm sorry. The church is completely locked down at night."

"What about the grounds? Maybe just being on the property would be helpful."

"Oh, I'm sure that's fine. You may run into the night security just checking the place out, but they won't bother you much unless you're a troublemaker." The woman let out a small, sweet laugh, causing immediate guilt to fall over Keating as he surveyed the joint. He knew the reality. He was casing a graveyard.

"Thank you."

Exiting the church and turning back toward the headstones and a small round tower marking the resting place of another Stratfordian, Keating felt slightly ashamed of and massively disappointed in having explored the possibilities of grave robbing. His morality remained intact, but he knew his larceny skills were weak. The setting was perfectly absurd, another dead end.

Rosalind slowly moved away from the others and followed Keating out into the cool, early afternoon air. Matt and Dave remained inside, searching the church and their own minds for possibilities.

"Hey. Are you OK?"

"Fine. Why?" Jim noticed himself answering too quickly.

"You seem a little distant," Rosalind replied.

"Didn't realize you knew me well enough to feel distance."

"Oh, God." Rosalind looked across the cemetery toward the river beyond. "Not distant from me, distant from Matt and Quotes."

"Quotes?" Jim flinched at the familiar reference, but his voice remained even.

"That's what you call him."

"That's what I call him because I've known him forever. What about you?" Keating should have been embarrassed by his childishness but never thought of it. Somehow a Grail quest steals humility.

"Got it." She paused for a moment and considered walking away, but there was something fragile about Keating, forcing her to remain. "Not sure precisely what you dislike about me, but it's not like I'm trying to marry David. So if you have a problem with me, you just have to make it through a few more days, and then you'll probably never see me again. This whole thing will be over, and you can forget me, my father, and this ridiculous search for a book we all know doesn't exist."

"You think it doesn't exist?"

"Jesus, Jim," she exclaimed.

"Awful close to the church for God and Jesus segues."

"I'll take my chances. Of course I think it doesn't exist. I have no faith in my father—and with good reason."

"So you're here for Dave?" Keating asked.

"Why does that matter to you?"

"It doesn't."

"Seems like it might," she responded.

Keating needed to shift. "Then why are you here? If you don't believe the book exists, you're here for another reason."

"Look, Jim, I don't really know anything about you, but if you grew up with a father in your life, I'm not sure you would understand. This trip isn't belief in my father, but it's my first real look at him in over twenty years. I had a great relationship with my mother. She was perfect. She was more than enough. And when I lost her a few years ago, it was devastating, but she did everything for me her whole life. She was beautiful. When Jack died, I really didn't give a shit, but at least I can take a look. There was no other woman. There were no irreconcilable differences. There was Will and a tall stool. That's what my mother always said. She could never make my father as happy as Will and a tall stool. That's why I have no father. So if this little trip can prove to me that my father gave me up for something more important, maybe I can finally have some closure."

"Seriously?" Jim asked, incredulously.

"Not a good enough reason?"

"No, I mean you think William Shakespeare or Mary Sidney or anything from the fucking English Renaissance might be more important than you?" Keating's voice softened. Churches and graveyards, both historical markers for death and taxes, also make wonderful places for the truth. "I'm sorry Jack left you. And based on the reason I'm here, I'm guessing he was too. He gave us the clues to find the fictional or real *Cardenio*, but he also left a picture of a young girl with a bright red circle around her. I've wondered about the *real* search every day for the last six weeks when I wake up. Is it happiness for us," and then Jim hesitated for perhaps too long a moment before adding, "or for you?

"Before he walked out of that bar for the last time he said to us, 'Figure out what's important.' I can't possibly imagine he meant anything but you, Rosalind. I have no idea why he walked out of your childhood, but I guarantee he regretted it."

Rosalind never looked away to gather herself or paused to contain a lump in her throat. She didn't find some point in the middle distance as a distraction to find words in lime trees, or steeples, or headstones. Instead she stared right into Keating's eyes the whole time. "I'd love to believe that's the truth."

"Hard to tell if you're as tough as you pretend," said Keating.

"No one is."

"You didn't deserve it," he paused. "You don't deserve it."

Rosalind leaned in quickly before Keating could really react and kissed him gently on the cheek. "Thank you, Jim."

"DP, come check this out!" Connelly yelled from the corner of the churchyard on the far side beyond the entrance. Naturally, he shouted louder than acceptable for any cemetery, and the few other visitors in the outdoor area stared in his direction. Dave's discretion belonged in bar rooms and nowhere else.

"Love the fire," said Jim.

"Have to," responded Rosalind.

You don't have to, thought Keating.

When they reached the far side of the church, Connelly reduced his volume immediately, worrying Keating, as it meant Dave had hatched a plan to get them into the church and, more likely, an English prison.

"Check out this door," said Connelly in as near to a whisper as he'd ever attempted.

"What about the door?" Jim responded unenthusiastically.

"If you look at the level of the church, this door goes right underneath the altar. If we can get in that door at night, we might be able to get to the grave."

"Is he out of his mind?" Jim looked to Matt for help.

"Definitely. You're just realizing this now?" asked Matt.

"Quotes, you have no idea what's on the other side of that door, and it's sixty feet from the other side of the church where Shakespeare's actual grave is located. I'm assuming you also know that the people of Stratford take this place pretty seriously and would frown upon grave robbing—"

"Stratfrown-upon-Graverobbing! Nice!" Dave laughed at himself without anyone joining in.

"Glad it's amusing you, Dave, but there is no way we're breaking into a church. We need to ask someone for help and see what they say." Keating said it rationally and with mirthless finality.

"Why were you asking the money lady about the church after closing?"

"Hopelessness," responded Keating.

"Bullshit," Dave retorted.

"We're not breaking into a fucking church, Dave."

"Jesus Christ, Jim, there is no way anyone from this town is going to let us break into his grave to expose the fact that Shakespeare didn't write Shakespeare. What do you think would happen to this town if we proved the actual bard lived ninety miles from here? The whole place would shut down. Not to mention the fact that it took them years to let someone perform a radar scan of a grave with a warning over it to never disturb the bones. No one is going to help us open that grave. Like everything else in life, we either do it ourselves, or it doesn't get done."

"Then it doesn't get done." Keating made the statement clearly, leaving no room for debate. He kept his voice calm and even but authoritative, in a way that forced Dave to realize the futility of rebuttal. "We can continue to investigate, brother, but no one is breaking into a church. I'm with you all the way on the radar scan. It makes no sense. There is definitely something down there—whether it's *Cardenio* or some other obscure piece of history. The only thing I know for sure, is that it's not Will's head. But no one is going to jail."

"Then what do we do?" Matt asked, momentarily breaking the tension.

"We make up a lie." All three men looked at Rosalind surprised she would interrupt their little squabble. "Let's go sit down, grab a drink and make up a whopper. We need a lie the town of Stratford will embrace. If we can use Jack's research to come up with something that would help the town, rather than hurt it, we might be able to get them to at least consider it."

"Perfect," said Keating, gesturing toward her. "And no one has to go to jail."

"I'll go in and see if we can meet with someone tomorrow." The self-assured look on Rosalind's face convinced Jim, but one question still remained unanswered.

"What are you going to say?" Dave inquired.

"Just that we have a couple of questions, and if someone will meet with us, we'll be happy to make a donation to the church. One thing we know for sure about the church, they respond to money." Rosalind turned and walked up the small hill toward a sign above a sign on a door.

"Damn," said Matt.

"Damn true," said Connelly

"I know but still a little harsh," added Matt.

36
CHAPTER

Approaching the Rose & Crown Pub, Keating was reminded again of the different world they now inhabited, as a marker by the entrance explained the history of the pub dating back to its original existence. Sadly, records for the property didn't go back past 1596, so the lineage could only be traced just two centuries shy of the American Revolution. The malt house on site existed as far back as 1703, seven decades before Madison, Jefferson, and Adams poured pints in their faces and started pounding out the future of America. In 1792, the pub officially became the Green Dragon owned by Edward Paine, no relation to Thomas Paine, who'd penned *Common Sense* sixteen years earlier. The Rose & Crown came to life on the current site in 1858, allowing Keating to push through a 150-year-old door and head for the bar.

Over and over, Keating and his friends were surprised to see no chairs or stools at the bar. It made sense to prevent crowding where the drinks were poured, but Jim wanted to belly up. The emptiness in the various seating areas throughout the front two-thirds of the restaurant made the room feel massive. Couches, loungers, and stools covered the six-inch-wide warped floorboards leading across the vacuous room to the beer garden outside the back door. The room begged for a loud crowd of thinker drinkers, mingling singly or, at the very least, a few contentious drunks lashing out before passing out. Instead, a lone couple sat quietly on a couch along the wall across from the bar with a contented harem of three large dogs at their feet.

"Why don't you guys find a seat outside, and I'll grab drinks. What does everybody want?" Rosalind took charge yet again.

"There's actually waitress service out there," said the barman, overhearing.

"OK, great. Wasn't sure; it seems a little quiet."

The beer garden—not much more than six picnic tables, a dumpster, and the faint promise of a little sunshine—drained beauty from the pub's welcoming interior. No one spoke up quickly, so Jim grabbed a side and hid his surprise when Rosalind slid in next to him, forcing Matt and Dave to pile in opposite them.

"All right. Ideas?" said Matt, plopping down ready to get to work.

"Well, I agree with Dave that we can't say anything about Mary Sidney." Rosalind spoke first. "We have to convince whoever's in charge at the church something vital to Stratford is buried where Shakespeare's skull used to reside."

"Hamlet." Matt almost shouted, looking across the table with satisfaction on his face. "I can't believe I get to use my entire English literature skill set again. The skull. You said it, Dave. The most famous image from all of Shakespeare is Hamlet holding the skull. What if we can convince them the skull was stolen and replaced with something important to the play *Hamlet* or Shakespeare himself? Something of value to the town."

"OK, but none of us know a damn thing about *Hamlet*, Smitty," said Keating.

"Don't be a hater, Jim. We have Google, nearly two days, and probably the most researched work of fiction in history. We have to be able to find something."

"Plus a high school English teacher." Normally it would have been Dave who harassed Matt about his ex-wife, but Jim took aim this time.

"Shot's fired, Smitty," Connelly laughed.

"Not really. She'll be happy to help."

Jim and Dave both fixed their gaze on him while he finished the sentence and then quickly and instinctively looked away. Keating knew Matt and Tracy's initial split had imitated a good thing for a few weeks. Their relationship, stressed to the point of violent argument, left Matt in a furious funk, nearly unrecognizable to Jim toward the end of the marriage. That initial rupture seemed like freedom from a great weight, but soon Matt knew it was an emaciated emancipation, thinly veiling the loneliness taking hold afterward. He and Tracy were right at the wrong time, an unoriginal historic episode.

. "There's only one problem." Rosalind broke Jim's moment of introspection over his friend's divorce.

They all looked to Jack's daughter now, hoping she would throttle the Hamlet gambit.

"I don't think there's any damn waitress service out here."

Naturally, this prompted laughter from the testosterone section, and they rose collectively, making their way back to the bar.

In Connecticut, Jim would have insisted they abandon the establishment with Hall of Justice speed, but more than four hundred years of history begged a second chance for the kid behind the taps. They succeeded in the small mission first, grabbing beers, before settling in for the tall task. With a quick draw of personal electronic devices, each of them placed "Hamlet" in their search engines, except for Matt, who did a quick time change calculation, figuring 8:30 a.m. was acceptable for a call.

—◆—

"I got nothing, guys," said Rosalind of her mad Internet search. Her struggle, born not from any lack of information but, rather, limitless amounts, was shared by each of them. Instead of one succinct strategy, they found what the author would have called "argument for a week, laughter for a month and good jest for a year." They had thirty-six hours. Despite newfound interest in the life and works of William Shakespeare, the four novices lacked both the acumen and the vernacular to find clues in a play running a full four hours, line by line.

Tracy Smith remained the best hope of finding an entrance into a grave sealed and cursed for hundreds of years. Unable to reach her, Matt left a message much too long to be discerned without an actual conversation, rambling between gravediggers and authors, trickery and truth. He vowed to call back in the evening, but until then, they would drink a while. As they continued thriving through one shift change, the young lady now pint-mongering behind the bar had poured several rounds already. Dave Connelly had a lean and thirsty look. Such men are dangerous.

"Nothing yet, Smitty?"

"My bad, DP. I forgot to mention that Tracy called, and she figured out how to break us into the all-time Fort Knox of graves. Also of note, I bought a shovel, hit the church, sold an argument, and I have the quarto edition of *Cardenio* in my room as we speak—all while drinking three feet away from you for the last few hours. Impressed?"

"Dick."

"You tell him, boy," laughed Connelly.

"Jesus, how long have we been drinking?" said Rosalind. Imbibing with these men for hours, she finally felt the palpable strangeness of spending all afternoon with three men she hardly knew. Despite the closeness of their group, these guys let you in amiably with a simple warmness, never holding the world at arm's length. She'd also learned over the last few hours that sitting with them did not mean she could successfully drink with them. "I need to head back to the hotel."

"OK, we'll walk you back," said Keating.

"No way. I never break up a party—firm and fast rule. It's rude." A slight slur in her voice made rule and rude sound a bit like the same word. "Besides, we're like an eighth of a mile from the hotel, and we're in the city of Stafford-upon-Avon. Oops. That didn't sound right. I think I'll be OK." Her glossy eyes conveyed a lie, but it was a small town. "When we get drinks together in Compton, I'll let you walk me home; 8:30 a.m. in lobby good?"

Rosalind handed her credit card across the bar to the second shift bartender, an attractive twentysomething brunette, and Connelly raised his arm to protest. "Shut it, Dave. I can pay for my own drinks."

"Don't take that card."

The bartender looked at Connelly. "The way she just dominated you, there is no way I'm letting this lass on my bad side."

"Well, whatever side you want me on, just say the word." Dave looked into his beer, unsettled these two women had gotten the better of him. He hated to lose—always.

"Clever," Rosalind mumbled, retrieving her check, signing,

and stepping toward the door. "I'll see you boys tomorrow. Good luck with Tracy, Matt."

—∽—

As a few more glasses emptied and the world grew blurry, the call finally came, their last shot in Stratford. What a strange road—a national championship, hockey movies, a religious debate, and the ire of an English Renaissance expert leading them to this phone call from a high school English teacher Matt Smith once loved dearly. The dark room, now filled with a thin layer of smoke, smelled the way to dusty death, and Smith's cell phone offered a brief candle.

"Hey, Matt. I got your message. It was a little hard to understand, but I did a little looking."

"Tracy, let me put you on speaker here. We've had a few too many cocktails for me to rely on my own memory." Matt held the phone out away from his ear. "All right, go ahead."

"Well, before I start, just try and explain to me one more time what you need."

"Oh, Lord." Matt had forgotten already.

"I got it, brother." Jim grabbed the cell phone from Matt's hand, placing it on the table in front of him. "Hey, Tracy, it's Jim. Thanks for the call back."

"No problem."

"Well, we keep getting stuck trying to follow Jack's little trail of bread crumbs. He's taking us on a tour of England, but we can't get anywhere near the spots where the quarto might possibly—"

Jim was cut off by the sound of laughter at the other end of the line. "Sorry to interrupt, Jim, but you said *quarto*. God bless Jack Taft."

"I guess that's a fair point," offered Jim, while Connelly pointed two fingers down at the telephone and fired his thumb forward, letting fly a silent round of ammunition at the telephone on the table.

"Next thing I know, Quotes won't be giving me the finger." She was close.

Jim smiled at Connelly. "So anyway, Matt had an idea, Tracy. Because we're at Shakespeare's burial place and there's clear-cut evidence the skull is missing from his grave, we could possibly parlay that into opening it up."

"Using *Hamlet*?"

"Yep. Matt made the point that the most famous image from Shakespeare is Hamlet holding the skull. If we could find something from that play to possibly convince the church an important secret lies with the body of the bard, then we might get them to agree to open the grave."

"OK. So, Matt's message was a little clearer than I thought, but you guys know about the curse, right?"

"Read it this morning. Feel like we can circumvent that. We don't want to move his bones. We just want to look at them," said Keating.

"It's going to be harder than that."

"We figured," said Connelly. "But we're here, we're Lear, and the ripeness is all. Besides, it seems these guys are a little nervous about breaking into a thirteenth-century church and cracking open the floor on our own. I'd front for the ski masks and crowbar, but they're not budging."

Tracy remained silent for just a moment, wondering if Connelly was really ready to bust into the grave himself. "Well I can look into it further, but I have one possible idea that you could use already. It's thin, but I'm not sure you'll find anything much better."

"Shoot," said Matt.

"The scene with the skull you guys are talking about is in a graveyard where two clowns are digging Ophelia's grave. The first clown is rather famous because, in a world where Hamlet seems to get the best of everyone through language, he kind of humiliates the prince in the very same way—so much so, in fact, that the lines between Horatio and Hamlet are typically ignored, often even cut from modern productions. Right before that, the two clowns discuss the value of a grave.

"The first clown asks who builds stronger than the mason, the shipbuilder or the carpenter. The second clown gives a good answer, and they have a laugh, but then the first—"

"Why are clowns digging graves?" Matt interrupted.

Tracy laughed on the other end of the line. "Not big shoes and wigs, just men who are supposedly uneducated yet somehow manage to steal all the great lines from their scenes. Clowns in that time relied on wit to entertain as much as anything else. Shakespeare's fools and clowns were like that but on steroids. So anyway, I'll call them grave diggers instead, which is actually what they are. The first one tells the second he likes his answer, but the correct answer to who is the strongest builder is the grave maker because 'the houses that he makes last till doomsday.'

"So that should get you started. The grave would make a great place to hide something because according to the man *in the grave*, it will last until doomsday. You guys said from the beginning that, obviously, the author wouldn't be writing the story ahead of time. The men who hid *Cardenio* would be using Shakespeare's plays as a map to hide it, rather than writing their own map. This would be a great scene to use because of the often overlooked dialogue between Horatio and Hamlet. I have it here so I can read it to you":

Hamlet. This fellow might be in 's time a great buyer of land, with his statutes, his recognizances, his fines, his double vouchers, his recoveries: in this the fine of his fines, and the recovery of his recoveries, to have his fine pate full of fine dirt? Will his vouchers vouch him no more of his purchases, and double ones too, than the length and breadth of a pair of indentures? The very conveyances of his lands will hardly lie in the box, and must the inheritor himself have no more? Ha?

"Just checking here, Trace," interrupted Connelly. "We're not supposed to understand a single word of what you just said are we?"

"I'll get there, David. I promise. Just listen first and I'll explain after":

Horatio. Not a jot more, my lord.

Hamlet. Is not parchment made of sheep-skins?

Horatio. Ay, my lord, and calf-skins too.

Hamlet. They are sheep and calves which seek out assurance in that.

Dave, Matt, and Jim looked at each other in a brand-new state of confused inebriation. When they'd watched Jack's lectures, the professor had offered explanations and direction. To hear the language across a phone line minus inflection and emphasis left them all wondering where the hell Tracy was taking them.

"There are a few more lines at the beginning and end, but that's basically it."

An expected, confused pause came from a public house in Stratford-upon-Avon.

"Tracy?"

"Yes."

"What the hell does any of that mean?" Connelly queried before letting his head rest on his forearms.

Laughter filled the other end of the line.

"Still laughing at us?" Jim asked.

"Still not at all sorry."

Finally, they could all laugh together.

"But I understand. Hamlet talks about what a man may have

done in his life, his holdings and acquisitions he's garnered. Statutes, conveyances and indentures meaning contracts and deeds. You can own and manage these things all your life, but obviously not after you're dead. All makes sense right?"

"Yes, but—"

"What does it have to do with the book?" She cut Keating off.

"Yep."

"The last couple lines before he speaks to the grave digger are the most important. Sheepskin and calfskin were used to write on all the way back to the eleventh century. It definitely sets up the next line for Hamlet's humor, but it doesn't totally fit. Hamlet is saying the holdings of a man can't be taken to his grave. The author would have loved the irony of hiding some manner of holdings, like a valuable book, precisely where you're not supposed to take it with you—beyond the grave. And I'm guessing the church board would love it as well."

"Wow. That's amazing, Tracy. Pretty solid work for four hours." More than Matt's words, the tone of his voice best conveyed his appreciation, not so much for her help but for her intellect and unselfishness. "I have no idea if this will work, but it really is just what we needed. We'll bring it to the church tomorrow."

"There's one problem." A look of strange sadness crossed Dave's countenance even as he too appreciated Tracy's help. "What's in the grave? We can't tell them we think Mary Sidney's *Cardenio* is in the grave. They'll never open it. What's in there?"

"A First Folio." She said it naturally, almost condescending without the intent, as if it were arithmetic for a particle physicist. "Stratford-upon-Avon's folio, brought back to them as a gift from their bard."

Keating knew that David Connelly didn't usually feel inferior, but this was twice in one night now. Dave had everything he needed to figure it out himself, and in the past, missing the obvious would have angered him, even with his limited knowledge of the subject. Rather than any furrowed brow or angry scowl, Jim saw something else on his friend's face. "Thanks so much, Tracy." It looked like appreciation.

"Sorry, guys, I must have a bad connection. That sounded like Quotes saying thank you. Must be losing you. Either that, or he's losing *it*."

With yet another unfamiliar step down an unknown road, Dave responded. "Tracy, this is David Connelly of the Glastonbury, Connecticut, Connellys. I just wanted to say thank you." His sarcasm oozed through the phone, but his tone changed when he added, "We really appreciate you helping with this. It's really become a big deal to all of us."

She paused, likely contemplating another shot at Dave but followed suit instead. "You're very welcome, Quotes." The second familiar *Quotes* resonated with all of them.

Keating looked over to Matt who swept his phone and pint from the table. Matt gently tapped the phone, switching off the speaker, and walked away from the others. Keating grabbed his pint from the table and took a long quaff, finishing it off. Change was coming for Matt Smith.

"We should probably roll too, Dave. We might have actual work to do tomorrow."

"Grab Smitty on the way out. I'm on vacation," said Connelly, remaining firmly in his chair.

Keating knew his friend, the thirst, and the futility of coming between the two. Dave wouldn't be talked out of the bar, and Jim didn't feel like wasting time. Dave Connelly could never be talked out of doing exactly what Dave Connelly wanted to do. A still fairly empty bar and a short walk made for little reason to worry, so Jim stepped away into the cool evening.

37
CHAPTER

Rosalind Taft stared blankly at the ceiling of her room in the Mercure Shakespeare Hotel, a victim of time change, a captive of natural ubiquitous sleeplessness, and a hater of all eighteen channels of British hotel television. In the bedroom of her condominium, she could turn to 2:30 a.m. episodes of real estate shows, cooking shows, and even an occasional late-night sitcom. She never really fell into reading and never wondered if it was a rebellion against her father. If he'd been in the house long enough to require reading hours or mandatory homework, perhaps she could consider it an objection, but she felt no such resistance. She'd inherited his intellect but never his proclivity for reading or his curiosity. She studied to win. Grades in undergraduate and graduate school afterwards were a path to a paycheck.

The one connection to her father, the bibliophile, lay in the barely tenable memory of Jack reading to her as a child. Despite long days of work during the school year and massive writing projects and research in the summer, he had found time to read to his only child at night. Their pattern was almost religious, even if a bit foggy to Rosalind all these years later.

—⟋⟍—

While the memory of her father reading aloud was blurry and faded, her recollection of him leaving never existed. The-nine year-old girl was sheltered from it intentionally, because Jack Taft knew Shakespeare well, and that was bad news for fathers and daughters. When Mrs. Taft finally tired of Jack's long hours, she sought entertainment elsewhere and with more than one man. Jack caught on fairly early but never blamed her. He'd been a decent father over the years but a terrible husband. He would have allowed her indiscretions go on for all time, but his wife angered beyond the limits of cohabitation when she still failed to get his attention. Jack arrived home late each day, and the arguments grew a little more heated, until she finally left with her young daughter in tow.

The man from Stratford and his addiction to strong women finally had the professor's full attention. Caught in the paradox of wanting to do right for his daughter and wanting to do right by his wife, Jack had let go—secure in the overwhelming heartbreak of the truth that young women need their mothers. Like so much of his professional conjecture, Jack knew this answer wasn't right or wrong, just a feeling based on knowledge acquired in his young life. At first, he tried to stay in touch, sending money, letters, and gifts along the way but had received no contact in return.

It finally occurred to him as an overwhelming truth that, if Rosalind always blamed him for her parents' split, then she would never blame herself or the woman raising her. He cried nearly every day for two years straight.

As technology changed in the latter stretch of Rosalind's formative years, he was able to follow her life closely through social media. Her graduations, birthdays, dates, and friends were all available to an old man on Twitter. But eventually, even this stream of information ran dry, perhaps his daughter's wisdom recognizing a superfluous pool of self-aggrandizement. He wondered often about the path leading to a different fulfillment of the phrase *life's work* but had maintained his distance and his heartbreak.

—⧗—

Rosalind should have been sound asleep hours ago, but the inability to sort out her place in this new world kept her eyes open—not the cliché of her place in the world, which grew more secure every day, but her actual geographical location. Her first trip to Europe had been haphazardly thrown together in search of a piece of her father she may not even want, in the company of three men she just met. Rosalind got out of bed.

The knock at such a late hour echoed down the quiet hallway, making Rosalind a bit self-conscious, a rarity. She could hear some shuffling from inside the room, and it suddenly made her question whether this was a good idea. Dave opened the door of the small hotel room and froze instantly. Rosalind Taft said nothing. They'd spent a few memorable nights together over the three weeks since that initial late afternoon, but this was still a surprise to both of them. She'd walked intrepidly out of the pub hours ago and should have been sound asleep. It would have been so much better if she were sound asleep.

Rosalind couldn't help looking past Dave, feeling quite ridiculous now. With the exception of some major cities, hotel rooms in the United States generally offer at least a little bit of space beyond a bed and a bathroom, but it's rarely the case in Europe, where just getting into the room often requires some dexterity to squeeze between the bed and the in-swinging door. This fact, more than anything else, gave Rosalind a direct view of the second shift bartender sitting fully clothed on Dave's bed.

"Hey," said Dave. Though he would never believe it, he actually blushed.

Rosalind laughed innocently in his face before she turned and walked away.

"Wait," said Dave, stepping into the hallway, still frazzled.

"Yes." When she spun around to face him, Rosalind was already over it. They were grown-ups who'd slept together a few times. He owed her nothing, and she knew it better than Dave. More than anything, she felt anger for the instant of shock she experienced seeing the young woman in Dave's room. She knew lots of men like Dave, what they were good for, and the low expectations that came dragging along behind them.

"Sorry, I just—"

"Oh, please, David. You have nothing to be sorry about. I couldn't sleep and figured you'd just be rolling back in. Get back to it. I'll see you tomorrow."

Rosalind turned away for good this time while Dave stood motionless. Her arms swung loosely by her sides as she shuffled down the hallway carelessly, and each of her strides sent a clear message—no problem. Connelly had invited Rosalind on this trip and that fact alone meant she probably deserved a little better than the lonely walk, but she never considered that. Her father had taught her early on in life that, if you give them the chance, men will disappoint you. She didn't give Dave the chance.

—⟋⟍—

Jim watched Connelly skulk into the lobby last, never knowing about the mild confrontation or the late-shift bartender. Matt and Rosalind stood next to him by the Quill entrance. They all followed Dave out the door with a smattering of good mornings. At currently 3:30 a.m. in Connecticut, none of them felt strong.

Matt fell into stride on the sidewalk alongside Dave and gave a brief recap. The other two meandered along two steps behind. "Hey. So, a couple other things Tracy mentioned last night when I spoke to her. I told Keating on the way home, but he was hammered, and I was struggling with the English language myself, so it's worth explaining again. I figured you guys would want to know as well." Smith looked like an amateur tour guide speaking in uncomfortable lecture format, with Connelly ahead and the other two lagging behind. Swiveling his head back and forth, in a manner more common at Wimbledon than Stratford, he continued educating.

"I guess there is something called the *age problem* that happens in the scene with the grave digger."

"The age problem?" asked Rosalind.

"Yep. For the entirety of the play, Hamlet is perceived to be somewhere between eighteen and twenty-five years old. Then in the graveyard scene, he is suddenly thirty. It happens pretty much overnight. Hamlet asks the clown how long he's been digging graves, and he says he started the day Prince Hamlet was born, thirty years ago."

"Sorry to interrupt again, Matt," said Rosalind, "but how does Tracy think that will help?"

"That's exactly what Matt said." Keating responded. "She doesn't think it will help with the folio. We need to suggest the people who hid it thought the discrepancy would make a good marker. It's a very minor scene that has been poured over because of the problem with Hamlet's age."

"Wasn't really expecting you to remember that, DP," said Smith.

"Little faith," responded Keating

"Much alcohol."

"Looks like you win."

"*Tombstone*, kinda," said Dave.

"Really, pretty clever." Matt said it with obvious pride in his ex-wife's acumen. "She wants us to convince them the clue has actually become subterfuge over the years, because no one pays attention to the part with the sheepskin and calfskin. Whoever hid the folio left a hint so clever everyone missed it. At least, that's what we need to convince the folks at the church."

"Do you think we'll need an argument for who actually put the book there?"

"Ha. We're on the same plane, Rosalind. I asked Tracy that, too. The First Folio was published posthumously. Shakespeare never saw it. We can make the argument it could have been anyone from his crew in England. His acting troupe, the publishers, or a younger writer would all make sense because they were replacing Shakespeare's *head* with Shakespeare's *mind*. She read me the one part of the quote again—'to have his fine pate full of fine dirt.' What better resting place for all his plays then right where they came from, the eight inches above his shoulders."

"Damn," said Connelly, "not bad. Anything else?"

"She just said to vaguely mention that it's a play filled with death and questions, two more things that could serve as clues."

"Dude, is she fired up?" asked Keating.

"She is." Matt squeezed out the lie quickly, not wanting to spoil the mood of his fellow archaeologists. Tracy was a huge help to him and his friends, but the truth of the matter came in her final warning that no one would open Shakespeare's grave under any circumstances. She actually told Matt it would be easier trying to flood the Avon River up to the church steeple, forcing the floating body out of the grave, than convincing anyone from the church to crack open the floor.

Turning left into the street entrance, the group walked off Trinity Street through the tunnel of lime trees, past the headstones, and toward the ridiculously low wooden door at the entrance. Keating took a deep breath, nervous this whole wild swan chase would end without one piece of tangible evidence to prove Jack's theory.

As he exhaled, Rosalind reached over, squeezed his hand briefly, and whispered, "If nothing else, it's a beautiful town to visit." More than the squeeze, her awareness astounded Jim.

The vicar of the Holy Trinity church in Stratford-upon-Avon was a tall, lean bespectacled man named Steven Cavanaugh. Approaching the four of them in the back of the church, he smiled and introduced himself. His hollow, amiable face made all of them more comfortable to tell the story of a First Folio. Jim began with Jack Taft, an erudite English professor who left them a map of discovery. He led the vicar through the details of the initial meeting, Jack's death, and how four complete amateurs had come to arrive in his church on the eastern side of the Atlantic Ocean.

Matt Smith chimed in, taking the lead when it came to the details of Hamlet and how it seemed this church was the best final resting place for the folio. Mentioning the monument or Wilton House seemed counterproductive, lacking any connection to the man from Stratford. Matt nailed his brief presentation, even quoting Hamlet directly, however briefly, to make his point.

He leaned heavily on his practiced oratory skills in concluding, "If this folio is found, it would be more important than any of the other two hundred or so in existence. It would be the most important work of literature ever discovered. This would be Stratford-upon-Avon's folio; Holy Trinity Church's folio; and, most importantly, William Shakespeare's Folio—not just as author, but as owner."

Vicar Steven Cavanaugh nodded his head patiently in appreciation, embracing their passion as they wove through the labyrinth spanning the last four centuries. He feigned interest, as if this group rather than countless, nameless others had found the answer to the enigma of William Shakespeare's grave. Brother Cavanaugh was a good man, a shepherd of a man, and a man who had heard this story before.

"Thank you all for taking the time to come and visit with us. It's an amazing story. The problem, however, is that the church wardens have entertained stories like yours for a hundred years. Some believe no one is in the grave. Some believe they know exactly where Shakespeare is buried in the walls. Some are motivated by his last will and testament, while others have proof from the sonnets. And a few, while all God's children, are just a little crazy.

"You folks are definitely not the latter, and I know you're offering us a gift in the form of Stratford's folio." Cavanaugh hesitated, looking past his visitors and into the vastness of the church beyond them. "Imagine if that folio were there? It would indeed be truly incredible. But if we dug up our church every time someone submitted a new theory, there would be no church, just a huge excavation site. You see, William Shakespeare made a very special contribution to humanity. But here, in these walls, he is everyman. If there really is some great mystery, I fear no one will ever get to the bottom of it. Thank you for coming in to see me, and God bless you."

Jim noticed the semantics of the vicar's words in his circuitous, polite, emphatic *no*. *In these walls, he is everyman*, just like Bottom. He'd even continued on, *Get to the bottom of it.*

"I notice you have some projects going on." Dave Connelly had sat quietly the whole time before uttering that one simple sentence.

"Always," responded the vicar, turning his attention to Dave.

"The Friends of Shakespeare's Church is a very helpful organization I understand. Started in 2003 with a donation of five pounds, and they've raised over a million more since then to help with church beautification."

It was now Dave's turn to peruse the church. "You can see it. It's gorgeous in here." Dave was looking across the church, but Jim thought he could see him counting zeros in his bank account.

"Thank you. I agree." The vicar smiled at Dave's perfunctory comment.

Jim knew right where he was headed.

"But always more to be done. What are you working on now?"

"Oh, they are working on refurbishing the wall on the south transept." The vicar nodded in the direction of the Chapel of St. Thomas Becket.

"Do you think the wardens would be willing to open the grave of one of God's children if we donated a million pounds to the church? Seems like fourteen years' worth of projects for a look would be a bargain. No disturbing the bones, just a little digging in the dust." Dave's eyes continued to drift casually across the expanse of the church and then fell abruptly and heavily on Steven Cavanaugh.

Brother Cavanaugh stared silently at Connelly. Jim knew Dave had quickly inferred the nature of the vicar's rehearsed speech. He had likely regurgitated it a hundred times, practicing the cordiality to the point where it felt like doing a favor when he turned people away. He'd delivered it impeccably, but they were off the script now. He'd never been countered with a million pounds before.

While vicar Cavanaugh stammered and contemplated, Jim did the same. *How much damn money does Dave have?*

"That would be a question for the wardens."

"Would it be a terrible trouble to ask them?" Dave handed a card to the man with oversight of religious services in the Holy Trinity Church—the same card he'd handed to countless martini-soaked women in bars. Two words were on the front— David Connelly—his cell phone number written on the back.

—⧟—

"You guys eat anything this morning?" Connelly asked, exiting the church and beginning down the path toward the road.

"Hotel room coffee," answered Matt.

"That was kind of fucked up," said Keating.

"Yes, it was," Rosalind agreed. "I think I may need a shower."

"What's that, DP?" Connelly asked sardonically with his answer at the ready. "That a church can break its sacred tenets if the price is right? Dude, you should consider opening a history book."

"I don't know if it's worse that they might agree or that you offered. Something just felt wrong about that, David."

"Seriously, Rosalind?" Dave spun to face her. "I'm offering a million pounds to help a church. Not only that. But if Jack was right, they get a book that would then be worth ten or twenty times that? I did something wrong?"

"Just didn't feel right," she replied.

"Well, sorry I hurt your feelings."

"Don't be a dick, Quotes," Keating said very calmly.

"Oh Jesus, DP, not you too."

"Hey, brother, I don't care what you do with your money. More power to you. More projects for them. Didn't really like your tone though. She's entitled to her opinion."

"Don't worry about it, Jim. It's just his default mode. He doesn't mean anything by it." Keating was a little surprised to hear the words come from Rosalind, but much like the previous night, she made it clear immediately. She didn't care at all.

"Default mode?" asked Jim.

"Let's get some food," she responded.

"Fine. Fuck it." Dave ended the protestations, turning and striding down the path through the lime trees. "Wish they had a Corona tree," he mumbled to himself.

The waitress placed small cups of coffee in front of them and motioned to Dave. "Your Guinness will be up in a minute."

"I appreciate the proper pour. No worries."

"Don't know how you continue to do it, brother," Matt said with admiration. "I got a bit of a dinger, and I was down hours before you I'm guessing."

"Quite a few hours," interjected Rosalind.

Dave glanced at her, offering no retort. Jim and Matt remained clueless. Rosalind smirked carelessly.

"Mother's milk, kid. A Guinness will get you right."

"It's amazing how different this town is compared to London. Jesus, I'd kill myself if I had to live in London. But I'd love to shelter up in one of those row houses for a decade or two. Work a counter, buy a dog, and disappear for a while. Wouldn't be too bad." Jim looked across the restaurant and out into the street.

"Well I'd have to say, New York City is a little different than

Glastonbury, Connecticut," Matt challenged. "Pretty much the same everywhere, right? Big towns and small towns."

"This place has a different feel," said Jim.

"All right then," said Smith. "What's the nicest city you've ever been to?"

"Killarney, Ireland," Connelly answered quickly. "Easily the most fun I've ever had, and quite possibly the nicest people on earth. Irish breakfast every morning, a few chops at the golf and fishing club, and the best nightlife in the history of starry evenings. Phenomenal pints. The people take pride in her too. The streets are clean, and the homes are beautifully maintained. They even have a little competition against other towns to see which is the most aesthetically pleasing. Great place." Dave made a mental note to get back there soon.

"NYC for me," Matt followed. "Anything you want day or night. Exposure to everything. It's—"

"Brother, the question was nicest town. You're gonna get put in a Riley Shaunessy time-out," Connelly said to Smith.

"Boston beats New York any day," said Rosalind.

"What?!" Matt fired back.

"Not even close, Matty."

"I knew I didn't like this girl. Broadway. Empire State. Yankee Stadium. Broadway. Wall Street. The city that never sleeps. Not even close."

"Jesus, Matt. You named a stadium that sucks so bad they had to replace it. At least Fenway is still open. And a street that caused the collapse of the American economy to kick off the new century. Are you arguing for it or against it? You're talking about a group of people who use their middle finger as semaphore and the word *fuck* as every possible part of speech, other than adverb, but only because they can't define it."

"You are fuckly lying," said Matt perhaps acknowledging a truth known to everyone in the world other than New Yorkers.

"Ha. You did modify a verb. I stand corrected on one count," said Rosalind.

"You spend much time in Boston?" Connelly almost instantly realized his thoughtless slip.

"I live there."

The weird twist brought simple truth to the English morning more than anything that had happened before or after—three great friends and a traveling companion none of them knew. An uncomplicated conversation starter benignly intended, and once again, Connelly felt like an idiot.

Over the past weeks, the time he'd spent with Rosalind could not be described as intimate, but it sure as hell was familiar. When they weren't horizontal, they spoke of this project, this enigma, slowly starting to define them all. It was just a brief twinkling to let them all know to keep looking forward, something the boys in the booth rarely, if ever, brought into their conversations. Their friendship was a monotony of pastimes revisited. This whole thing helped them grow, but hell if Connelly didn't wish he'd remembered where Rosalind lived.

Thankfully, the compassionate waitress broke the tension, setting the Guinness on the table and opening with another harmless query. "Are you folks ready to order?"

"Definitely," said Rosalind.

38
CHAPTER

Rather than holding up the lobby walls again, they agreed to meet in the Quill this time. The subtle difference between meeting inside or outside of the hotel pub meant Dave arrived first; early; and, as always, thirsty. The others all filtered in behind him—first Matt and then the party crasher and finally Keating, who took a little longer than normal getting ready, though Matt didn't notice. There were no dogs, good Samaritans, or oddly pacified giants, but it still felt warm in the small space.

"Looking particularly handsome, James," said Connelly.

"Thanks, Dave. Coming from you that means absolutely nothing, but you're looking sharp too, my man."

"You guys want Matt and I to bag out so you can be alone?" asked Rosalind.

"I don't think Jim is the kind of guy who puts out on the first date, so no, you guys are good. A couple more shoulders for me to sleep on during the play."

Keating looked toward Rosalind while trying not to look. She wore a loose-fitting beige blouse with a long floral-patterned maxi skirt. She was both beautiful and surprisingly unaware of it. It wasn't just the fit of her clothes exuding comfort; she was overwhelmingly relaxed in her own skin amid the group in a Stratford hotel pub.

When she rose from her soft leather chair on Keating's arrival, Connelly instinctively piled down the remainder of his drink. The four of them neatly filed out the door, limping toward the first Shakespeare performance any of them had ever seen.

—◌◌◌—

Twelfth Night is the perfect starting point for all Shakespeare rookies. The play involves many of the typical Shakespearean devices, including a shipwreck, separated siblings, and cross-dressing women but, most of all, three great scene-stealers. Across the canon, the author inserted minor and major characters who dominate every scene they enter but are only rarely a part of the resolution of the story. Audience favorites are most often the ones who bring a laugh rather than profound thought. *Macbeth*'s porter, *Much Ado About Nothing*'s Dogberry, and *Two Gentleman of Verona's* Launce are all minor characters who elicit laughs every time.

Twelfth Night rests on the shoulders of its three scene-stealers—a strongly played Malvolio, a likeable clown, and a well-directed Sir Toby Belch. Malvolio almost always delivers, but Sir Toby can fail if he misses a few lines. While he is only one small thread in the fabric of the future Jack Falstaff, the character he anticipates, he grabs a lot of laughs. The clown gets the first few chuckles of the play, reminding the groundlings, and quite possibly Robert Greene, "It's better to be a witty fool than a foolish wit."

Three first-time playgoers attempted to lock in as Connelly yawned in unison with Orsino's opening line, "If music be the food of love, play on." It made sense for the creators of the movie *Shakespeare in Love* to jump ahead to scene ii, showing

Joseph Fiennes putting pen to paper, as they needed Viola and the sea coast to be the opener for relevance. Like many of the love stories, the triangulation of desire takes center stage, as the lovers go unloved for most of the play. Orsino pines for the fair Olivia, before the lovely Viola, obviously disguised as Cesario. Olivia, of course, desires the disguised Cesario, before falling miraculously for Sebastian in the last few lines of the play. Like Emerson's grief hundreds of years later, love is shallow for the author:

> We men may say more, swear more, but indeed,
> Our shows are more than will, for still we prove
> Much more in our vows, but little in our love.

Viola, still presenting as the male Cesario, offers this sentiment echoing the disguised Rosalind in *As You Like It*, who opines, "Men have died from time to time and worms have eaten them, but not for love.

Playgoers enjoying either show are reminded that Shakespeare's women, stronger in so many other areas, are stronger lovers as well, according to the author. Viola is no exception, far exceeding the clunky, meatheaded Orsino. Only Rosalind noticed the line, "Our shows are more than Will," when Cesario delivered it in Act II. She hoped so.

"Dude, are you following this?" Matt whispered to Connelly.

"For the most part. We'll compare notes over a beer at halftime."

"I think it's called intermission."

"Whatever."

Before the lights went up for intermission, one last case of mistaken identity amused the audience, as Antonio, servant to Viola's brother Sebastian, believes the subterfuge. Seeing Viola dressed as a man and ready to fight Sir Andrew, he is quick to jump in and defend Viola-Cesario-Sebastian in the fight. With good direction, the beauty of the play is an audience laughing for a full five acts without a complete understanding of the language. This edition's director did well, as Matt and Dave remained smiling for a few minutes after the curtain dropped and they moved torridly toward the bar.

"OK, here's all I got. Toby wants to sponge and drink. The servant guy is an asshole, so Toby and Maria are going to mess with him. Everyone believes Viola is Cesario, except the guy at the end, who thinks she is her twin brother. And the fancy girl is in love with the disguised girl. How did I do?" Matt pushed both arms out to his sides in a motion that could have become a bow, but the concession line moved forward, and he followed along.

"Sounds good to me, brother," Keating replied.

"It's funny. I always thought that quote about, 'Some men are born great, some achieve greatness and others have greatness thrust upon them,' was from a president. I had no idea it's from Shakespeare. Makes you wonder how many other lines have been plagiarized from his writing."

"*Her* writing, Dave," Rosalind said. "If we want this whole thing to break right, then they need to be Mary Sidney's plays, right?"

"Most certainly," Dave replied.

Connelly was correct. The list of cliché's, quotes, and speeches plagiarized from Shakespeare went on almost infinitely. "What's done is done," "Love is blind," "spotless reputation," "Sweet are the uses of adversity," and "The better part of valor is discretion" are all found in the plays, along with countless other axioms. Of course, it is no shock the expressions folded into the language, but it's amazing they persevered so long.

"This is it," said Dave, looking at his phone.

"This is what?"

"I'm getting a call from Stratford," said Connelly. "Hello?"

Capitalism is a flexible, evolving mechanism with seismic shifts from time to time. Products become obsolete, ideas are outdated, and stable markets become volatile. Blockbuster becomes Netflix, MapQuest becomes GPS, and bulls become bears overnight. One monetary offer pushed the wardens into fast-forward simply because there was enough cash on the line. Could the church possibly ignore a curse on a Bard's bones because the price was right? Maybe they would allow a late-night inspection: *The better part of valor is discretion.* Connelly continued to nod his head in ascension without saying a word in response.

"OK, I understand," said Dave as he pulled the phone away from his ear.

"No dice, kids. They're keeping it locked down. Said they appreciated such a generous offer, but it would go against pretty much everything they stand for if they opened the grave."

"Wow," said Jim. "I hate how it all went down, but I never believed they would turn down that kind of money for one peek."

"Maybe we found something that can't be bought," Matt offered.

"Does anyone else think it's weird that—"

"Jack started in with religion?" Keating finished Dave's sentence without intent or any forethought whatsoever. He didn't even know for certain he'd said it aloud.

Despite their initial trepidation, Jim could see each of them enjoying the second part of *Twelfth Night* as much as the first. The director made great use of the area below the stage to have Toby, Maria, and Fabian spy on Malvolio and Olivia from all manner of places. As they surfaced and disappeared behind trees, shrubs, rocks, and benches like a giant, stage-wide Whac-A-Mole game, Malvolio danced around in yellow stockings with a ridiculous smile, the victim of their practical joke. The audience laughed harder and harder without necessarily considering the universality of the Man from Stratford but, of course, enjoying the show.

"Well, guys?" asked Connelly.

"I can't frickin believe I'm saying this, but it was hysterical," said Jim.

"I'm with you, DP," said Smith. "I didn't understand half of what they were saying, but I chuckled my ass off."

"Jack was right," added Keating, somewhat quietly, "well at least in this play. The duke wasn't good enough for Viola. I just couldn't see them together. He really didn't talk much about her in the lecture, at least not that I remember, but she dominates. Jack talked more about the women of Shakespeare in general. Olivia and the duke should have ended up together. Viola's too clever for him. She survives the shipwreck, dresses as a man, controls the plot, ducks everyone with her language, brings everyone together, and all she gets is the goon?"

"He's a duke." Connelly said it with passing interest, but at least he paid attention. "Maybe it's all you ever need."

"Times haven't changed much then." Smith laughed.

"That's a real possibility," Connelly agreed.

"You guys want to grab one more before we turn it off?" asked Matt.

"Yes!" Connelly exclaimed.

"Shit, I wasn't asking you, Dave. I know you're in. I was asking DP and Rosalind."

"Out tonight," said Keating.

"Me too," said the professor's daughter.

—⚋—

The street noise dropped to a whisper, and the evening air begged for a walk or a smoke, depending on inclinations. England offered the best of late summer. Reaching the split at Church Street, Connelly and Smith turned left for one last drink, or four, while Keating and Rosalind trekked back to the Mercure.

"See you in the morning," said Matt

"Yep. We headed for that castle tomorrow?" Rosalind asked.

"Indeed," Connelly replied.

"Peace," Keating responded.

Less than twenty paces apart from the other men, Rosalind offered the sentiment Keating was thinking, "God, it's gorgeous out here tonight."

"You ain't lying," said Keating with an exaggerated sigh.

"I can't even believe I'm here."

"Because you're on a fruitless mission with three idiots or because you're running down your father's life work? I'm guessing they're equally improbable at this point."

For a breathless moment, she offered nothing, instead tilting her head back looking skyward as if the fault lies not in ourselves but in our stars. Hell, maybe it did. Reentering the conversation, she put her hand on Keating's shoulder in a familiar way for just a second and responded. "I guess I'd have to say both, but somehow, I'm actually glad I'm here. I'm not even sure I could say why, but I know I'm glad. For the moment I'll call it good company and change my mind later. Let's get that drink after all."

Keating looked over his shoulder, unable to spot the other two in the late evening street. "Not sure which way they went."

"Nah. Fuck Dave! Let's find our own spot."

—ɯ—

Past the Mercure, the twosome made a right turn toward Loxley's Restaurant and Wine Bar. A glass of red and a small outdoor space presented the combination Rosalind sought. The tight outer courtyard along the building's east wall felt perfect. The structure's white brick caught just enough of the streetlight to make the table their own secret hideaway. They were hidden, and they were exposed. Six minutes later, the waitress set the wine on the table next to Keating's Carling and dropped one menu on the table.

"Thai food in the bard's birthplace. Not exactly what I would have guessed," said Jim.

"You're the one who asked for a menu," Rosalind returned.

"I can always eat, but this combo may keep me hungry."

"Oh, what's the matter? Afraid to stretch out and try something new?"

"Afraid to vomit up Thai food in central England."

"Fair enough." Rosalind smiled at Keating, making him extremely thankful the other men had broken away for the night. "So how do you feel about the trip so far? You seem like much more of a realist than David, but you were still willing to come to England."

"I don't know if I was willing to come to England or just so damn excited to leave Connecticut. You know the highlight of most of my days is time spent in a bar with three grown idiots telling the same stories over and over again."

Keating exhaled briefly, debating whether to continue on, not knowing if he was willing to pour his life out onto the table. "I know this isn't real, but damn if I don't want it to be. You know Smitty has the law, Quotes has money, and Shaunessy has the gym. When your father handed me that envelope, he gave me something that was mine." Keating noted the word *mine*, feeling selfish and needed to clarify. "Not a possession, but a vision. It was something I could actually sink my teeth into and awake with a purpose every day. I guess that's the real reason I'm here."

"Policing douchebags isn't getting it done anymore?"

Keating laughed. "Dave told you about that?"

"I was a little curious how Jim Keating gets the initials DP. He expounded."

Keating's lifelong hobby obviously brought him both pride and embarrassment, but a person really needed to dislike other humans in general to think him righteous. Most anyone would see his antics as childish, simply because they were. However, it's a rarer person still who never even considers policing all the selfishness seen in the course of a day. Watching someone throw garbage on your earth, disrespect his elders, pull a child's arm just a bit too hard, or steal your time to add to their own makes everyone angry. Keating thought of it as a definition of degrees.

"I guess I earned them." His emphasis on *earned* conveyed the pride he felt, despite his often ridiculous methods.

Keating and Rosalind fell into conversation naturally and comfortably, as if they were old friends. They laughed at the expense of others, shared small pieces of themselves, and drank a little later into the evening than planned. They talked of the world they lived in, the people they'd met, and occasionally just leaned back and looked skyward, enjoying the cool evening. Perhaps more than a mysterious quarto or a magician's prestige, this conversation in a Stratford back alley was Jack Taft's goal.

39

CHAPTER

The sprawling Kenilworth Castle grounds are incredible even as ruins. They had entered through the main entrance from the car park, experiencing a full view of the vast landscape. The small stream they crossed was once damned, creating a huge lake filling the now grassy valley. The gateway gave way to a massive hillside and myriad hundred-year-old oak trees that appeared even older. The formidable castle beckoned them up the hill toward the church in the distance. A wedding ceremony was underway in Leicester's Gatehouse to the northeast, so they continued upward to Elizabeth's garden and the keep.

Entering the flower garden of Kenilworth Castle, Jim led the other three toward the ruins of the tower at the edge of the courtyard. A small child, perhaps three or four years old, wailed incessantly into the sunny morning. His father clearly held some object of affection away from the child as the boy pursued him, arms and lungs outstretched. There were no discernable words, just loud screams of agitation echoing deep into the countryside beyond, sending birds into flight and serenity into hiding.

The construction of Kenilworth Castle dated back to the early 1120s when, in its infancy, Geoffrey de Clinton built the original tower and priory on the site where castle ruins are still visited today. The property exchanged hands over the next three hundred and fifty years from King John, when the massive lake was dammed, to John of Gaunt and the construction of the Great Hall to Henry V and, ultimately, to Robert Dudley, the Earl of Leicester who nearly bankrupt his considerable fortunes creating a retreat for Queen Elizabeth.

Dudley's eighteen-day pageant held at Kenilworth was the reason for the group's visit and Jack's fascination with the castle. Leicester's building was designed to equal the original ancient tower. The top floor brought the building up, literally and figuratively, to the elevation of the original. Robert Langham, who attended the Kenilworth pageant in 1575 as part of Elizabeth's entourage, wrote a description of the room where Mary Sidney stayed for the pageant.

While Taft loved the idea of the bedchamber as an appropriate resting place for Mary Sidney's play, he accepted the unlikelihood that a quarto could survive the outdoor conditions for four centuries. If the castle ruins, where Mary's love affair with the theater began, were the play's final resting place, the group would need a bit of luck to find it.

"This place is unbelievable," said Matt.

"How would you even build this without modern tools?" Keating responded.

"Brother, you could give me every tool ever invented, and I couldn't begin to build this place." Dave pointed up at the architecture as they moved past the north side of the keep. Some of the stone stairways in the Great Hall had caved in over the years, and wooden replacements led them up to the top level and more amazing views of the countryside in the distance.

"Tight quarters," Rosalind stated, making her way down the original spiral staircase toward the kitchens and the ground level.

A couple in their early fifties stopped in a small alcove to let them pass as the screams of the same angry child still echoed throughout the thick stone walls. "Somebody just muzzle it for Christ's sake," the man suggested.

Keating almost apologized as his policing extended just shy of loud children with bad parents.

Reaching the ground floor, Matt turned to Dave again as his tour guide. "What's the story here again, Quotes?"

"As a teenager, Mary Sidney visited Kenilworth along with the queen in 1575. She would have seen a play performed for the Queen and perhaps even fallen in love with the theater. She—"

"'It is an honour I dream not of,'" Keating interrupted, speaking to himself and looking out toward the center of the grounds rather than his friends at his side.

"What's that, Jim?" Rosalind looked at him quizzically.

"You can almost hear her saying it," said Jim to no one in particular as he mentally moved away from Dave and Matt. "She's fourteen years old, just returned from Ireland, watching a play where a war is settled when the women save the day. One of the great patrons of Renaissance literature is inspired on these grounds. She loves the theater and writing, but it's not proper for her to be a part of it all. When her marriage is arranged for her as a young girl, you can almost hear her anticipating Juliet. 'It is an honour I dream not of.' It's pretty amazing."

"Anticipating Juliet?" Matt smiled.

"When her mother tells her she's to be married, that's how she responds." Keating looked back toward Matt, though he may have honestly forgotten to whom he was speaking.

"Looks like you're not the only one who studied, Quotes." Matt laughed.

"And where did my father propose the quarto might be?" asked Rosalind.

"Top floor of Leicester's building," Connelly answered.

"Just sitting there?"

"Not exactly."

—⁂—

The metal staircases and walkways were anachronistic within the confines of the stone castle walls. Naturally, the juxtaposition was less objectionable than falling three stories to the earth below, so they moved onward up the stairs to Mary's bedroom on the top level of Leicester's building above Queen Elizabeth's bedchamber and anteroom.

Ultimately, they stopped in front of a placard describing the room as it had once existed, literally a hollow shell of itself as the floor fell to the ground hundreds of years ago, and only three walls remained. Looking across some ten yards of vacant open air, Connelly pointed to the far wall stretching up from the castle floor three stories down.

"He thinks it could be there," Connelly pointed.

"Where?"

"That little alcove and shelf on the far side was a fireplace. Jack thinks the pages could have been placed in some sort of iron strongbox and hidden in the fireplace. I think he called it a dispatch box—something used to protect important documents back in the day."

"That's ridiculous," said Keating, frustration clear in his voice. "If it was there, one of the Herbert kids would have needed to guess exactly how the building would decay over the years. There's no way someone hid paper in a fireplace. No one is that dumb. And no one is dumb enough to believe it."

"I wish Riley was here," said Matt to no one in particular.

"Because he is dumb enough to believe it?"

"Not exactly. You know that dude climbs like a frickin' squirrel. Remember we went to that rock climbing wall with him as a warm-up for Sharon's business retreat. He's a freak. He's a better rock climber than footballer. He'd be up that wall in three minutes."

"C'mon, Smitty," Keating said. "You can't believe there's something hidden in the fireplace. I don't mind getting arrested if we get some solid proof and have to bust open a wall, a floor, or a church door. But I'm not getting dead."

"Riley really is a good climber," Connelly echoed.

"Jesus."

"Why didn't he come with you guys in the first place?" Rosalind asked without really thinking about him climbing a castle wall. She thought more about four great friends, four more than she'd ever counted in her own life.

"He's on a second honeymoon." Dave smiled.

"It doesn't matter," Keating snapped. "He's not here."

"Not yet," said Matt.

"Quotes, there's no way you're shipping Riley across the Atlantic to climb a wall. We're here because the research is solid, but Jack didn't make one good argument for *Cardenio* in a fireplace. If we come up with all blanks, we can revisit it, but Riley isn't going up that wall for you. We'll assume Jack was wrong."

"I miss Riley." Matt summoned the very best of his sarcasm.

"You guys are fucking with me."

"Yes we are," said Connelly, now belly laughing. "It's really, really fun. Riley is a hell of a climber, though."

"Damn." Keating glared at Rosalind as she futilely attempted to conceal her smile.

40
CHAPTER

The A343 winds through the hillsides of England the second half of the way from Stratford-upon-Avon to the town of Salisbury. More than a road, the thoroughfare is a combination roller-coaster / petting zoo, where the endless looping roundabouts often give way to all manner of animal crossings. Ackerley's heavy foot hammered equally on the gas and brake as the terrifying treks up and down the midland hillsides left his passengers white-knuckled and sweating Jamesons.

Fighting off the urge to vomit, Keating looked jealously at Dave rolling and bouncing easily with the van, chilly can of breakfast beer in hand. The futility of grave robbing may have bothered Connelly, but he appeared undaunted. Buzzed, both from his midmorning souse and the shampoo from their last night's cocktails in Stratford, he was lucid.

The road itself presented plenty of danger, but when a family of small ducklings followed their proud, strutting mother across the road just outside Newbury heading for a small stream and a big world, the ride turned life-threatening. The fowl following forced a familiar pull of inertia, leaving Keating regretting the previous evening's last two whiskeys. A kennel just north of Andover greeted them with a dog crossing just south of what seemed to be the two hundredth roundabout on the journey to Wilton House. Finally, a group of a dozen young girls in the requisite khaki riding pants and boots forced the van into a skid. Jim now fervently believed the traversing of A343 led toward a welcoming ark and away from an oncoming flood.

Matt Smith's knuckles briefly returned to a familiar fleshy tone, rather than the bone white accompanying each grasp of the *oh shit handle* above him. He stared out over the countryside into the endless fields of barley around each deadly curve on the road to Salisbury. The English countryside was gorgeous, but Keating knew Matt couldn't feel any better than he did. Despite that knowledge, Matt still looked fairly content on the jaunt through the countryside with two of his best friends and Jack's daughter. Jim did wonder if perhaps Smith's thoughts were drifting to another woman, on another continent.

"Great news, fellas. When we die on this ride, we'll never know for sure that my father sent us across the pond for no particular reason at all." Rosalind reached for levity and balance.

"Is that really what you believe?" Dave snapped.

"I do." Keating responded before Rosalind could. "And so do you, brother."

"Maybe you guys just lack the imagination for this." Dave said it with eerie calm.

"For a while, I was hoping, or at least trying to hope, it was real. I sit behind that stupid desk every damn day assessing claims, pouring through emails, and debating whether a bullet would be tasty until the bell rings and I can get the hell out. This is a nice break from reality, Quotes. It's not reality." Keating peered from the back seat at Dave in the middle row, as if he could find a way to see around that corner. "But thanks for making it all possible." Jim ripped open a beer of his own as loudly as possible in an effort to sooth Dave.

Somehow, Connelly looked straight through Keating when he turned, leering over his shoulder, to the back row. The look was the equivalent of the tone in his voice when he'd convinced his friends to make this trip, an increasingly familiar look to Keating—Dave Connelly with a purpose in life. Keating smiled at his friend, prompting his retort.

"Yes it is, Jim. It's absolutely real."

"I love the confidence, Quotes. But how do you know? More importantly, how could you?" Jim asked.

"I just do." It wasn't much of an answer and Keating's expression begged for more, so Dave continued without really knowing where he was headed. "You believe in God?"

"You know I don't," said Jim.

"Nor do I, but somehow 95 percent of people on this earth are convinced of a higher being they pray to and devote themselves to. People are willing to blow shit up or hand over their life savings. They kneel and dance and sing. Somehow, they just know. I'm not an expert on Shakespeare, and I'm not an expert on archaeology, but I'm getting damn close to becoming an expert on Jack Taft's research. And I'm telling you. This is real!" Dave paused and Jim could see him searching for some kind of segue to persuade them. He found it quickly, and as usual, in numbers. "You know what the divine ratio is?"

"Absolutely not," Keating answered honestly.

"It's a number."

"Yeah, I've heard of it. It's like the ratio the human body relies on right?" As usual, Rosalind felt free to speak up.

"Correct, to a degree," said Connelly. "It's much more than the human body, but that's definitely one example, or several. The actual number is roughly 1.62, and in the human body, it relates to the phalanges in your fingers, the symmetry of your face, the cochlea in your ear, and the uncoiling of the embryo. But it goes way beyond that. It's present in seashells, sunflowers, and planetary alignments. The ratio is so visually enticing, it's a part of thousands of works of art, paintings, drawings, the pyramids. But the repetition in nature is impossible to ignore without acknowledging some sort of higher being pulling the strings and manufacturing consistencies. Now I'm not saying there is or isn't a God. I'm just saying something as pervasive as that simple number is compelling.

"That's how I feel about Jack's research. I'm not saying we have the means or all the information to find a four hundred-year-old stack of papers, but hell if I don't find the evidence compelling. Does that make sense?" Dave leered around the van at each of them.

"It absolutely does, Dave. And I'm man enough to admit I don't want to match my intellect or even my damn instincts against yours. I would have never found Judas in the argument. It's just a whole lot, brother," said Keating.

"There's something else. I just can't believe the professor intentionally and knowingly started all this with us for no reason whatsoever. He's got the light on in his office scratching his head and hatching a plan to manipulate four chumps he hardly knows so they suffer through disappointment a couple months after his death. Just doesn't add up for arguably the smartest guy we've ever met."

"Smartest guy you've ever met." Smith smirked.

"What's the diff—" Dave caught himself reacting to Matt's expression. "Ha, well played. *Beware of flatterers.* If you really believe that, Smitty, then believe me. This thing is absolutely real. I just don't know if we have the resources to find it."

"There is another problem, Dave," Matt followed.

"What's that?"

"I love your argument for why he wouldn't mess with us. It makes a lot of sense to me, and I argue for a living. The problem is the other side of the coin. Why the hell would he give us the map to a $100 million discovery? That doesn't make sense either."

"I don't think he gave it to us," Dave answered quickly.

Connelly craned his neck farther, looking back toward Rosalind. The other men naturally followed his gaze—a red circle around a young girl you would have noticed first anyway. Was Jack paying a long overdue debt to his estranged daughter? Keating thought back to the day Jack handed him the envelope in Kelly's. *A great reckoning in a small room.*

"That's not bad, Dave."

"You keep saying that."

"Now we just need someone to let us tear down a wall or pull up a stone." Rosalind smiled at Connelly.

"We'll get there."

As if the God Keating and Connelly refused to believe in now watched over them closely, a deer fired out of the shrubs lining the road, forcing Ackerley to slam on the brakes one final time along the A343 zoo. Water once again slushed out of the cooler, spilling onto Dave's sandals this time, reminding each of them they preferred cold beer to dry feet and offering a jolt he didn't seem to mind.

"Jesus. Maybe we won't."

41

CHAPTER

The road into Wilton House intentionally leads visitors up to and past William Chambers' Corinthian Triumphal Arch. The beauty of the passageway to the North Forecourt is undeniable and completely closed off to guests. Like much of the structure and architecture of the house, the arch shifted locations over the years to make the country home more aesthetically pleasing. The gateway existed as a wonderful philosophical contradiction, where function followed form. Rather than enter the forecourt through the arch, cars passed by, snaking through orange traffic cones into the gravel parking lot on the far side of the gift shop.

When Ackerley skidded to a halt, stones flying in multiple directions, the car's occupants caught their collective breath and maneuvered out of the vehicle with dexterous thrift, happy to once again put foot to terra firma. Walking along the outer wall, they found signs directing them to the actual main entrance. In the great tradition of funding museums, this road *more traveled* led them through the gift shop and, ultimately, to the ticket desk.

The house offered grounds passes for £5, house passes for £18, house guides with vivid descriptions of everything but the artwork for £8, and finally the artwork guides for another £8.

Keating handed over four £20 notes with more doubt than enthusiasm. As was the case with seemingly every place in England, the two women working the money drawer exuded friendliness and offered every manner of cliché. *If you have any questions ... If you're in need of direction ... Be sure to visit the ... The gardens are surely my favorite.* Conditioned by a lifetime of ball games and concerts, Jim stared blankly at the duo. This warm welcome differed immeasurably from the normal grunt and point directing him away from a ticket window.

When the foursome made the right turn out of the gift shop toward the forecourt, Connelly echoed Keating's thoughts. "It's going to be a bit of an adjustment when we get back to the States. Not sure I've ever had anyone in the service industry smile at me."

"Damn, I was just thinking the same thing," echoed Smith.

Keating led the group through the main gate and into the spectacular North Forecourt. The arch ascended on their immediate right with the replica statue of Marcus Aurelius atop the incredible stonework. To the left, separating them from the front entrance of the house, a symmetrical formation of boxwoods and lime trees grew, coincidentally the same trees leading the way to Trinity Church. The Vicary Fountain, added in 1971, spewed water up above all the greenery, creating a centerpiece for the house beyond.

Stepping onto the stone pathway through the garden, Keating's gait shortened, and the others instinctively slowed behind him. The idea that this place existed as a home to anyone seemed impossible.

"Holy shit," said Smith succinctly.

"You got that right, Matty." Rosalind had hardly spoken on the ride to Salisbury, and this was her first utterance to any of the men since exiting the car.

Jim looked at her and could tell that this place, this

spectacular view made the whole trip worthwhile. The entire building was erected as an exercise in detail, where every single glance, every pause, every sigh was a chance to miss something. The whole house stood as a reminder of what visitors failed to see, rather than what they observed.

"DP, can you crack open that book once we get inside and tell us what we're looking at? Guessing there might be something important in there," said Matt.

"You bet."

When animals are cold, the small muscles under their skin contract, causing other areas to raise up, thickening their layer of fur and creating greater insulation. The phenomenon called goose bumps are absolutely useless in humans, but at least Jim knew he was in the right place. Walking into the front hall, Keating felt the punch directly in the face, as there in the center of the room, surrounded by various paintings mapping the history of the Earls of Pembroke, stood a six-foot high statue of William Shakespeare. Created a mere two hundred years ago, this entrance still reminded him of the ubiquitous connection between Mary Sidney and William Shakespeare. He looked down at his arms, sans fur, and shook his head.

Keating read from the opening page of the guidebook, chuckling as he orated, "The room is dominated by the statue of Shakespeare, designed by William Kent and carved by Peter Scheemakers. It is a variant of the monument in Poets' Corner at Westminster Abbey commissioned by the earl in 1743. This statue's presence recalls the 2nd Earl and his wife, Mary Sidney's, patronage of literary men and of Shakespeare above all."

"Shakespeare above all?" Connelly asked.

"Jesus, man." Matt looked at Keating in a now familiar way, where the small tumblers in the lock continued to line up.

"Or Judas," Keating said, smiling at Dave.

"Anything else of particular interest, Jim?"

"Art is mostly family portraits. They name a designer for that suit of armor over there but not for who it belonged to. And the statues are all from Greek mythology."

"See Mary in any of the pictures?" Matt asked.

"Just the big statue in the middle," said Rosalind, forcing the others to turn their attention back to Shakespeare in the center of the room. "It's kind of hysterical the face of the man Shakespeare in Wilton House looks nothing like the one in Trinity Church. I mean you, wouldn't have any idea that was the same guy."

"That's because no one knows what Shakespeare looked like." The voice came from behind them as a small woman who appeared to be in her late forties walked through the main doors of the house. She wore a red polo shirt and khaki pants and spoke with unmistakable confidence. "That statue was commissioned 120 years after William Shakespeare died, so certainly this sculptor never got a look at him. And the one in Trinity Church, while likely perfect at one point in time, was destroyed by someone trying to clean it. That's why Shakespeare looks like a cartoon character on that wall."

Connelly looked to Keating, allowing him the room to speak first. So Jim turned his gaze to the five-foot tall woman and thought of the divine proportion. "Sounds like you're an expert on the subject of Shakespeare."

"Ha, hardly. I'm an expert on this house, the family who lives here, and almost nothing else in the world."

"Almost?" asked Rosalind

"Well, I'm in the Premier League of Scotch drinking. Never sure if that counts, but dealing with the current earl has lost me my amateur status for sure."

"Do you want to be best friends?" asked Dave, smiling.

"I'm pretty sure I just told you Scotch is my best friend, but I'm patient with the slow-witted. They amuse me."

"Yep, we're best friends." Dave, always happy to be in the presence of someone who spoke his language, moved toward the small woman, perhaps to give her a hug. But Keating got to her first.

"Then only fitting I should share my name. I'm Reva Clarke."

"Pleasure, Reva," said Jim, offering his hand. "I'm Jim Keating. That's Matt Smith, Rosalind Taft, and the slow-witted guy is David Connelly, but you may call him the slow-witted guy."

"So are you the curator for the house, Reva?" asked Rosalind.

"I would say half curator, half archaeologist. I move a lot of the artwork around from the house to various museums and back, but I also have been doing quite a bit of digging the last few years. As you make your way through the house, you'll see a couple of areas where glass floors or walls expose original parts of the foundation all the way back to the monastery. The house has changed so much over the years, and we've uncovered a great deal. But the real mysteries go all the way back to the eighth century. I balance both."

"How's your Mary Sidney scholarship?" Matt spoke to Reva, but he was still staring at the statue of the man from Stratford.

Reva looked at the four of them separately, glancing from one to the next and wondering exactly who had just entered her house. "Not just here on holiday?"

"No ma'am. We have some work to do," said Dave.

"How can I help?"

Jim suddenly thought of Dr. Shubert placing the manila folder on the table in front of him at his office back in Connecticut.

It represented the only time in this whole fiasco he'd felt any sense of real guidance from someone with information to provide. That information was simply the address of a dead expert, now roughly ten weeks and three thousand miles away. But suddenly they were in the company of a living breathing aficionado. And she was willing to help.

"Any chance you have time for a quick tour of the house?" asked Jim.

"I'm not sure I can provide such a thing."

"A tour?"

"A *quick* tour. Of all the trinkets, stories, history, and magnificence of this home, I'm not sure I've ever felt a greater affinity with any part of the history or any person than I've felt for Mary. Simply put, she was amazing. Writer, linguist, countess, magician, and on and on and on—a Renaissance woman when she was allowed to be no such thing. Its' very difficult to even fathom."

"A lengthy tour then?" said Rosalind.

"Cheers, then. I will warn you that this little girl will buzz every so often." She said pointing to her handheld radio. "If duty calls, I'll have to break off for a while, but I'm happy to keep moving back and forth."

"Sounds perfect."

"OK, well it seems like you've got a grip on this room. And as you know, it didn't exist when Mary lived here. The only thing I would point out is on the wall behind you. The painting to the far right is of Mary Sidney's brother, Philip. He was killed in battle from a wound to the leg. He died a few days later."

"Can honor mend a leg?" Dave inquired of Sir Philip Sidney.

"Pardon?"

"Sorry. You just reminded me of a friend. You don't by chance know if Philip Sidney died on a Wednesday, do you?"

"That's one I've never been asked before, David. I'm sorry I actually don't know the answer."

"No worries."

Reva moved up the few stairs at Shakespeare's back and motioned for the group to follow. "So this area here is considered the Upper Cloisters. This whole hall also postdates Mary Sidney, but if you look closely at the stained glass windows, you'll see small pink flowers in a few of them. Those are remembrances for Mary and the 2nd Earl of Pembroke. Many of the windows were created in the early 1800s, but a few of them were saved and reset from as far back as 1507."

Looking through the windows, Reva pointed down toward a small square courtyard, bereft of any visitors. "What's of particular interest outside these windows is what you don't see. This whole area in the center was, at one time, the entrance to the house. Visitors would come in from behind that wall on the far side and into this courtyard. The Upper Cloisters did not exist at the time, so the open area was obviously much larger. At ground level was the Holbein porch, a huge rectangular entrance inside the tower. The porch was moved during the redesigns and now sits in the Pembroke's private garden. But Mary Sidney would have welcomed guests right there." Reva pointed to the shrubbery below as if disclosing some valuable secret, and the four guests leaned in, looking at nothing.

"Was she by chance holding something called *The History of Cardenio* in her hands when she met them?" Smith whispered, almost silently to Connelly.

"Reva, do you have any idea where Mary's writers' group would have met?" Rosalind asked, ignoring Matt and Dave.

"Her writers' group?"

"Yes, there's fairly extensive proof that Mary Sidney met with a group of artists who later garnered the name the Wilton Circle. I know there is some speculation about which of the more prominent writers attended, but the group itself is real. My father tracked it in various letters from her time."

"We'll, it seems I'll be taken to task today." Reva appeared thrilled with the prospect, rather than embarrassed by her inability to answer the question. "I'll have to look into that one, Rosalind. I've certainly heard of the group but have no idea where they may have met, if it was even in the house, or who participated. If I can't find tangible evidence, it doesn't always warrant much digging."

They meandered through the dining room and library before arriving in the Single Cube Room. The symmetry of the thirty-by-thirty-by-thirty room fought helplessly for their attention, as family paintings adorned with golden frames jumped off the walls. The central ceiling panel showed *The Fall of Icarus*, a boy flying too close to the sun. Jim Keating could relate. Red velvet chairs with gold legs and backs were scattered throughout the room, forcing the word *ostentatious* to run for cover.

"This six-room stretch was designed and completed by Inigo Jones and John Webb in the mid-seventeenth century, not long after Mary's time. The fire of 1647 destroyed most of the existing house. The redesign, intended to host King Charles I, missed its mark, as he was executed before ever seeing the completed rooms. This first room is appropriately known as the Cube Room, measuring a perfect thirty feet in length, width, and height.

"I'm not sure how much detail you want about the family or the history, but I'll start with the Sidneys. The dado shows twenty-six paintings detailing various scenes from Sir Philip Sidney's *Arcadia*. All the paintings are by Emanuel de Critz. There isn't a terrible amount of evidence either way, but most believe Mary completed *Arcadia* after Philip's death. Either way, the epic was written right here at Wilton House."

Keating's eyes were still locked onto the incredible ceiling of the room, but he finally reconnected to Reva. "I'm sorry. The dado?"

"Yes. The area on the lower portions of the wall underneath what you would know as a chair rail. Most of the paintings on the upper walls depict the family years after Mary, around the time of the 7th and 8th earls."

"Reva?"

"Yes."

"Is there anything else you can tell us about the dado?" inquired Jim.

"Well, what would you like to know?"

"Anything at all you might care to share."

"Oh, hell, DP, just ask her if there is a book hidden behind the wall." Staring at Jim, Dave missed the sideways glance from their host.

"Have you heard that story?" Reva asked, returning to Dave.

"Which story?" Rosalind asked quietly.

"Well, for years, there was a rumor that a copy of Shakespeare's First Folio lay hidden behind one of the panels in the *Arcadia* series. To an extent, I'd like to believe it just because it drips with so much romance and mystery, but I also feel fairly certain that Lady Clifford, wife to the 4th Earl, took the folio back, pilfering it for her own collection so many years ago. She was another patron of the arts along the lines of Mary. Lady Clifford commissioned an amazing painting known simply as *The Great Picture*, and that painting is the reason I know she stole the folio. In the painting, there are some two hundred books in the background, but none of those books are William Shakespeare's *First Folio*. It seems like quite an incongruous oversight or, more likely, an intentional one, as Lady Clifford certainly would have wanted a copy. Its absence reveals its presence to me.

"As it relates to my work, this is certainly a nonissue. However, it's hard to reconcile. Mary was considered one of Shakespeare's greatest patrons. The First Folio, as well as the sonnets, were dedicated to her children. One of the playwright's acting troupes was even sponsored by the Earl of Pembroke, yet there is no copy of the folio belonging to the family. It really doesn't sit well. The Herberts owned a copy of that book for sure. Maybe it sat behind the wall, and maybe it sat on a desk, but Lady Anne Clifford stole that book away, and it's never been seen again."

"So they've checked behind the panels?" asked Matt.

"Oh, gracious no." Reva gasped.

"Then how do you know the book isn't there?" asked Connelly.

"How do you know *a book* isn't there?" Keating corrected, looking at Dave.

"You'll pardon me, gentlemen, but you do understand the dado is 370 years old. No one is really excited to take a sledgehammer and smash them through to search for a mythical book."

"What if we could convince you it's not a myth?"

42
CHAPTER

"Let's just get fucking hammered." Clearly, Matt Smith was done with history lessons for the day.

"You got it, Smitty." Connelly could never argue with one of his favorite sentiments, especially after another empty trip through British history.

The Cathedral Hotel in Salisbury is one of the better venues in England for Matt's mission. More of a night club than a pub, the hotel slowly packed parched patrons in until roughly ten o'clock, when space ran out and a queue formed out front. Hard to explain a line for drinks in a town with countless watering holes, but as always, when people were in need and had money to donate, the Cathedral found a way. The pink neon sign behind the bar read, "Cocktails and Dreams," an exact replica of the sign in the window of Flanagan's at the end of the film *Cocktail*. Finally, they were in the right place.

"Blink, blink, dinkity-blink," Keating offered, staring at the sign.

"Maybe we could reinvent the flugelbinder," said Smith.

"A what?" Rosalind asked.

"C'mon, girl," said Dave. "The flugelbinder is the little thing on the end of your shoelace that makes it easy to thread through the holes. You've never enjoyed a poorly acted Tom Cruise movie? You're just letting the best in life pass you by."

"AFGM!" Matt screamed it with a certainty that almost made sense.

"Are you boys drunk already?" she inquired.

"Quotes, that's a faux pas," Smith stated before turning to Rosalind. "He was explaining the movie *Cocktail* but then shifted gears to *A Few Good Men*. 'You're just letting the best in life pass you by' is a Jack Nicholson line. I won't elaborate on the reference. But one poorly acted Cruise movie at a time, David."

"You called me David." Connelly laughed.

"Probably is a first, Quotes."

"Definitely."

"Means it must be my turn to buy," said Smith.

"Fact!"

"What's everybody having? Car bombs?" Matt asked.

"Dude, I don't know if you can order Irish Car Bombs in England," said Connelly. "I would think folks might be sensitive about that, given the two countries' histories."

"Ha." Keating chuckled. "Depends on who is doing the bombing, but I always enjoy Quotes as the voice of reason, Matty. This trip really has made him grow up. When's the last time anything registered on his sensibility radar? Perhaps that was the point of this whole shit show. Maybe Dave needed to grow up."

"Never," interjected Connelly.

Lost in yet another inane conversation, each of the three men failed to notice Rosalind step to the bar until she came over Keating's shoulder with four small rocks glasses filled halfway with brown liquor. "I figured you idiots might stand here all night talking about Tom Cruise so I took the liberty. Jamesons. Doubles."

"Could be the two best words I've heard this whole trip," said Keating. "Nice work there, young lady."

"I'm not that young."

"Couple of these, and you'll never be young again," said Connelly.

"I'm hoping for the exact opposite—at least in the short term." Holding the rocks glass in one hand and flipping her hair out of her eyes with the other, she appeared more honest than flirtatious.

It looked a lot like perfection to James Keating. That look, the wry grin on her face took him back to the photograph with the red circle over and over again. The funeral home may have been the perfect place for them to meet, because the woman in that room grew weary with the world, beaten by its imperfections. This Rosalind Taft looked ready and determined. As Jim watched her pour the brown liquid into her mouth, he knew a crappy world would slow this woman as much as a small glass of whiskey would. Both subtle and somehow brash, she naturally and carelessly wiped her mouth across her sleeve when finished.

That was it, thought Keating. *The last little charge at proper.* He didn't need heels or nails, thongs or pushup bras, no sense or sensibility, just a woman who would whack down a glass of whiskey and wipe her mouth on her sleeve.

Connelly and Smith disappeared, seeking more beverages for the perfect expanse of time, and Jim enjoyed each second the two of them shared alone in the hotel bar. He wished for a stagnation of time, perhaps a wormhole or Well's work to engulf a small bar in Salisbury, England, so they could dangle like this indefinitely.

"Are you going to drink that?" Just like that it was over. "Or are you locked into the middle distance, deeply contemplative." She chuckled. "Because I'll drink it."

"I can do both."

"Well, get cracking," said Rosalind. "You're no good to me sober."

Keating looked down at the whiskey, and the glass felt heavy in his hand. It felt heavy. That heavy feeling and a countess from Wilton House were his last thoughts before he set the glass to his lips and pulled the trigger. *Not this way*, he thought. *I'm not going to let this be another moment of regret.*

—⁂—

"There is no way in hell we're getting into that wall, Matty."

"OK, so you won't find this mysterious manuscript that no qualified person has found in the last four hundred years. You can go back to piles of money, piles of one-night stands and know that you did your very best." Smith's perfectly helpless response dripped of futility.

"No, I can't." It was perhaps the saddest sound he'd ever heard from his friend David Connelly.

Matt Smith had witnessed apathy from Dave Connelly the way fish witness water, but the look on his face and the sound in his voice were completely new. It was pure sadness. Concrete walls, stone floors, and priceless oil paintings made Matt helpless. He didn't know what to do for Dave other than the same thing he had always done—be his friend.

"Brother, at least you're here. I mean, I know DP pushed from the beginning, but you got us all here. Hell, we may never find a damn thing, but we're not back at the bar spewing irreverent trivia and checking out Dakota's jean shorts." Matt paused laughing at his surroundings. "We're actually here in England, at the bar, spewing useless trivia and staring at that blond girl's jean shorts." Matt pointed across the bar toward no one in particular.

Connelly joined in on the laughter. "You make a good point. Damn, you really are a hell of a lawyer, Matty."

"Duke educated."

"Oh, fuck that."

"More shots?"

"Deal."

As Matt turned toward the bar, Dave grabbed him by the arm to slow his purposeful first stride. "One last thing because I'm curious. After I explained our whole story to Reva, and she politely told us no one was ripping those paintings off the wall, I slept through the rest of the tour. But there was something in Wilton House I actually paid attention to, and I was wondering if you noticed it as well."

"Big house, Dave."

"All right, never mind."

Matt felt torn, not wanting to raise his friend's hopes from the ashes only to have them explode in flames again. He guessed what Dave spoke of and knew this internal debate would eventually end with a forfeit. Sometimes there really is no choice. It sat in a glass case in the center of the very last room of their tour of Wilton House—the exact same thing Jack said would hold *Cardenio* safe in the walls of Kenilworth Castle.

"The dispatch box?" Matt asked.

"Duke educated!"

Keating awoke to the sound of the street traffic rolling down Main with much higher volume than expected at 6:15 a.m. The open window offered no buffer from the sounds of the morning, and despite his best effort to pull in some cool air, the room remained sticky. He slid the sheet off his body, and that sound hurt his head as well. Now realizing the Jamesons and not the traffic below pounded through his cranium, he uttered a barely audible, "Fuck."

"You said no."

Jim shot up straight in bed, moving way too fast for his present state of hangover and paid the price again as his skull erupted. There, propped up on top of a blanket in the corner of his room, lay Rosalind Taft.

"What are you doing here?"

"You know just how to make a girl feel special," she said facetiously. Her eyes were still closed, but she smiled, curled in a ball on her side.

"Sorry. Obviously didn't mean it like that. Still not in any way coherent." He was back in the funeral home, apologizing. "I didn't even offer you the bed?"

"I said no."

"And nothing happened?" Jim asked incredulously.

"*You* said no."

"Damn, that doesn't sound like me."

"Bullshit."

"You have a tremendous capacity to make me feel uncomfortable you know. Somehow, I'm a seventh grader around you at all times." Keating futilely rubbed his temples as if that minor movement would combat three-quarters of a bottle of whiskey. The traffic seemed to get louder.

"Wow, that was shockingly honest." She rolled off her side, getting her arms underneath her and began rising to her feet. Her white linen blouse was a wrinkled mess, but her pants remained pristine, folded neatly on the hotel room floor.

"I'm not honest?" asked Jim.

"I meant surprising for a man, not for you."

"I'm not a man?" Keating smirked.

"How absolute the knave is."

"Ha. Hamlet. I know that one."

"I didn't. Some jackass made me study it in a bunch of lectures offered up by a father I hardly knew." Rosalind slowly raised one leg up after another and knelt on the edge of the bed at Keating's feet. "I can't decide if it makes no sense or perfect sense that an author dead for four hundred years took my father away from me and then brought him back. So in the meantime, I've decided that you and your idiot friends brought him back to me."

"Did you even want that?"

"I would have said no a month ago—hell, five days ago." Her voice cracked, and her solid resolve almost splintered. But Keating knew better than to wait for tears she would never shed. Instead, he pulled back on the sheet now covering little more than his knee and rolled his arm back in invitation. Rosalind slid forward lowering her head on his chest in what Jim would later describe as the most intimate moment of his life. "Now I don't know. But I'm glad I'm here."

"So am I."

43
CHAPTER

Jim sat quietly across from Connelly in the corner pew of Declan's bar. Friday lunches in that very spot were a favorite tradition of the four friends, anticipating another long weekend. Riley and Matt missed this one, and it bothered Keating a bit, as he was headed out of town for a few days. The four of them had not found a single time to meet up since the return from England a few weeks ago, and it weighed on Keating a bit. Maybe times were changing a little for each of them.

The theme song from the '80s TV show *The A-Team* interrupted his thoughts when it reverberated from Dave's pocket. Lethargically, Connelly pulled the phone from his jeans, assuming the latest internet mess he'd swiped had decided to reach out for rectification. Immediately the *+1* in front of the number revealed an overseas call and sent those same goose bumps running in a gaggle down Dave's arms. He showed the number to Keating before answering.

"Hello?"

"Mr. Connelly?"

"Yes."

"It's Reva Clarke at the Wilton House." The long pause forced a follow up. "Mr. Connelly?"

"Yes. I'm sorry. I wasn't exactly expecting your call. What can I do for you?"

"I have some news I thought you might find interesting. The earl couldn't take it anymore. He needed to know for sure. I think the combination of family pride and insatiable curiosity forced him to action. We went in behind the *Arcadia* panel as you suggested—"

"Sweet Jesus, I hope you didn't damage any of the paintings. I'm sorry. It's my fault. I feel terrible if anything happened to the dado."

Jim immediately noted Dave's use of the word *dado*.

"No, you don't understand. We found something."

"What?!" The few patrons scattered around Declan Kelly's bar all looked in his direction.

"Yes. And we didn't have to touch the painting. We were able to find our way in through the cloisters below. If you remember from your trip, that room is an addition to the original building—the Inigo Jones wing. Well, that's not necessarily important. Anyway, we were able to get in through the space between the walls. It wasn't easy, but it certainly was productive."

"How productive?"

"We found a dispatch box behind the wall."

"What? You found a dispatch box behind the wall?" asked Connelly for Jim's benefit.

"A dispatch box is really just a sturdy container." Rather than cutting her off, Connelly let her continue with the definition, and switched his phone to speaker. "These days, it refers to a box holding papers at Parliament, but starting in the reign of Elizabeth I, they were used to transport various papers and documents to keep them safe. There is actually one on display in the very last room of the tour. It sits just in front of the doors before you head out to the garden. I doubt you would have noticed it." It never bothered Connelly that people underestimated him. It made life so much easier.

"Holy shit!" Dave spoke to Keating more than Reva.

"Pardon?"

"Nothing, I'm sorry. It was there, wasn't it? The quarto was in the box." Connelly and Jim waited anxiously. "Miss Clarke?"

"I'm sorry, Mr. Connelly. The box was empty."

"What!?" It was only the third time he'd offered the exclamation in the two-minute-old conversation.

"Yes. I'm afraid it was empty," said Reva.

"Sorry. You found a box used to protect documents, hidden behind a wall, exactly where we told you to look, and the damn thing was empty?"

Jim motioned to Connelly pushing both his palms downward toward the table, signaling him to lower his voice.

"I'm sorry, Miss Clarke. I didn't mean to yell; it's just that my friends and I have been chasing this with quite a bit of passion. Realizing we were both right and wrong is a little difficult to swallow."

"I do have some good news," she responded.

"Ha. Not sure it could be good enough, considering what we were hoping for, but I'll take anything I can get right now."

"Well, I think I mentioned this on your visit. It was rumored for years that a copy of Shakespeare's First Folio was hidden in that room. There are myriad theories about what happened to it—if it even existed. As we discussed, the Earl of Pembroke and his wife, Mary, were huge patrons of the arts, and it always seemed shocking that no Herbert copy of the folio had ever been discovered. There was a leading theory that Lady Anne Clifford knew about it and had stolen the copy. Do you remember all this?"

"Of course," said Connelly.

"Well, there is currently a painting in Abbot Hall showing

various stages of Lady Anne's life. And in the panels behind her are all manner of references to her patronage of the arts, including books by Ovid, Chaucer, and Cervantes, among others. Shakespeare's First Folio is conspicuously missing, despite her devotion to the arts. This box could be the link needed to prove that a Herbert copy existed at some point. And while it's a dream, it could even lead to the discovery of an extant First Folio."

Two months ago, none of this would have registered to Jim or Dave with any resonance. When Reva had recounted it just weeks ago, they'd hung on her every word, thanks largely to a four-minute lecture on Mohammed, delivered by the best teacher they'd ever met. Now, they just wanted the damn quarto, but Dave thought of Professor Taft anyway.

"Jack would be thrilled," said Connelly.

"I'm sorry. Who is Jack?" Reva asked.

"I was thinking out loud. Our friend Jack Taft got us going on this ridiculous quest a little while back before he passed away, and this was really all his doing. It would have made him happy."

"Did you say Jack Taft?"

"Yes ma'am," said Dave.

"Jack Taft from Wesleyan University?"

Jim's heart skipped a beat, and Dave looked at him incredulously. Why would his name have come up? They were on their own mission, searching for their own answers. There was no need to discuss the fruition of the project with someone outside of Kelly's Pub, but now they needed answers.

"Yes. That Jack Taft."

"Oh dear, I'm so sorry to hear he passed. I didn't realize you knew Jack. What an amazing coincidence."

"Goddamn, Freud."

"Freud?" Reva asked.

Jim had no idea what the reference meant either.

"Yes. It was Freud who said there are no coincidences, and he was correct."

Connelly processed information faster than most anyone Jim had ever met, particularly when having lots of it. Jack had led them to a place he'd already searched, already investigated. He'd sent them to the one person who knew more about Wilton House than virtually anyone in the world, a person he'd already met. There were no coincidences.

"I'm not following, Mr. Connelly"

"Not important. How did you know Jack?"

"He was here for nine or ten days a few years ago. I worked pretty closely with him on his research at the house—went all through the grounds, took a close look at the Holbein Porch together, as well as the house. Actually, we made a few new discoveries together while he was here. Brilliant man."

"No doubt," said Dave.

Jim noticed the precision of Dave's words. The last few months had been filled with doubt.

"I guess that leaves one important question."

"What's that?"

"Has anyone taken a close look at the box?"

"No one but I. Why do you ask?"

"Well, I couldn't agree more that Jack is a brilliant guy. Certainly the smartest guy I've ever met, but this new development creates a kind of fork in the road. It's possible, and even likely, that Jack possessed both the knowledge and the desire to make an incredible discovery that could change the entire nature of the name Shakespeare—or, at the very least, spearhead the discovery of another elusive First Folio. If the two of you had found the box, I wouldn't even think of another possibility.

"The problem is four knuckleheads from a bar in

Connecticut. Our involvement worries me because he was also brilliant enough to manifest an incredibly elaborate hoax. If he left all the bread crumbs for us, isn't it possible he could have found a way to leave that empty box when you were all over the house together? I'm sure he built enough trust to earn a little autonomy around the place over a week and a half."

"Oh, dear," mumbled Reva.

"He could have found a dispatch box anywhere. Hell, he could have made one, but he wouldn't be able to find one that was 370 years old. I'll believe it when someone looks at the box. Is that possible?"

"Perhaps you misunderstood me, Mr. Connelly. I'm not concerned that Mr. Taft somehow stole into the walls of the Cube Room and hid a mysterious fake box within the innards of a centuries-old home. I'm concerned you would think so. The box is real. My area of expertise is antiquities. The box wasn't made of titanium. This box was hidden in that wall when Inigo Jones built the additions. The only question to answer now is what the box contained." Reva paused momentarily. "I'm terribly sorry that you think your friend might do something so terrible to you."

"He wasn't my friend."

44

CHAPTER

"Are you fucking kidding me, DP? Did that really just happen?'

"Brother, I'm not sure this isn't a good thing. She found the actual box, and she's saying it's over three hundred years old. Let's just wait and see what happens now." Jim waited for Dave's response. The relationship between Reva and Jack was difficult to reconcile, but it wasn't an ending.

"If Jack found a copy of *Cardenio* in the wall, then why all the damn subterfuge? Why not just give it to us if he ever wanted us to have it?" asked Dave.

Keating stared at the empty plate in front of him, and he could not manifest one concrete fact for his friend. He ultimately looked up, unsure if this would break Dave. It was honestly the first time he'd ever known Connelly to care about anything other than his close friends.

"Maybe you were right."

"About what?" asked Dave, exasperated.

"You said it in the car on the way to Salisbury. Maybe this whole thing was about his daughter, and we were the path to her. Jack may have been a crotchety old man teetering on the edge of his career, or even his mortality, but there's no way he screwed us on purpose. Whether the story is real or not, I know in my heart that Jack believed it was real.

And you do too, Quotes." Jim leaned in now. "Let's examine the worst possible case, brother. It was all fake. Wasn't it a hell of an adventure? Have you ever learned more in your life? About anything? And now that I'm saying it, I know something else. It was, at least partly, about us—partly about you and your uncontrollably brilliant mind. I think Jack wanted us to be better than we were. I think he was sick of the drivel. Was he wrong? Look at Riley's marriage. Smitty's reconciliation. Could you honestly say any of us are worse off than we were two months ago? Whatever the outcome."

Connelly refused to answer, simply polishing off the last of his pint, perhaps hoping to ignore Keating's truth. Jim bailed him out when he made the mistake of checking the time on his phone.

"Need to be somewhere?" Connelly asked.

"Yes, actually."

"You were early for lunch. Didn't catch that until now. You're usually last man in struggling to get off the desk."

Usually, Keating would have tried to ignore him, but he needed to get going. "Headed out of town."

"The daughter?"

Keating didn't answer but gave himself away when he stood up from the table and reached for his money clip. He dropped two twenties on the table. "Your next pint is on me." He said it as he started to walk away.

"Jim?"

"Yes, Dave."

"Thank you for this." Connelly never actually looked up.

Jim knew that the unsolved mystery had not broken his friend, but looking up for just a second may have. "You're welcome. I'll see you next week."

"Next week," replied Connelly. And then more quietly he said, "It's the daughter."

—m—

Declan Kelly set the pint in front of Dave as Keating exited the bar. Connelly couldn't help but feel his barman had an answer for everything. Somehow, brevity and timing came together in almost everything Kelly did, like holstered pistols just waiting for ten paces and a problem needing solving. He wouldn't utter a word to begin the conversation, but he'd heard enough to know David surely would. Those weeks were a hiccup in Connelly's life, but they'd changed everything.

"What, Dec?" asked Dave as Kelly continued to leer. "Fine. You want to know. Just found out the boys and I studied plays, lectures, and journals and traveled across the pond all for an empty box that will end up on a shelf in a house I'll never see again, thank God. I don't know what the hell this whole thing was about, but—"

"Dumbass," Kelly interrupted.

"Say again."

"Ever consider it wasn't the box that was empty?"

Dave saw the look of impatience on Declan's face. He knew that explaining himself was Declan's least favorite pastime.

"What I heard in your last sentence was, 'The boys and I studied plays, lectures, and journals and traveled across the pond.' That doesn't exactly sound like a colossal waste of energy."

"Even if it was all for nothing?"

Declan glared. "Really?"

"Really! We did all this for nothing."

"Jesus, David. Why don't you tell me about the hottest supermodel of all time so you can do something productive with your life instead of wasting energy learning about

Shakespeare, the Renaissance, and a woman so far ahead of her time people still don't understand her. Maybe you're a bigger fucking idiot than I thought."

As Declan walked away, Connelly put his head in his hands letting out an exasperated gasp, but despite his best efforts, there really was no looking away from it. Jack had expressed it well weeks ago, and Declan had reinforced it now. David Connelly was a prolific waster of time. Finally armed with a quest and a purpose, his complaining stemmed only from the lack of closure. Over and over in his lectures, Jack promised his students that Shakespeare's greatest gift in his writing stemmed from the limitless interpretation and conjecture offered up to the reader. Existence, the canon, and David Connelly were incomplete sentences coming alive anew every time, searching for a purpose.

"Fuck that," Dave said quietly enough to make certain Declan couldn't hear him, though the barman probably did.

Reaching down to his shoulder bag on the floor at his feet, he pulled out two books. One, depending on the accuracy of the Stationers' Register, was over four hundred years old and known to the world around. The other was a leather-bound journal purchased just one day ago. Dave set the journal full of blank pages on the table in front him and opened *Hamlet*, by William Shakespeare.

ACT 1, SCENE 1. Elsinore. A platform before the castle.

Stand and unfold. Francisco and Bernardo.

David Connelly could almost hear the clock strike midnight, but to him it was still noon everywhere.

45
CHAPTER

Jack Taft laughed. The professor loved to teach, and as he walked away from the post office in Oxford, England, he felt pride in his life's accomplishments in a way he'd never allowed himself. With no expectations, the package he'd mailed five minutes ago represented all his work—an author; an impostor; a lifetime of study; and, most importantly, one daughter with a profound decision ahead of her.

He never properly understood his twenty-plus year relationship with Declan Kelly until he asked a favor bigger than any friendship should allow. The ridiculous became necessary because of 'the will of a living daughter curbed by the will of a dead father.' If he couldn't learn from Lear and Cordelia, Polonius and Ophelia, or Shylock and Jessica, then it was possible he couldn't learn anything at all. The last few years of his life had taught him about a lack of certainties—a short time upright to fix what he could before the universe stretched on without him.

Declan still harbored a few less than reputable friends making their way in and out of Boston from time to time. When Jack needed out of the United States, out of *this great globe itself*, and some remnants of a sailing accident, Declan's friends were happy to help. Detours purchased as needed.

Crawling around the innards of the Wilton House as a lesson in the Renaissance was exciting and mysterious. The Pembroke family history made for great reading. Speculation about the Wilton Circle had created dissertations, novels, and papers throughout Jack's life and many lifetimes before. However, the relics of an eighth-century monastery and a great fire were touchable, like blood on the back of an elevator. Reva Clarke welcomed him with open arms to her life's work, and together they dug. That Jack had been alone when he'd found the dispatch box was pure luck.

Quite naturally, he grappled with the issue of trust when he found *The History of Cardenio* by Mary Sidney hidden in a wall, but whose trust? Reva Clarke, a guardian of antiquities at the Wilton House, or Mary Sidney, the creator of antiquities at the Wilton House? He'd uncovered the greatest secret in the history of literature, but the secret belonged to Mary—no one but Mary. Her story. Her writing. Her signature.

Mary Sidney, Countess of Pembroke, had always aspired to write but had never aspired to fame. To find her audience, she called on a desperate owner of a playhouse in need of stories to fill his stage, a man willing to invent an identity to protect his muse. She needed a glover's son, an upstart crow, so she made a kind offer.

He could never know for certain, but in Jack's mind, a prince and a gentleman tracked the Count of Gondomar's quarto into Spain to protect the identity of a great mind, not reveal it. Two young earls, two loyal sons, two young men to whom the First Folio was dedicated hid this lone piece of evidence to protect a woman outside her time and a phenomenal story the world still believed. It was one more story she crafted in an effort at anonymity. Should a professor of English literature be the judge and jury on the unearthing of such a secret?

Jack pondered a great many questions, along with one overwhelming certainty. His daughter Rosalind deserved a priceless gift. The gift would never explain why he'd left her, only that she'd never left him. Inexorably, Rosalind Taft was his daughter.

As the old man stumbled through the age of information searching ceaselessly for details of his daughter's adult life on Twitter, Instagram, Facebook, and any other ridiculous self-indulgent social media site, he came up empty. And he came up empty. He knew where to find her simply because the details of her work life were readily available, but her personal life was nonexistent. He always suspected an early betrayal had left her shut off emotionally and never doubted his ownership of that betrayal. No matter what had happened in his marriage, he'd left his daughter, the person he cared for most in the world.

When he'd brushed past them at Wilton House, he confirmed all his decisions. He could have continued to ramble about a Danish Prince or a coup d'état in Scotland, but things finally felt right. He'd found his purpose once and for all. He'd reached out from time to time with a phone call to his old haunt, Kelly's, and Declan had kept him up to date and even shouted out across the bar to keep them on point. Perhaps, "All the world's a stage."

His daughter ambled through the house and gardens, laughing occasionally with men he'd known for years, looking most comfortable in conversation with Jim Keating. Jack felt sad Riley had missed the trip. Each play needed a clown, but he guessed Riley needed to play the lover. The professor never knew Tracy Smith taught high school English and enjoyed the surprise as his own guilty pleasure. David Connelly wasted no time that gorgeous afternoon, walking stride for stride with Jack's old friend Reva Clarke, a man on a mission for the first time in his life. He kept a safe distance, but quite honestly, how often are you on the lookout for a dead man?

—⟋⟋⟍—

He bought a boat and named it *The Terence,* going against the time-honored tradition of christening her a woman. Instead, the great Roman poet accused of plagiarism seemed perfect. He loved learning to sail.

Christening an actual woman was much easier for the professor. All through high school, college, and his life in academia, he'd heard arguments for Shakespeare's greatest play—*Hamlet*, *Macbeth*, and *Lear* got all the noise, in that order. He rarely heard another play mentioned. Above all others, Jack loved the great Harold Bloom's case for Hamlet, sighting his "inwardness" as his greatest attribute. Jack agreed completely when Bloom made the same argument for Rosalind.

More than anything else, Jack loved Rosalind's ability to *do.* The Danish prince and the banished niece were opposites, where Hamlet represented procrastination and Rosalind represented action. He let things happen; she made things happen. Intellectual equals, they were the center of their plays, the center of their world, one shaped by his world and the other shaping hers. Hamlet dies, whereas Rosalind gets the last word:

> It is not the fashion to see the lady the epilogue;
> But it is no more unhandsome than to see the lord
> The prologue. If it be true that good wine needs no
> Epilogue; yet to good wine they do use good bushes
> And good plays prove the better by the help of good
> Epilogues. What case am I in then, that am

Neither a good epilogue nor cannot insinuate with
You in the behalf of a good play! I am not
Furnished like the beggar, therefore to beg you will not
Become me: my way is to conjure you; and I'll begin
With the women. I charge you, O women for the love
You bear to men, to like as much of this play as
Please you: and I charge you, O men, for the love
You bear to women—as I perceive by your simpering,
None of you hates them—that between you and the
Women the play may please. If I were a woman I
Would kiss as many of you as had beards that pleased
Me, complexions that liked me and breaths that I
Defied not: and, I am sure, as many as have good
Beards, or good face or sweet breaths *will, for my
Kind offer, when I make curtsy, bid me farewell.*

Critics marvel at the repeating ironies of Rosalind's apology in William Shakespeare's *As You Like It*. She begins by stating outright, "It is not the fashion to see the lady in the epilogue," a sort of suspension of disbelief, offering up the joke for an audience to consider. The anonymous sixteen-year-old boy assigned the part tells the crowd, "If I were a woman" provoking another laugh and ending William Shakespeare's play. A boy, dressed as a woman who is no longer cross-dressed as a man explains everything and nothing.

"*Will*, for my kind offer, when I make curtsy, bid me farewell." Jack Taft looked over his shoulder, back toward the post office building, bidding Mary farewell. He looked back toward the accidental discovery of a lifetime, back toward a canon of endless interpretations and finally forward, toward a superfluous red circle drawn carefully around a beautiful young girl in a photograph.

ABOUT THE AUTHOR

William Sullivan is a 1995 graduate of The University of Connecticut. He is a retired college basketball coach living in Connecticut with his wife and children. As the world's greatest collector of friends, he can also be found hoisting the occasional pint in the corner pub. *Tilting with Lips* is his second novel.

Printed in the United States
by Baker & Taylor Publisher Services